USA TODAY bestselling auth[or]
is read in multiple languages[...]
her sweet romances writing as Emily Murdoch, and
steamy romances as Emily E K Murdoch. Emily's
had a varied career to date, from examining medieval
manuscripts to designing museum exhibitions,
working as a researcher for the BBC to working for
the National Trust. Her books' settings range from
England 1050 to Texas 1848, and she can't wait for
you to fall in love with her heroes and heroines!

Also by Emily E K Murdoch

The Wallflower Academy miniseries

Least Likely to Win a Duke
More Than a Match for the Earl
The Duchess Charade

Discover more at millsandboon.co.uk.

THE PRINCE'S WALLFLOWER WIFE

Emily E K Murdoch

MILLS & BOON

All rights reserved including the right of reproduction in whole or in part in any form. This edition is published by arrangement with Harlequin Enterprises ULC.

This is a work of fiction. Names, characters, places, locations and incidents are purely fictional and bear no relationship to any real life individuals, living or dead, or to any actual places, business establishments, locations, events or incidents. Any resemblance is entirely coincidental.

Without limiting the author's and publisher's exclusive rights, any unauthorised use of this publication to train generative artificial intelligence (AI) technologies is expressly prohibited. HarperCollins also exercise their rights under Article 4(3) of the Digital Single Market Directive 2019/790 and expressly reserve this publication from the text and data mining exception.

® and TM are trademarks owned and used by the trademark owner and/or its licensee. Trademarks marked with ® are registered with the United Kingdom Patent Office and/or the Office for Harmonisation in the Internal Market and in other countries.

First published in Great Britain 2025 by Mills & Boon, an imprint of HarperCollins*Publishers* Ltd, 1 London Bridge Street, London, SE1 9GF

www.harpercollins.co.uk

HarperCollins*Publishers*, Macken House, 39/40 Mayor Street Upper, Dublin 1, D01 C9W8, Ireland

The Prince's Wallflower Wife © 2025 Emily E K Murdoch

ISBN: 978-0-263-34531-5

08/25

This book contains FSC™ certified paper and other controlled sources to ensure responsible forest management.

For more information visit www.harpercollins.co.uk/green.

Printed and Bound in the UK using 100% Renewable Electricity at CPI Group (UK) Ltd, Croydon, CR0 4YY

For Stephanie Booth. We're rewriting the story.

And to PB, PB, BB, and BB.

Chapter One

There was probably nothing wrong. Nothing wrong at all. And, even if there was, Miss Daphne Smith was almost certain it wasn't her fault.

But she wouldn't know until she opened the door. The trouble was, the act of opening the door would bring her closer to the problem, whatever it was. That was why tendrils of panic were curling around her heart, why her stays were so painfully tight, why spots were flickering in the corners of her vision, dancing and dark.

Daphne took what she had intended to be a long, deep breath, and only succeeded in feeling stifled, her corset suffocating. The door of the Pike's study remained resolutely shut. As it would—Daphne had made no move to open it.

This is ridiculous, she tried to tell herself in the privacy of her own mind—the only place where she felt comfortable to voice her thoughts. The very idea of opening her mouth and sharing them with the world... *No.*

And now, on a perfectly ordinary Thursday afternoon,

she was expected to stay calm when summoned—by a footman no less—to the Pike's study?

Miss Pike. She really must remember to call the woman by her proper name.

Daphne swallowed. Her mouth was dry, the action scraping painfully across her throat. Still, her fingers did not leave her side.

The door opened.

'What are you doing out there, Miss Smith?' snapped Miss Pike. 'I sent for you ten minutes ago. Come in.'

Though it was tempting to fold gently onto the carpet and feign a faint, Daphne found herself completely unable to do so. She was shy, yes, but she was not ridiculous.

'My apologies, Miss Pike,' she murmured as she stepped past the irate proprietress of the Wallflower Academy and into the small room.

What she wanted to say was, *Ten minutes is typically insufficient time to traverse from the croquet lawn to your study, Miss Pike, as you well know!*

But those were inside thoughts—what she thought but was not permitted to say.

Daphne swallowed hard, trying to put out of her mind the towering governess who had terrified her as a child.

Inside thoughts. Inside thoughts. No one wants to hear your true opinion, Daphne Smith...

It was many months since she had last been in here. This was not a room that many of the wallflowers currently in residence at the Wallflower Academy wished to enter. Doing so typically meant that their proprietress, who had taken on the status of some sort of god while living here, was displeased. To have earned Miss Pike's displeasure was to have transgressed—although Daphne had to admit that sometimes it could be something as simple as having an un-darned hem or an opinion about…well…about anything.

The Pike was not wholly supportive of opinions. Namely, other people's…

Daphne knew her cheeks were reddening as Miss Pike slammed the door behind them, and equally knew there was nothing she could do about it. She could also do little to stem the flow of Miss Pike's tirade.

'I don't know, Miss Smith—you have been a resident with us for so long, I would have thought by now you would have gained at least the very basic understanding…'

Daphne rather supposed she would. Because it was true; she had been at the Wallflower Academy an awfully long time. Painfully long.

I have only been a resident with you so long, Miss Pike, because my father is ashamed of me.

Inside thoughts. Mustn't let out the inside thoughts.

'Descended as you are from one of this nation's most prominent families…'

Doing her utmost not to wince, Daphne tried not to think about what her father would have said at Miss Pike's description: 'one of the nation's most prominent families'.

Yes. That was what made having an illegitimate daughter so difficult for her father.

'Done my best, really I have, but to be quite frank with you, Miss Smith, you have never given me much to work with.'

Heat blossomed over Daphne's face at Miss Pike's words. Yes, she was a wallflower—a true one, unlike so many of the other ladies sent to the Wallflower Academy by their families when unwanted, too awkward to keep around.

She was shy—a word that Miss Pike detested and had come to forbid, though the pronouncement could not alter Daphne's character. Even Daphne could not do such a thing, try as she had when she had first arrived.

'And so I was delighted to receive your father's letter!'

Daphne's eyes sharpened and she focused on the older woman who had settled in the seat on the opposite side of the impressive desk. 'I beg your pardon?'

'Your father's letter,' repeated Miss Pike, gesturing at a piece of paper lying on her desk. 'I presume he wrote to you also?'

Daphne swallowed hard before replying.

Well, yes, he did write to her. Once a year, near her birthday—never actually getting the date right, but the month was always correct. Almost always...

Inside thoughts.

'Yes,' she said slowly, mentally scanning each word before she uttered it to ensure she was, technically, telling the truth. 'Yes, my father writes to me.'

Miss Pike beamed—an expression with which she had rarely treated Daphne during the years they had known each other. 'Then let me be the first to say… congratulations!'

Daphne blinked.

The room was silent, save for the longcase clock that merrily ticked just off-key. The words Miss Pike had uttered echoed around Daphne's mind and she desperately attempted to understand them.

Congratulations? For what?

'I…' *Say something, Daphne, say something.* 'I…'

Congratulations? Mind whirling, desperately attempting to understand what on earth the Pike could be referring to, Daphne could only think of two possibilities, each as unlikely as each other.

Perhaps—and it was a very doubtful perhaps—her stepmother was with child. It would be unusual; her stepmother had a child already grown to full manhood. He had, in fact, married one of Daphne's close friends. Still, it was not impossible. She'd experienced plenty of inside thoughts about that, though thankfully none had slipped from her tongue.

Or perhaps… No, her father would not do such a thing…

'Ah, here he is!' Miss Pike rose with a pretty curtsey as the door opened.

Turning, Daphne saw her father. She examined him, just for a moment. How often did one get to look at the Earl of Norbury up close? He looked…older. That was hardly surprising; it was nigh on six months since she had last seen him, and he was of that age now where a hard year could roughen one's skin quite drastically.

The summer months had come and gone, and she had not seen him. The leaves were just starting to golden, and now here he was.

'Daphne,' said the Earl of Norbury with a smart nod.

Daphne knew there was little she could do to quell the heat that would rise through her chest and across her neck to her cheeks, so she did nothing to avoid it. Curtseying low to her father, as befitted his rank and station, she allowed the chatter to wash over her.

'Most exciting, my lord. I must congratulate you...'

'Impressive, I must say so myself, though I knew I would be successful...'

Daphne listened closely, as was her habit, but could distinguish little in the way of clues within their speech. Why were they to be congratulated? Why had she been summoned to the Pike's room?

'And I suppose it is Daphne we must celebrate,' her father said with a broad smile.

William Prendergast, Earl of Norbury, was not an unkind man. Daphne knew this, as she knew that the earth spun round the sun. With both, warmth changed over the seasons.

'Celebrate?' she repeated, hating how quiet her voice was but finding no inclination within herself to strengthen it.

'Yes, for your... Does she not know?' said Miss Pike, turning to Daphne's father.

The Earl of Norbury drew himself up as though about to announce a success on the field of battle—and for a shimmering moment, just before the words left his mouth, Daphne knew. She knew what he was going to say. She just couldn't believe it.

'Daphne, my girl,' he said proudly. 'You are getting married.'

And that was when Daphne's mind entirely ceased to work.

Married. *Married.* Married?

Her—married—at a wedding. Gaining a husband, being married...

'No,' Daphne breathed.

No one was listening. Miss Pike was delighting over the fact that the Wallflower Academy would have another wedding to celebrate, her father was congratulating himself on the impressive connections of the groom, and Daphne...

Daphne merely stood there, unable to understand what had happened.

Married? She was a wallflower, not a wife. She stuttered and stammered in the presence of those she did not know. She coloured and blushed at the merest look from a gentleman—any man! She hated attention, dreaded entertaining and had once accidentally trodden on a man's foot so heavily that he had been forced to retire not only from the dancing, but from the ball itself. Sylvia had said the man had been forced to have his shoe cut away from his foot.

An unbidden smile crept across Daphne's face. Sylvia really was most ridiculous. The smile disappeared almost as soon as it had arrived. Sylvia was gone now, married, like Daphne's two other friends. She was alone.

Though, by the sound of it, she would not be alone for long…

'Three or four weeks, that is all that is required,' Miss Pike was saying. 'I will assist in any way I can.'

'Married?'

It was only when her father and the Pike both turned that Daphne realised she had spoken aloud. Cheeks flaming red, she said awkwardly, 'I mean…married?'

'You are the daughter of an earl,' her father said stiffly. 'Did you expect to find your own suitor, my child? I am your father, and I am a peer of the realm. I have arranged your marriage.'

An—an arranged marriage? Daphne was not sure why she was so surprised. It was a perfectly logical thing to happen. Daughters of great houses were paired off with sons of great houses every week. She read about them in the newspapers.

It was just, she had never expected…

And then the words she was thinking accidentally spilled out from her mouth. 'But why would a gentleman wish to marry me? Marry an illegitimate daughter?'

The Earl of Norbury's face reddened, and Daphne was reminded just from where she gained that particularly powerful colour.

Miss Pike gasped, her eyes flickering between the two, waiting for a pronouncement from her father.

Daphne swallowed. *Ah.* Yes, that was probably one of the inside thoughts that should have remained on the inside. *Oh, botheration.*

'You are my daughter,' the Earl of Norbury said stiffly. 'Do you think I should be ashamed of you, is that it?'

No, of course it wasn't, Daphne wanted to say in a strong, clear voice. *But I would be absolutely beyond the realms of sense if I did not enquire as to what gentleman—who presumably has a good name and character, by the way Miss Pike is celebrating—would want to marry a woman who can barely string two sentences together in public, who has no name save Smith, no true birth due to a stain of illegitimacy and, moreover, he has never met!*

Perhaps another woman could have uttered those words—another Daphne, in another time. A Daphne free of the restrictions beaten into her.

This Daphne merely muttered down at her feet. 'N-no. I shall obey you, Father. I will marry whomsoever you choose.'

What choice did she have?

When she was brave enough to lift her eyes, it was to see that her father appeared mollified. 'Well, good.'

'As any daughter should,' Miss Pike interjected.

'Yes, yes, I quite agree, Miss Pike,' said the Earl of Norbury quietly. 'But...but my daughter has an enquiring mind, and I can forgive her for that.'

A flash of anger made heat once again seep into Daphne's cheeks. 'How dare you—forgive me for having a mind? The arrogance! Should a woman merely cease to have opinions in the presence of men?'

At least, that was what she would have said, if she

could have been certain her father would not immediately berate her for being an ungrateful child.

Inside thoughts.

And so she just stood there, meek and mild, waiting to see what her father would say next.

The Earl of Norbury sighed. 'Daphne, it will not surprise you to learn that, after a year of marriage, it has become clear to me that your stepmother and I... She has left her childbearing years.'

It did not surprise her, but Daphne was far too circumspect to make that obvious. Widening her eyes carefully, she murmured, 'I am sorry to hear that, Father.'

'Not as sorry as I am,' the man said gruffly. 'I always thought an heir would come along, one way or another. If only you had been born a son...but there it is. I married for love, in the end, more fool me. Perhaps I should have married a younger woman, planted an heir in her, but as it is I do love...'

Daphne swallowed hard as her father cleared his throat. It was an unusually open speech, one she had not heard him give in all her years.

It appeared Miss Pike was just as surprised. The older woman's eyes were goggling, and she gently lowered herself onto a seat by her desk.

'As it is, I have no other choice but to do it,' the Earl of Norbury said, his voice gaining strength. 'Others may think me mad, but there it is.'

And now Daphne was utterly lost. No other choice but to do...what?

Within moments her unspoken question was answered, and not in the way she expected.

The Earl of Norbury grinned ruefully. 'Daphne, you are now my heir. Well, my financial heir, as you know the title will go to a distant cousin—but you will inherit my entire private fortune. I settled with the solicitors a week ago.'

It was fortunate indeed that there was a chair just to Daphne's left. When her knees gave way, she was—almost elegantly—able to collapse onto it.

Her...her father's heir? No. No, she must have misunderstood in some way. It was not possible.

'That means you now have a dowry,' her father said quietly.

At least he spoke quietly, Daphne thought. It could just have been the whirling, pounding rush of her pulse drowning out the strength of his voice. It was all she could hear: the thrum, thrum, thrum of her increasingly pacing pulse.

A dowry? Her?

'Daphne?'

No, it was not possible. Dowries did not just drop into the laps of illegitimate daughters—unless her father was truly in earnest and he did not intend to betray his wife. That would mean no other children...

She would be his only child.

His heir.

'Daphne, are you listening to me?'

Daphne blinked hurriedly and looked up. Her father

was still standing, his hands folded behind his back now in a posture of business.

Yes, that was all this was—she had to remember that. This was money, inheritance and alliance. That was all.

But it would also give her a future.

Mere minutes ago, she had been standing outside this room, terrified about what she was going to find within it. Now here she was, seated by Miss Pike's desk, an heiress.

An *engaged* heiress.

'Daphne,' her father said quietly, sharpness gone from his tone. 'Daphne, you now have a dowry of sixty thousand pounds.'

Daphne fell off the chair.

'Miss Smith, oh heavens!'

'Daphne—are you quite well?'

Strong yet gentle hands manoeuvred her from the floor and back onto the chair. Daphne's head swam, the dizziness which had overcome her still lingering in the corners of her mind.

'I do apologise,' she said quietly, needing to ascertain whether she had been momentarily dreaming. 'I think you said—you said I had a dowry of six thousand pounds.'

She blinked, her father's wry smile coming into focus.

'Not quite,' said the Earl of Norbury lightly. '*Sixty* thousand—and, when I die, you will inherit my twelve thousand a year. I will make provision for the support of my wife if she outlives me, naturally.'

She was dreaming. Yes, that was it. Daphne was not

sure why this dream appeared so realistic, but it was a most strange one. It was only a dream. 'Oh, naturally, naturally.'

She almost laughed, a strange, hysterical squawk trapped in her throat. This was madness. Madness! Sixty thousand pounds? Twelve thousand a year? How on earth her mind had managed to concoct such a fantasy, she would never know!

Besides, this man—whoever he was—would surely be disappointed to be presented with a wallflower like herself. She was no beauty, no great wit. She had a poor singing voice and played the pianoforte very ill. Her painting was acceptable, but not remarkable, and she had no talent with a needle...

And she was a wallflower. What man would want a wallflower for a wife?

'Your father is being very generous, Miss Smith,' Miss Pike hissed from the other side of the desk. 'You might wish to thank him!'

'Thank him?' Daphne repeated, still dazed.

Thank him—for riches beyond anything most duchesses could imagine? For arranging a marriage to a man she'd never met without consulting her? For making her his heir, and therefore transforming her life into something she could never have predicted?

Her temple throbbed, the light-headedness still present.

This cannot be anything more than a dream...can it?

'You may thank me, if you choose,' said her father stiffly.

When Daphne blinked and her father came into greater focus, it was to see the Earl of Norbury looking...hopeful. Perhaps she had knocked her head when she had slipped off the chair. She could certainly not recall her father ever being hopeful in the past for any sign of favour from his daughter.

'Th-thank you, Father,' Daphne managed. 'But—but sixty thousand pounds! It is a king's ransom!'

'Yes, I suppose it is,' he said, with a smile she did not understand. 'Heed me well, Daphne. The man who has asked for and been granted your hand is a gentleman, with all the sensibilities of a gentleman. But he is, well, shall we say, a tad low on funds...?'

And just when she was starting to believe the fairy tale, believe her luck had finally turned, believe a happily ever after might actually be possible for her, Daphne was brought right back to earth...

Low on funds. So, her future husband was what—a gambler? A spendthrift? A wastrel? All of the above?

Do not ask, do not let the questions pass your lips, do not speak up...

'He is more than happy to keep the, ahem, exact nature of your birth a secret,' the Earl of Norbury continued. 'He is a very kind man, a very good one—at least, his letters certainly make him appear so.'

And that was when Daphne stopped listening.

Of course. Her father might preen and congratulate himself on securing a husband for his embarrassment of a daughter, the one he had kept hidden away at the Wallflower Academy, but he had never actually met the man. Her future husband could be hideous! A monster! Cruel and distasteful!

And it would not matter.

The thought was painful, but Daphne could not deny it. She would marry this man, whoever he was, and she would be grateful. He surely could not be as dull as living at the Wallflower Academy for another twelvemonth…?

'So, off you go,' said Miss Pike brightly.

Daphne stared. 'I—I beg your pard…?'

'I knew you were not listening! Honestly, Miss Smith, you are going to have to do much better than that when you are married,' Miss Pike said with a shake of her head. 'I said, they will be expecting you at afternoon tea. Off you go.'

It appeared there was no more for her to say or do. Rising slowly to her feet, gingerly hoping her knees would hold her, Daphne curtseyed low to both the Pike and her father.

Only the latter responded, and it was with a very slight incline of his head. 'No need to fret, Daphne. Everything will be organised to my expectations.'

And that was why Daphne Smith left the room in a complete daze, knowing she was going to get married—and with absolutely no idea to whom.

Chapter Two

There was no need to fret. Everything had been organised to Christoph's expectations, and so...he would marry her, this woman he had never met.

Perhaps this was a mistake.

The thought had flitted into Christoph's mind before he could take it captive—which was unlike him. Rigid control was the way he had managed to keep himself alive this long. Was he truly going to give up on that restraint now?

The English countryside shimmered past the window as the carriage rumbled along the roads. It was not as he had imagined it. It was wider, and greener, even with the gold and red that were starting to flicker past the windows as the carriage picked up speed going downhill.

Do not think about it. Do not think about her.

Easier said than done. Ever since he had intercepted the letter from the Earl of Norbury agreeing to the match, Christoph had wondered about this woman who was going to utterly change the course of his life.

Miss Daphne Smith. It was a pretty name. He would

have to hope she was amenable to his proposal. He was doing the right thing, he knew he was, but even Christoph could admit his plan was quite extraordinary. If it wasn't for the danger...

But, no. Christoph shifted in his seat, the discomfort from the long journey starting to make his bones ache. He could not do a thing about his brother now, save marry, and he was doing all he could to hasten that along. He would just have to hope his brother would not find out in time to prevent the wedding. Anton's spies were everywhere.

Christoph steeled himself. This was his plan, his very own, careful plan, concocted over time and designed for his betterment.

'You are in charge of your own destiny,' Christoph muttered to himself in the privacy of the rattling carriage. 'You are not going to let your brother control you. You are going to return one day and show him what it means to be a man—be a leader.'

Besides, the plan was going perfectly, was it not? He had managed to leave Niedernlein; he had made his way safely to England; he had agreed to the marriage contract with the Earl of Norbury.

All he had to do now was marry the woman. Anything to save Laura.

His fingers tightened on the letter he had been attempting to get through since he had left London. Each line was splattered with marks that could be tears. The capitals shook, as though the hand that had inscribed them had been unsteady.

But Christoph knew the truth. Laura was writing with her left hand.

I heal nicely from that ridiculous accident—how silly of me to slip on that step!

Christoph's jaw tightened. He knew precisely what his sister truly meant: how silly of her to anger Anton to such an extent that he would break her wrist.

The weather is poor here so sadly I am hemmed inside most of the day.

He knew what that meant, too: Laura was not permitted her daily rides.

But thankfully I have sufficient books to entertain me—though I would appreciate some new titles.

Barred from the library, too. Christoph's pulse throbbed at his temple. Unable to spill her true thoughts, Laura was being careful in her letters to her brother in England. As well she should.

And I hope to receive good tidings from you, dearest brother.

Please, please rescue me: that was what his sister was really saying.

The carriage lurched, taking a corner at speed and attempting to slow simultaneously. Christoph's head bumped against the door, his gaze twisting towards the window.

His mouth fell open. It wasn't as though he had not lived in impressive homes in the past. The Winter Palace in particular had always been heralded as one of the most stirring displays of architecture in the whole of Niedernlein.

But this? It was a tall building, perhaps three or four storeys, and wide; wider than could be properly seen from the carriage. The red brick glowed in the afternoon sun, blazing as though it were on fire, the gleam of sunshine on the many windows adding to the impression. The chimneys were tall, towering, spiralling up into the brilliant blue sky.

Christoph swallowed. He knew the woman was wealthy, yes, but this? This was akin to one of the royal palaces he had seen in London.

When his carriage finally came to a stop, he discovered much to his discomfort that the rattling sensation was from inside him, not thanks to the rumbling wheels. His legs felt strange; not weak, not quite shaking, but not too dissimilar.

Well, this was it.

He had come a long way, and he was not going to veer from his plan merely because he was intimidated by the woman's home. This was what he had come for.

Not waiting for the coachman to open the door, Christoph jumped down and relished the crunch of gravel under his feet. It was grounding, earthing, reminding him his journey was almost over.

The bell jangled loudly when he tugged the pull, and the man who opened the door looked none too impressed at being summoned.

'Yes?' he said, peering at him.

Christoph plastered his most charming smile upon his lips as his focus took in the large hall, the elevated ceiling, the paintings and the...women?

Yes, women. Several.

True, he had hoped to be gifted a glance of the elusive Miss Smith—her father had refused to send any portrait, as was his right, but still, it had been frustrating. But Christoph did not see a single woman, but many. Far too many. Six, seven, eight...they poured down the staircase as though summoned by a bell, some of them drifting lazily across the hall to another doorway, some lingering and chattering, some whispering, a few glancing in his direction.

Christoph could not help but stare. The Earl of Norbury had mentioned a daughter, yes, but this many? The man must have been prolific in his day...and had several sets of twins. The ladies were surely all too close in age to be...?

'Yes?'

Christoph started. The aggressive tone of the footman was perhaps not entirely warranted, but then he had been terribly rude, standing in his mute state. 'I—I am here to see Miss Smith and Miss Pike.'

Miss Pike—the governess, he assumed. The Earl of Norbury had mentioned her several times in his letters but had given little indication as to her status in the household.

One of the ladies giggled and Christoph did everything he could not to turn his head.

'Hmm,' muttered the footman, as though unimpressed, unsure whether Christoph had earned the right to enter.

'Ah, our honoured guest!'

His attention jerked to the right as an older woman floated towards him with a beaming smile. She curtseyed low and simpered as Christoph bowed.

'Are you expecting him?' the footman asked in a quiet voice.

'Miss Pike, I presume?' Christoph asked, ignoring the footman as, to the best of his ability, he attempted to ignore the stares of the women now clustering at the foot of the stairs and whispering. One of them pointed.

What was going on here? Surely these could not all be Miss Smiths? The Earl of Norbury would bankrupt himself to marry them all off! So what was this—a house party? A house party of…only ladies? Well, that was certainly one way to ensure no gentleman had their way with His Lordship's daughter…

'I am Miss Pike and I am delighted to welcome you to the Wallflower Academy,' said the woman brightly. 'Come in, come in.'

Christoph did indeed enter, though gingerly. The woman had said… 'Wallflower Academy?'

'Oh, yes, only the very best send their daughters here to refine their accomplishments,' said Miss Pike happily, stepping back as he moved into the centre of the remarkable hall. 'We help the ladies find the right suitors if they are not particularly forward in their courtships, as you can imagine. A nudge here, an introduction there...'

She trailed off as she gestured with one hand in what she probably thought was an elegant way.

Christoph's jaw tightened.

Ah. So a school, then. A school for ladies no one wished to marry. The Earl of Norbury had not been so descriptive.

Well, the whole thing had been far too good to be true. He should have expected something like this; earls did not attempt to marry off illegitimate daughters with a dowry like *that*, and with the help of a school, unless there was something distasteful about her. But he needed the dowry—desperately.

Was she unpleasant to look at? Or was it unpleasant to be in her presence?

'Miss Smith awaits us in my private sitting room,' Miss Pike said, gesturing to a door to her left. 'She is most anxious to meet you, as you can imagine.'

Christoph's charming smile was starting to waver. 'Undoubtedly.'

You made this decision before you had ever met the woman, he told himself sternly, *and, no matter what she is like, you will go through with it.* There was no other option.

'Come, let us not leave the young lady in suspense.' Miss Pike strode to the door and opened it, pushing it open but not stepping through. When she turned to face him, there was a glittering in her eyes. 'After you, of course.'

Of course. Inclining his head and bracing himself for a truly unpleasant encounter—one he would have to charm his way through—Christoph stepped into the room and discovered a light, bright sitting room elegantly decorated in pastel blues and gold with sparse furniture, save for a settee and three armchairs. On one of those armchairs sat a woman, a woman who rose to her feet as he entered the room.

And she… Christoph's lips parted.

She was beautiful.

No, 'beautiful' was not a sufficient description. Perhaps there was not the vocabulary in the English language to fully encapsulate the woman's appearance.

She was of middling height, with a sweeping bust restrained by good quality muslin and a shawl of silk that was tucked over her shoulders. Her hair was golden, with few curls—it appeared this was not a woman who would sacrifice her own sleep to create a coiffure of the latest fashion.

And her face… Christoph's stomach lurched. There was fear there, hidden amongst the beauty. A shadow of concern darkened her otherwise blue eyes, and her shell-pink lips were pressed together in unmistakable nervousness.

'You,' he said, forgetting proper manners.

Miss Smith—for that was surely who she was—did not respond. Instead her cheeks coloured to a rich rose-red, her eyes dropping immediately to her hands, which twisted before her.

Ah. Shy, then. Well, Christoph had imagined far worse.

And then he hardened his heart—no, this was perfect. For his plan to succeed, he did not want a chattering, forward, inquisitive wife. He needed someone who would allow the marriage to go ahead with no quibbles. He must not permit himself to become distracted.

'Miss Smith, may I introduce you to Prince Christoph Augustus Maximilian Henricus…? You must excuse me, Your Highness, I have quite forgotten!'

Miss Pike's tinkling laugh filled the room but Christoph did not turn to her.

Instead, he kept his eyes firmly fixed on Miss Smith. 'Christoph Augustus Heinrich Maximus Anton Philip von Auberheiser, at your service, my lady.'

Although he had not considered it possible, Miss Smith's cheeks became even redder. When her lips parted, sound definitely came out. It was just that none of the sounds could be understood.

'Come now, Daphne, pull yourself together!'

Christoph jumped at the sudden snap from the woman behind him.

Miss Pike stepped forward between them and glared at her charge before turning to him with a smile. 'You must forgive Miss Smith, Your Highness. She is a mite shy with strangers but is quite gregarious…eh…when she feels comfortable.'

'Just "my lord" is fine.'

He should not have said anything. Miss Pike's brow furrowed. 'I beg your pardon?'

'Not "Your Highness", just…just "my lord" will suffice, thank you.'

Christoph was hardly going to explain it here. He wasn't his father. He wasn't his brother. He didn't demand ridiculous obsequiousness to prop up his ego. He didn't want to be part of that world any longer.

Miss Pike was rattling off a list of accomplishments, presumably all belonging to Miss Smith, whose attention was still focused on her twisting fingers.

Christoph swallowed.

Remain detached, he told himself. *Yes, being detached is not in your nature, but you have to try to keep to the plan. You cannot fail now. You've come too far, risked too much.*

'Miss Smith,' he said curtly, interrupting the paean about the gifts Miss Smith evidently possessed. 'You are how many years?'

Miss Pike's little gasp of concern evidently signalled her surprise at his rudeness, but Christoph could not afford to beat about the bush. He had to be distant. He had to treat this as it was: as an arrangement. Sympathising with her would doubtless make him vulnerable, weak.

Miss Smith did not raise her eyes as she spoke, but at least the words had formed this time. 'I—I am two and twenty.'

'And you have lived here how long?' Christoph said mercilessly, hating the coldness in his tone.

'Several years.'

How interestingly vague. He glanced at Miss Pike, who must surely be the owner or proprietress here, and saw her cheeks redden slightly in turn.

So...a long time. A very long time, if he was any judge. So why had Miss Smith been hidden away for so long? Illegitimate, yes—he knew that. But there was something more.

'And you have received no offers in that time?'

Christoph could have cooked an egg on the young woman's face, if he could have stepped closer. And knew how to cook an egg.

'No, my lord.'

At least she had not followed Miss Pike in giving him that ridiculous title. Christoph stepped closer, knowing it was beyond good etiquette, but needing to be nearer this woman.

She was shy, that much was evident. He rather suspected that, with Miss Pike in the room to intimidate the young woman, she would likely or not revert to nodding or shaking her head in reply. Anything to avoid direct conversation. Yes, it could not be more clear that she wished herself elsewhere.

'And your father has arranged a match for you. How do you feel about that?'

Even Christoph had to admit it was perhaps an unfair question: direct, sharp and deeply personal.

Miss Smith gasped and her eyes flickered uncertainly to Miss Pike, who stepped forward again and smoothly began, 'Oh, Daphne is most delighted by the kind attentions of both her father and yourself, Your High...'

This could not continue. 'Miss Pike, would you do me the honour of gifting me ten minutes alone with my future bride?'

Christoph had not intended to be so blunt, but he had to speak with Miss Smith without Miss Pike's interference.

'Alone?' The older woman blinked in abject horror. 'You—you cannot possibly...?'

'Miss Smith and I are to marry and will spend a great deal of time alone,' Christoph said harshly, ignoring the shocked gasp from his left. 'There are certain things that I would like to discuss with Miss Smith, as I can imagine you understand, and with Miss Smith only. Ten minutes will suffice.'

They would have to. From the disgruntled expression on Miss Pike's face, he could see he would be permitted no more—perhaps fewer. He would not put it past the woman to barge back into the room at any moment... but she did, finally, acquiesce.

'And not a minute more!' Miss Pike said over her shoulder before closing the door.

Right. Well, that was sufficiently awkward. Now to make things...hell...even more awkward.

Steeling himself, Christoph turned to the woman who would in a few weeks be his wife.

His wife.

He shook his head slightly to dislodge the thought and

gestured to the armchair Miss Smith had so recently vacated. 'Please.'

She appeared to fall rather than lower herself into the chair, but Christoph attempted to ignore that as he sat in the chair opposite. Her gaze was once again fixed on her hands, her cheeks still pink. The silence eked out, moment by moment, each passing second making it more difficult to break.

'Your accent is very good.'

Christoph's eyes widened. 'It is?'

Miss Smith nodded and asked her knees, 'Far better than my German.'

More silence. He hardly knew whether to remark that there was no need for her to learn German, enquire as to whether she had learned any German—unusual, for an Englishwoman—or ask just what part of his accent let him down...

Foolish questions. Questions a lover would ask, a friend. And he was neither.

Christoph cleared his throat. 'Miss Smith, I would like to learn more about you. Your past. Why you are here.'

To his surprise, Miss Smith looked up and spoke in a low, level voice that was perhaps more of a recitation than a response. 'My father sired me out of wedlock and my mother died when I was five or six... I am not sure. My father placed me here in the Wallflower Academy and this is where I have been raised ever since.'

'Your mother died?' It was not what he had intended to say, yet the words slipped out before Christoph could halt them.

Miss Smith looked a little startled at his directness. A pink flush tinged her collarbone. 'Yes. Consumption.'

'My mother died of the same thing,' Christoph said, his voice suddenly hoarse. 'It was awful. To lose such a person, and in such a way…'

'It never leaves you, does it?' Miss Smith said softly. 'The pain.'

It was not so much a laugh, as a bark of agony. 'I thought for a time I would never… That the sun would never… That I could never feel…'

Christoph swallowed hard. Dear God, where had that come from? One moment he was interviewing his future bride, the next she had his most private thoughts stumbling from his lips. The glimmer of vulnerability had to be stamped out. He could not allow himself to show such weakness.

'I am sorry for your loss.' Miss Smith's voice was still soft, but there was a curiosity in it now. A curiosity that he simply could not permit.

Christoph straightened, blinking back the tears that he would not shed. 'Yes. Well, let us not speak of that, but continue on. Your mother died. Your father lives.'

Miss Smith inclined her head. 'My father, the Earl of Norbury, has been very good to me.'

There was a mechanical nature to her speech that suggested she had prepared the answer—evidently she had expected to be quizzed in this way.

Well, perhaps not in this way. Even Christoph had been slightly mortified at how his questioning had begun so interrogatively. 'And you did not live—you have never lived—with your father?'

Miss Smith shook her head. Evidently no words were needed for that one.

Christoph bit his lips, trying to decide how to proceed. If to proceed. No, he had to. Miss Smith was his best possible hope, his only hope to gain a fortune and live independently in England, in safety. If he did not wed soon, his absence at home would be missed. God forbid his brother came after him before the wedding was complete…

But, once the vows were exchanged, that would be it. His brother would hardly risk upsetting the Regent of Great Britain over a marriage which could not be undone. He valued his reputation, at least the one that people outside his family had of him, far too highly.

This was Christoph's opportunity for a fresh start. A new life, a new beginning in England—and he needed an English woman at his side. She would…guide him. Propel him into English Society. Help him to…

'He…he…'

Christoph looked up. It was the first time Miss Smith had offered something as a statement, rather than responding to a question, and it was clearly an effort. Delicate fingertips tugged at her gown, pulling at a loose thread, and her gaze did not lift to meet his as she spoke.

'He…he did not want the shame of me,' she said in a rush.

After waiting for a moment for more, Christoph said quietly, 'The shame of you?'

Miss Smith shook her head, staring down at her knees. Her cheeks were a scalding red now, so bright a colour that her cheeks must be burning. 'It… I am not widely known. Most do not know the Earl of Norbury has an illegitimate child and…and he did not want… He wouldn't…'

When she had truly trailed off into silence and it appeared she would not be imparting any more, Christoph nodded curtly. Well, it was not too dissimilar from what he had expected. Every illegitimate child, after all, was a stain on one's respectability. Even an earl would not wish the knowledge to become widely spread.

'I see,' he said quietly.

Somehow he had come closer—he could not tell when. Something in this woman drew him to her. She was beautiful. Very beautiful. Why had this Norbury man not led with that?

'And I am shy,' Miss Smith said in a rush.

Christoph smiled as a rush of something poured through his veins. 'Shy?'

She *was* shy, wasn't she? And yet there was something… An archness to the mouth, an intelligence in the eyes. It was quite clear that, though this woman said little, she thought very much.

She was intriguing. *Attractive*.

Christoph pulled away from the thought as swiftly as he could. Not attractive…no. He could not permit himself to be side-tracked by such things. He was here to save his sister, no other reason. Mere attraction could lead to desire. Desire could lead to errors. Errors could see his sister killed.

He would not allow desire to sidetrack him from his only purpose. Even if she was...alluring.

'Yes, shy,' said Miss Smith, and for a moment her whole expression changed. 'Though I suppose some husbands would prefer a meek and mild wife, ready to obey whatever foolishness they—'

Her words halted in an instant, her hands at her mouth, horror in her eyes.

Christoph's stomach lurched. Oh, there was far more to this Miss Smith than met the eye. He'd had a glimpse, that was all it was, but a momentary revelation that below the quietness and obedience was someone who thought boldly.

He tried to stifle his smile. He did not manage it. 'You are a radical, then?'

Miss Smith shook her head, hands still covering her mouth, what little of her cheeks he could see flaming red.

'It is not my business to forbid my wife thoughts or speech,' Christoph said, far more gently than he'd intended. 'An arranged marriage cannot hope for love, but it should expect respect.'

Miss Smith's eyes were wide. When she spoke, her hands slowly lowering, it was in a breathless voice. 'Respect?'

A frown creased Christoph's forehead. Did these English not respect their wives?

'I... I will respect you, my lord,' Miss Smith added

hastily. 'And I will give you everything that a husband requires. Everything.'

And, before he could reply, before he could explain that he had meant that respect went in two directions, Miss Smith...looked at him.

What a look. Christoph could feel the burn of her gaze as it flickered up and down, taking him in afresh, and could see the ferocity, the sensual hunger, that flashed in her eyes, like those of a wanton woman who thirsted for the touch of a man.

Then it was gone, and the abject look of horror had returned to Miss Smith's face. 'You will not wish to marry me now.'

Christoph's breath caught in his throat. Miss Smith had smiled as she spoke, finally, a devastatingly pure defiance in her face as she did so.

Did she wish that...? Or was she afraid that he would walk out of this Wallflower School, or whatever it was called, with their arranged marriage broken?

'No,' he said quietly.

Best to get it done and over with. That was the plan. He had to follow the plan. *Do not get attached.*

'No, I wish to marry you. What date do you wish— Thursday in three weeks, or four weeks?'

Chapter Three

'Oh, isn't it darling?'

'Absolutely hideous.'

'How can you say that? Look at the lace, look at the stripes…'

'Look at the colours! You honestly want to put Daphne—our Daphne—in orange and pink?'

The raucous laughter of Daphne's friends filled the renowned modiste Madame Lavigne's shop and Daphne attempted to smile, trapped as she was in a seat that was far too stuffed, and weighed down with five different fabric samples in her lap, two bonnets to examine, a half-open parasol, a pair of elegant dancing shoes, a rack of ribbons that she apparently had to choose from and the burden of her friends' expectations.

Perhaps this had not been a good idea.

'This was such a good idea,' declared Sylvia, Duchess of Camrose, hands resting on the swell of her stomach. 'I haven't had this much fun in ages.'

'What, getting tired of that husband of yours?' asked Rilla, Countess of Staromchor dryly.

The women's giggles echoed around the entire modiste's establishment. That would have been mortifying to Daphne, had her father not insisted on booking the entire place for the whole day. His note to the modiste, via the footman who had escorted her, had explained that his daughter was extremely private, and that, with her wedding to a prince, they would need to be careful to keep it discreet, and would not need to be 'gawped at by all and sundry, as a lady of similar taste like yourself is sure to understand'.

And the modiste did understand. Daphne was sure the clink of coins passing from one hand to the other had helped.

Still, she should not complain. She was here, with her good friends…and she was getting married. After years of having lived together at the Wallflower Academy—laughing together at the Pike, suffering through the awkward Society dinners, and then Daphne being left behind by first one, then the second, then the third—it was pleasant to spend a little time with them.

Even if Daphne thought them all incorrigible.

'This silk embroidery truly is exquisite,' Rilla was saying, her unseeing eyes unfocused before her as her attention centred on the delicate feel of the blue silk in her hands. 'I shall have to have some for Florence. She may only be a few months, but she deserves beautiful things. You should choose this for your wedding gown, Daphne.'

'Blue? Absolutely not. Our girl suits green,' Gwen, Duchess of Knaresby, said firmly. 'I mean, look at this!'

In her hands was a bolt of delicious forest-green silk. There was no pattern, no embroidery—it did not need it. The shimmering colour alone was sufficient.

Daphne swallowed. It all seemed very...excessive. She could hardly recall the last time her father had given Miss Pike additional funds for a new pair of gloves, let alone a silk gown. Parasols, gloves, bonnets, reticules, pelisses, two types of riding boot and stockings adorned the plethora of tables to her left and right. She had ignored them until now, hoping she could almost forget they were there.

'Why restrict yourself?' Sylvia was grinning, having thrown herself down on a *chaise longue* just to Daphne's right. She was holding a very stylish bonnet trimmed with golden feathers to her breast, a perfect match for her glowing black skin. 'Have a gown made of every colour, Daphne. Your father can afford it!'

Her friends' laughter rang out and Daphne tried to smile. She should be smiling. She knew she should. What woman would not wish to be welcomed into Madame Lavigne's and told she could order whatever she wanted? What woman would not wish to be married?

What woman would not wish to be married to a prince?

What date do you wish—this Thursday in three weeks, or four weeks?

Swallowing again, and finding to her discomfort that it did nothing to calm her nerves, she tried to smile. 'It's...it's all so much.'

'And not half of what you deserve, either,' Sylvia said

sternly, before breaking out into a smile. 'And, if Rilla is ordering a tiny gown for her Florence, why are you not considering a matching suit for little Perce?'

Gwen's face went soft at the thought of her son, but eighteen months old. 'He would look particularly dapper in something like that—but I am here for myself, not for little Perce.'

'Gwendoline Devereux, put that down!'

'You don't think it suits me?' preened Gwen with a laugh as she held the most stupendous corset to her chest.

'I think you would have to sell off one of those houses of yours to afford it! Are those...? That cannot be diamonds embroidered around the edges!'

'Such extravagance,' muttered Rilla with a wry smile. 'After all, diamonds are such cold, harsh things. Now feathers, on the other hand—'

'That gown of yours you wore to the theatre last week was outrageous.' Sylvia cut across her as Daphne watched her friends chatter. 'The way you had those feathers sewn into the cuffs!'

'I like to feel them—what do I care what colour a gown is?' retorted Rilla. 'Give me a velvet gown with feathers any day.'

'I think...' began Daphne quietly.

She was not exactly ignored. Her friends were too earnest for that particular cruelty. No, they simply did not hear her. Did not expect to hear her.

I think, she wanted to say, *that it doesn't matter what I wear. I'll be marrying a devastatingly handsome man, who caught me looking at him with lust, and I can never speak to him again!*

'Are not feathers considered gaudy these days?' Gwen pondered.

Sylvia snorted. 'Not the way Rilla wears them. Now that stepmother of yours, Daphne—your mother-in-law, Rilla—'

'It is a little incestuous when you put it like that,' quipped Rilla with a grin.

'The way she wears coloured feathers in her hair and bonnets, it's obscene!' continued Sylvia, entirely ignoring the interruption. 'I don't think it should be allowed.'

'And what about you, with you wearing breeches at home? Yes, I heard that particular bit of gossip!' Gwen laughed as she and Daphne saw Sylvia's pinking cheeks. 'You think I don't know? My lady's maid's sister is one of your under-maids, and she said you go about the place wearing breeches! Duchesses shouldn't wear breeches!'

'I am not a typical duchess,' Sylvia said, winking.

'Why would you…?' began Daphne.

'Good for you,' said Rilla firmly, putting down the embroidered silk she had been stroking and picking up a reticule embroidered with small pearls. 'Far more practical than skirts, I say.'

'How can you say that? As though Sylvia isn't scandalous enough…'

And so the conversation continued, with very little effort on Daphne's part. In fact, she seemed immaterial to it. Her three friends chattered on about silks, gown styles and the way one's bust changed over time; they pondered the suitability of bonnets made from Spanish straw, not English, and whether or not red could truly be coming back this Season; and, of course, whether their husbands would happily foot the bills they were swiftly running up with Madame Lavigne.

Daphne smiled wanly.

Why aren't you all listening to me?

She should be grateful. She knew she should. She had three friends who truly cared about her and did not fuss if she preferred to be silent, quiet and unobtrusive—preferably unobserved.

They were all prettier than her, cleverer than her, wittier than her. Rooms silenced to hear what Rilla had to say. Crowds listened eagerly to the tales of what Sylvia had been up to. And Gwen? Gwen could command a room by her mere presence alone.

And then there was Daphne.

She tried to maintain her smile. She tried to remind herself that these were her good friends; that they had never critiqued her or compared her poorly to themselves. But it did not matter. The sense of inadequacy was strong, and it could not be overcome by the small matter of marrying a prince.

'Oh, no, she won't like that—put it in the "no" pile,' said Sylvia firmly, throwing a pelisse to Gwen that looked perfect to Daphne's eye, who placed it in an ever-increasing pile.

'What about this?' Rilla said, lifting up a headband of woven ribbons and what appeared to be emeralds.

'Oh, I don't—'

'Perfect match for her green wedding gown,' Gwen said firmly. 'Let me put it in the "yes" pile.'

Daphne sat back in her seat. It would be pleasant, just once in a while, to get a word in edgeways... But then, on the rare times she was able to gain the attention of the room, any room, her tongue most inconveniently stuck in her mouth and all words disappeared from her mind. It was as though she had never heard a single word in her life.

'So.'

Daphne jumped. She'd become lost in her thoughts, half-forgetting where she was, and now Rilla was fixing her with a most impressive stare.

'So?' she attempted softly.

It was no use. Gwen and Sylvia, arguing over the suitability of a buckle, glanced over and grinned.

'So,' repeated Rilla sternly. 'What is he like?'

Daphne's soul went cold. *Oh, no.* No, she really didn't think she could...

'Yes, we demand to hear everything about this groom of yours,' said Sylvia smartly, dropping the buckle precisely halfway between the two piles she and Gwen had been adding to, and moving to sit beside Rilla. 'This new husband of yours!'

'Sylvia! Honestly, you make it sound as though Daphne is shedding one husband to select another!' Gwen tutted, smiling as she sat herself down in a chair on Daphne's other side. 'Still, I would like to know about him. What does he look like?'

'Is he handsome?' Sylvia asked eagerly.

'Does he have a kind heart?' Rilla said, asking the far more important question to Daphne's mind.

Not that she could concoct a single answer to any of their enquiries. How was one supposed to describe a man she had only met once? Not that the encounter would have been much different had Miss Pike been absent for its entirety. No, she would have stood there, mute, unable to think of a coherent thought, her skin burning…

'You like him,' said Sylvia with a laugh. 'You're blushing!'

'Oh, that hardly signifies anything, Daphne is always blushing,' chided Gwen. 'Is he loud?'

'Is he clever?' Rilla wished to know. 'Does he hunt? Does he have any brothers?'

'Or sisters—I always thought having sisters improved a man to no end,' said Sylvia firmly.

Daphne tried to smile. They meant well. No, it was kinder than that—they truly cared. They were the only three people in the world who had bothered to get to know her, to push gently through her shyness and allow her just to…be. Still, the interrogation was most unwelcome. And reminded her of his…

'Look, let's start with the basics,' said Gwen calmly, cutting through the noise. Perhaps her panic had shown on her face, thought Daphne. 'What is his name?'

'Name?' repeated Daphne in a whisper, her chest tightening.

Her three friends nodded, evidently spotting that further questions would undoubtedly overwhelm her. As if she wasn't totally at sea already. Taking a deep breath, and knowing exactly what sort of response this was going to elicit, Daphne could not prevent her cheeks from burning as she said, 'P-Prince... Prince Christoph of Niedernlein.'

The shrieks undoubtedly could have been heard from several miles away.

'Prince Christoph of Niedernlein!'

'You never said that he was a prince!'

'Prince Christoph... Oh, what a name!'

'I absolutely insist on you selecting a monogram. Oh, Daphne, a prince—'

'Will you hush?' Daphne said in a sharp whisper.

It was perhaps the most direct thing she had said all day. Perhaps for several days. An inside thought had spilled from her lips and she flinched, the expectation of censure visceral. Thankfully her friends heeded her words, though Sylvia still squeaked, hands over her mouth, and Rilla was shaking with laughter.

'It's just a Germanic prince,' Daphne said, knowing full well that what she was saying was most ridiculous. 'There is no need to get so—'

'A prince!' shrieked Sylvia, which set off both Gwen and Rilla in excited squeals.

Daphne tried to shake her head in disapproval, but she could not help but laugh with them. It was all most strange. And wonderful. And ridiculous. Her marry a prince? Three days ago she was just the illegitimate daughter of an earl who had attempted to keep her existence a secret from the *ton*—not particularly successfully, from what her friends had said—and now...

'It sounds like someone is skinning cats in there,' came an unexpected voice. 'Surely the fashions of England cannot be so barbaric?'

All three of her friends gasped. Daphne gasped in turn, the memory of that deep, accented voice sending a jolt of panicked recognition down her spine. Rising hurriedly, fabric samples, bonnets, ribbons, parasols and goodness knew what else tumbling to her feet, she turned on the spot and saw...

Prince Christoph. Here. In the modiste's shop.

He smiled, and the cordiality of that smile cascaded into her chest like hot tea. 'Good afternoon, Miss Smith.'

'Good...' Oh why, oh why, was her voice completely giving up on her? 'Good...good...'

'It is pleasant to see you. Your father said I should endeavour to visit at some point,' he said charmingly, stepping around a pile of shoes that had been deemed unworthy of Daphne Smith and inclining his head at her. 'To ensure I selected a fabric for my wedding waistcoat and cravat that would complement your own choices.'

'I... I see.' Daphne stood there, hating her silence, hating that her cheeks were burning, hating that...

A squeak behind her reminded her that Sylvia had never been very good at controlling herself in public. Her smile softened immediately at the thought of her friend.

'Would you be so good as to introduce me to your companions?' asked Prince Christoph, charm itself.

He would be better off called Prince Charming, Daphne thought wryly as she glanced at her friends.

Sylvia's eyes were wide, Gwen's cheeks were pink—

and she the longest married!—and Rilla had tilted her head, as she often did when encountering a new voice.

Well, there was nothing for it.

'Her Grace, Gwendoline, Duchess of Knaresby,' Daphne said weakly, retreating into the standard pleasantries of social introductions. 'Her Grace, Sylvia, Duchess of Camrose. Her Ladyship, Marilla, Countess of Staromchor, who is also my stepsister-in-law. It's…it's complicated.'

There. That was the easy part done.

Daphne tried to smile and appear gracious at the same time—a challenge, for someone with her crippling shyness. 'Ladies, this is…this is Prince Christoph of Niedernlein—my betrothed.'

Sylvia let out a strangled sound, but Gwen nudged her hard in the ribs, for which Daphne was very thankful.

'A pleasure to make your acquaintance,' Rilla said graciously.

'I am delighted to admit that the pleasure is all mine,' Prince Christoph said with an amiable smile that slipped far too easily onto the man's lips, in Daphne's opinion.

How did he do it?

Before she knew what was happening, he was chattering happily to her friends, placing a befeathered bonnet on his head, with a twinkle in his eye asking their opinion and bringing a particularly soft shawl over to Rilla for her inspection.

Daphne sank slowly back onto her chair, ignored by the lot of them. He was speaking to her friends as though he had known them all his life. There was an easy manner to his attentions that did not cross any lines of propriety, but still, she could see that her friends were instantly taken with him.

How did he do it? How did anyone do it, these people who seemed to know instinctively how to speak to everyone they met? Daphne had always tried not to feel envious of the talent; it appeared to be something one was born with, rather than something one could learn. She had certainly never managed it.

'We thought green,' Sylvia was saying, picking up a ribbon from the 'yes' pile. 'With her golden hair...'

'And I thought these slippers,' Gwen said, picking them up eagerly and pushing them towards the gentleman. 'Rilla was wondering about feathers.'

'Feathers?' Prince Christoph blinked curiously.

Oh, Daphne could have died of shame. Did the man truly believe she was the sort of bride to come down the aisle in feathers?

'But then we thought, insects!'

'Insects?' Prince Christoph said blankly.

He glanced in her direction and Daphne swiftly looked away. She could not speak to him here—she was hardly sure how she was ever going to speak to him, which on reflection was going to make for a most interesting marriage.

Insects, honestly!

'Not live ones, you understand, but their shells,' Rilla was trying to explain. 'It gives a pattern of...what did you call it, Gwen?'

'Iridescence,' Gwen supplied as Sylvia tugged one

ribbon out of the Prince's hand and replaced it with another. 'What think you, Your Highness?'

'My lord, please, and I think you are all choosing very well,' Prince Christoph said sincerely. 'Much as I, though I say so myself, have chosen well.'

His eyes flickered over to Daphne again. She knew they had, even though she was not looking at him. She could feel the weight and ferocity of his attention, the heat of his eyes. Her chest tightened and her whole body flamed.

'But, as you ladies continue to consider the very best for my bride, may I borrow her for a moment?'

Daphne froze. *Oh, no.*

'Of course. You may have ten uninterrupted minutes as long as you promise to be kind to our dear Daphne,' Sylvia said, with almost a warning look across her brow.

If melting to the ground were possible, Daphne would have done so. Why couldn't Sylvia just…?

'Don't be daft, Sylvia, the man can surely see what a treasure Daphne is,' scolded Gwen, pushing Daphne forward, who was most unwilling. 'Go off and look at buttons, you two.'

Buttons? Was she supposed to think of buttons?

Prince Christoph smiled and took Daphne's arm before she could say a word. He strode purposefully towards the display of buttons and Daphne swallowed a great number of things she wanted to say, but couldn't.

Why are you really here? The modiste would have informed you about the fabric. Do you think I'm pretty? Do you have brothers? All the things I should know about you, and I don't know a single thing about you.

'One of your friends—she is your stepsister?'

Daphne nodded. Well, at least all she had to do was focus on facts. 'Technically, my stepsister-in-law. Her mother-in-law is my father's wife. We decided stepsister was the least complicated description.'

'Your friends speak highly of you.'

Daphne blinked. The Prince was still smiling, so it was not a veiled criticism, as she had come to expect from the Pike. 'I… I am fortunate to have them.'

'From what they say, they are fortunate to have you,' he said blithely, picking up a gold button and examining it. 'And I suppose, in turn, I am fortunate to be given you.'

Daphne swallowed down the retort that she knew would be unwelcome. Given? *Given?* She was not a possession, like a set of buttons, to be handed from one man to the next!

'What are you doing here?' she blurted out.

Well, it wasn't as bad as the 'possession' thought, but honestly! When was she going to learn to curb her tongue?

Prince Christoph, however, did not appear concerned. 'As I said, my cravat must—'

'I am not stupid.' Daphne's cheeks were burning, and she knew she would regret these words, but here they came. 'The modiste would have informed you of my choice. Why are you here?'

He put the button down and gave her a serious look. 'Is it so strange that I would wish to see you?'

Daphne's voice caught in her throat.

Careful, now. He had not said that he *did* wish to see her, just that it would not have been strange if he wanted to. It wasn't the same thing.

The last thing she needed was to get carried away, to start dreaming that this was a fairy tale. It wasn't. He wanted her dowry. She wanted an escape.

'I... I wanted to see you,' Prince Christoph said, his voice becoming curt. 'I thought it would be pleasant.'

And was it? That was the question Daphne wanted to ask, but her rigid control managed to prevent it. Instead, she tried not to notice how his gaze swept over her, lingering on parts of her that grew hot at his attention. Her lips. Her breasts. Her hips...

'But I make you uncomfortable.'

'Wait—no!' Daphne said hurriedly as Prince Christoph stepped away.

Regret pooled in her chest. The first time a gentleman had ever looked at her, properly looked at her, as a woman, and she had frightened him off! Perhaps her evident embarrassment was unattractive. Did he think her a prude?

'No, this was a mistake. I wanted to... I thought we could...' Prince Christoph's words trailed away and a slight tinge appeared in his cheeks.

Daphne could not help but stare. Was he...was it possible that this tall, physically powerful man was just as shy as she was?

'It does not matter. It was foolish. I should not have come. I apologise.' His words were stiff and there was an inflexibility about him now that drew him away.

Daphne wet her lips, desperate to say something to stem the change of this tide.

No, stay, I want to talk—I want to know you. I want to understand you. I want...

'And I hope you will all be at the wedding,' Prince Christoph was saying genially as he bowed to each of her friends. 'And your husbands, naturally. I must away, I am afraid—a prior appointment. Such a shame I cannot stay longer. Miss Smith, your health.'

Daphne moved hastily and managed to bob a quick curtsey as Prince Christoph gave a flourishing bow and took his leave of them.

The instant the doorbell clanged as Prince Christoph departed, the three women turned on Daphne.

'Daphne!' said Rilla, in a berating tone.

'What?' Daphne said defensively.

'Daphne Smith!' Gwen said, shaking her head and laughing.

'How could you not tell us?' Sylvia said accusingly.

Once again, Daphne was completely at a loss. 'Tell—tell you what?'

'Just how handsome your future husband is, you dolt!' Gwen said sternly.

'Handsome?' Goodness, this was the last thing she wanted to talk about. There he'd been, a picture of masculinity and charm, and she was already nervous as it was. That apology, his confusion—what had that been about? She needed time and quiet to think. The last thing she needed was…

'Handsome?' Rilla scoffed. 'Oh, who cares about that?'

'Easy for you to say,' muttered Sylvia with a grin.

Daphne could not help but smile as Rilla frowned, though with a look of mischief in her unseeing eyes.

'I merely meant,' Rilla said haughtily, 'That looks will fade, no matter how impressive they are in the moment. No, I meant to berate you for withholding from us just how genial and pleasant he is!'

'That Prince Christoph is a very agreeable man,' said Gwen sagely, nodding. 'He will make a fine companion for you.'

'Companion? Genial?' Sylvia scoffed and pushed Daphne down in her seat. 'Forget all that. Daphne Smith, he is very handsome. Handsome and charming. Are you not attracted to him? Are you not looking forward to the wedding night and a good bedding?'

'Sylvia!'

Three voices rang out in censure, but Sylvia merely shrugged. 'Well. The three of us all…well…had a taste before the wedding, if you take my meaning. You might not have the chance—the wedding is only in a few weeks. Are you truly telling me you have not thought about it?'

The day had gone from bad to worse. Desperately wringing her hands and trying not to think about slowly removing Prince Christoph's shirt from his delectable shoulders, Daphne only managed to stammer, 'N-no, I have never—'

'Not at all? The man is devilishly attractive, Daphne,' Sylvia persisted. 'Don't you think so?'

Daphne tried to prevent her shoulders from shaking. It was all too much. Three days ago she had been…well, not happy, but relatively resolved to accept the life that fate had dealt her. A sedentary, solitary one at the Wallflower Academy.

Now she was about to enter an arranged marriage with a prince, and her friends were quizzing her on… on…*that*.

'I had not noticed his appearance,' she lied, cheeks flushing at both the topic of conversation and the deception. 'I… Let us consider the "yes" pile. Please.'

It was difficult to ignore her friends' exasperated glances, but Daphne almost managed it.

This was an arranged marriage, not one to be filled with laughter, love and lust. That was just the way it had to be.

Chapter Four

'And this...this is usual here, in England?' Christoph asked delicately as he sipped his tepid tea. 'To take tea in this way?'

Miss Smith's blush threatened to draw his attention to her décolletage. Not that he was going to stare. Most definitely not. 'It is, yes. I myself prefer lemon. The Pike—Miss Pike requires milk. Do...do you not take your tea in either of these ways?'

He glanced over at the other side of the room, where a determined Miss Pike had taken up position in an armchair, eyeing them beadily, her own cup and saucer on a small tray.

The invitation from Miss Pike had been most welcome. Christoph's lodgings in London were not pleasant, the very little funds he had brought with him from Niedernlein, if eked out, just about enough to make it until the wedding. The opportunity to get out of the city, growing danker and colder with each passing day, was delightful.

But the invitation had said afternoon tea with Miss

Smith. That was why he had begged for a lift on the back of a mail coach going in mostly the right direction and had walked the rest of the way to the Wallflower Academy. Not for…this. Not for an awkward encounter with Miss Smith and an even more awkward one with the Pike. Miss Pike. Even more reason to select an English bride, Christoph thought. The customs of his newly chosen home were indeed most odd. Without a wife born of this land to help him navigate these unusual customs, how could he make a home here?

There came the gentle clearing of a throat. Christoph's eyes focused, and he realised he had completely forgotten what question Miss Smith had asked him. Something about tea…?

Miss Smith sipped her tea as her cheeks flushed. When she had placed the delicate china back in its saucer, she said softly, so only he could hear, 'Miss Pike requires her wallflowers to be chaperoned at all times.'

Yes, he could see that. More was the pity—he had hoped, perhaps foolishly, for a little more privacy.

'Are you sure you would not like a breath of fresh air, Miss Pike?' Christoph called down the room, shifting awkwardly in his seat.

'Oh, no, it's perfectly pleasant in here,' Miss Pike called over to them cheerfully. 'Besides, who would then ensure that nothing untoward occurs?'

Try as he might, it was not quite possible for Christoph to ignore the sudden flaming flush that swept across Miss Smith's cheeks. She was shy. The mere mention of something 'untoward', and her whole body appeared aflame. It was remarkable. Remarkably alluring...

Christoph pushed the thought away. It was not appropriate to think such thoughts. They were to be married, yes, but it was for naught but convenience.

'So we are...what? To converse while Miss Pike sits there and watches us?' Christoph asked in a low murmur.

There it was—a slight quirk of Miss Smith's lips. The moment was gone in an instant, only because his attention was so closely trained on her face did he notice.

Which was allowed. Perhaps even appropriate. If—when—he married her, Christoph supposed he should know the contours of his wife's face. Still, he supposed his stomach wasn't supposed to twist like that, desire to pour through his ribcage to collect around his heart.

'Yes, Prince Christoph, that is what we are supposed to do,' said Miss Smith quietly.

Christoph's jaw tightened. Prince Christoph. That was part of his life he had left behind, very much on purpose. There was no place for him in Niedernlein, no possibility of him returning. Absolutely all those bridges had been burnt.

The loss of his home was painful in a way he had not expected. Oh, it wasn't just the geography, though he would miss the mountains. No, it was his people. His nation, the people he had thought he would serve all his life.

There was one advantage, however: he would never have to be *Prince* Christoph again. He had always loathed that title.

'Prince Christoph?' came Miss Smith's quiet voice.

'Don't call me that,' he muttered, highly conscious of Miss Pike craning her neck as their voices remained low.

He had not intended it as a criticism. He had barely thought about the words at all, just his dislike of the title.

Miss Smith's expression became one of mortification. 'I—I am so sorry, I didn't—'

'It's quite all right,' Christoph said hastily, his voice a murmur. 'It's just... I don't like it.'

Confusion was written across her brow, and understandably so. 'It's your title.'

Blast. Did she have to be so logical about it? Christoph hesitated, considering precisely how much to tell her. Miss Smith looked at him, eyes wide, confusion now mingled with embarrassment once again as their gazes locked.

She was so very beautiful.

Concentrate, man!

'I am a prince, yes, but it is...an irrelevance,' Christoph said slowly. 'It is a small country—very small. The whole of Niedernlein could fit inside London, and quite comfortably. It...it hardly counts.'

'Better a prince than a wallflower,' Miss Smith said with a wry smile. Then the smile disappeared, the expression of panic returning.

Christoph could not help but smile. Every now and again Miss Smith said something unguarded, a part of her was further revealed and he liked what he discovered. This was a woman with a mind, not a staid, dull personality.

'I trust you are not speaking of anything indecent?'

The pair of them jumped. For a moment, just a few heartbeats, Christoph had managed to forget that Miss Pike accompanied them.

'We are speaking of Niedernlein, Miss Pike,' he called down, hoping his irritation at being interrupted was not too apparent.

'Ah, excellent!' came the warm words from the Wallflower Academy's proprietress. 'I am certain that Miss Smith will wish to hear all about... Oh, Matthews. Is all well?'

Christoph turned to see one of the servants enter with a bow before hurriedly stepping over to Miss Pike and muttering something in her ear.

'It really is very simple, Matthews,' Miss Pike started to say, clearly annoyed by the interruption. 'You'll need to tell half the wallflowers to wait their turn, and then organise the remaining wallflowers into two groups of... Look. I'll show you...'

With an apologetic look, the footman inclined his head to Christoph and Miss Smith as Miss Pike rose to her feet.

'You will have to excuse me, Your Highness,' said the proprietress as Christoph winced. 'An urgent matter that requires my attention, and my attention alone. I hope I can trust you to sit in absolute silence?'

Christoph blinked. 'I... I beg your pardon?'

'That way, I can be assured that nothing untoward occurs, you see,' said the bustling Miss Pike as she walked to the door. 'Come along, Matthews.'

The footman gave Miss Smith a look that spoke potently of their shared exhaustion with the woman, then retreated to the corridor. The dining room door closed. They were alone.

The silence that fell on the moment was intensely hushed. Christoph could not recall a silence like it—save at Katalina's funeral.

He would not think of it.

Hands clenching into fists in his lap, tension sparking across his shoulder blades, Christoph took a moment to breathe. *Just stay calm. Just don't think about it. Just stay calm.*

When he focused, it was to see Miss Smith picking at the cucumber sandwich that she had placed on her plate several minutes ago. Her attention was on the food, her cheeks slightly pink, as they always seemed to be.

Christoph cleared his throat. 'We are not actually going to sit in silence, are we?'

Miss Smith appeared startled. 'Aren't we?'

'I thought you would wish to take advantage of the lack of Miss Pike in the room,' he said, attempting to inject cheerfulness into his tone. 'Ask me questions, perhaps. It is right that you know something about me.'

Before I become your husband. The last five words did not quite make it to his tongue, and perhaps that was all to the good. Miss Smith appeared humiliated at the idea of interrogating him, her lips parted and moving but no sound emerging.

'You do not like to break the rules,' Christoph said

gently, helping himself to a dainty-looking cake that looked most delicious.

It was not a question, and Miss Smith appeared to know that. 'Rules are there to be followed. I have always done so, ever since I came to the Wallflower Academy. The rules are there to be obeyed.'

It was a challenge for Christoph not to allow a mite of disappointment into his heart. Well, he hardly wanted a hoyden for a wife—it would be remarkably difficult to keep track of her, for one, and it would be scandalous to have a wife who could not behave.

But still. A little fire...

'Besides, if I were to break a rule,' continued Miss Smith in a low tone, her cheeks reddening with every passing syllable, 'it would not be for conversation.'

Christoph sat up in his chair. Well, now. That was interesting. 'And what would it be for, Miss Smith?'

When she lifted her eyes and met his own, he found a knot tangled in his throat. There was something about this woman. Something that tempted any man to linger a while and see if something more could be discovered about her. She was like a jungle, waiting to be explored. Or a mine, diamonds within her just waiting to be carved.

A sharp jolt of need forced Christoph to cross his legs. *Focus, man!*

'I couldn't possibly... I mean, I shouldn't have said...' Miss Smith said in a hurried voice, her expression anguished.

He could not permit her to continue to tie herself in

knots. 'Forget my impertinence, Miss Smith. It was only a jest.'

Her breathing was irregular as she fell into silence, and Christoph did what he could not to notice.

Hang it all, though, he was only a man.

But he was allowing himself to get distracted from the plan.

The thought jerked Christoph back to his senses. He was getting too invested, too interested in the woman who was going to make his plan work. She did not matter; it was the plan that mattered. Back to the plan.

'Miss Smith, I would like to make it very clear that this marriage is one of convenience, and convenience alone,' Christoph said stiffly, before taking a bite of the cake.

He tried not to groan. How long had it been since there had been cakes like this in the palace at Niedernlein? His father's spendthrift ways had almost bankrupted the royal family, and his brother had hardly done much to improve matters. Goodness, he had almost forgotten what sugar tasted like. This was splendid—and it was included in a mere afternoon tea. What did they have for dessert at dinner?

When he looked up, it was to see Miss Smith had carefully arranged her face into one of calm passivity. Or was that just his expectation, that she was playing a part too?

'I quite understand,' she said quietly.

Christoph's jaw tightened. Did she? He would have to make it plainer, remove any possibility of hope within her. Only if she knew there was absolutely nothing of romance between them, and never would be, could he hold himself to the plan.

'It is... Well, when I wrote to your father, he was clear that... I need your dowry,' Christoph said aloud, hating the words but knowing he had to be brutal.

It was for her benefit—Miss Smith's. He did not wish to raise false hopes. He did not want her to tempt him.

Miss Smith nodded slowly. 'I see.'

'The royal family is willing to overlook your birth, as agreed with your father, due to the extensive dowry and impressive inheritance you are set to receive,' Christoph ploughed on, loathing himself with greater intensity with every word, but knowing it must be done.

And it was. There—he saw the moment Miss Smith gave up all hope of happiness in this marriage. Her lips pressed together and there came a slight lowering of her shoulders and a sigh.

Christoph wanted to pull her into his arms and show her how he desired her, but he would not—he could not. Not when he could not offer her some sweetness. He had to be hard, to be in control. He could not risk losing himself into the embrace of a woman who could make him feel so much without a single touch.

'My...my father said he had corresponded with the Prince of Niedernlein for several weeks,' Miss Smith said quietly. 'Anton was the name he mentioned. I presumed it was on just such a matter.'

A tendril of panic crept around Christoph's lungs.

Yes. He had known this moment would come, and he was prepared for it. At least, as prepared as any man could be. It would not be difficult to guess what his brother had said to the Earl of Norbury, after all.

'I have many names,' he said, which was the truth. 'Anton is one of them.'

'I see,' she said quietly, even though she did not.

Just so long as neither the Earl nor his daughter realised they had been corresponding with a different brother...

'Yes, it is crucial to ensure that we understand each other,' Christoph said carefully.

So far, so good. He had to assume Miss Smith had not read the letters from his brother. She would not have known what to expect of the Prince of Niedernlein. All he had to do was...

'I suppose that is why you wish to be married as soon as possible,' Miss Smith said lightly, finally taking a bite of her cucumber sandwich.

Christoph's pulse skipped a beat as he inadvertently found himself staring directly at her as she did so. At the way she wet her lips before a bite, the dainty way she nibbled at it, the slight hint of butter at the corner of her mouth...

'Prince... I mean, my lord?'

Christoph blinked. *Blast. What had they been saying?*

'Married as soon as... Yes, yes, I need your money,' he said before he could take a moment to think.

There were pink dots on her cheeks now, but Miss

Smith appeared relatively calm for a woman who had been told, at least discreetly, that her charms were nothing to her bank balance. 'I see.'

No, she didn't see. She didn't, and Christoph prayed she never would.

He had to get Laura out of there. His sister deserved to live a life…well, like this. This Wallflower Academy appeared perfection: a safe place for ladies to live without fear of harassment, bullying or violence. They spent their days embroidering or learning the pianoforte, from what Christoph could tell. Their greatest fears were whether they would make a match this year, not whether they would live to see the next one.

'My lord?'

Christoph started. There was a hand on his own, a warm hand, a comforting one. Miss Smith. She had reached out and taken his hand.

'You…you seemed very far away,' she said, scarlet blotches appearing down her neck. 'In a sad place.'

In a sad place.

Damn, but this woman was perceptive. Christoph had never encountered anyone who had so swiftly understood him with but a look. For a moment, he allowed himself the distraction. Oh, it was pleasant to have Miss Smith's shy fingers entwined in his own. He could feel her pulse—or was that his own, jumping and darting as they looked at each other, seated in silence at a dining table?

And then he recollected himself. No, he could not indulge in such behaviour—the last thing he needed was for Miss Smith to believe they could care for each other.

Christoph snatched his hand away. 'I was just thinking.'

Miss Smith did not appear offended, more disappointed, which tore at his heart all the more.

This Englishwoman... How had she done it? How had she seen within him the darkness that Christoph believed he would carry for the rest of his life?

'Tell me about your family,' Miss Smith said quietly. 'You have met my father, so you know mine.'

Family. Oh, hell, could she have chosen a more inappropriate topic? Not that she would have known. From the little he knew of English customs, Christoph believed discussion of one's family, both light-hearted and serious, was expected within polite Society. Not that the stories of his own family could be discussed in polite Society...

'I have a brother and a sister. My mother died five years ago and my father unexpectedly but a few weeks ago, that is all,' Christoph said curtly. 'Tell me, these cakes...'

'How pleasant to have siblings,' Miss Smith said softly.

Her words pulled him up short. Pleasant. Yes—that was one word for it. Yet, despite his own discomfort, Christoph could not be ignorant of the longing in his companion's words. Siblings—something she clearly did not have.

'Yes,' he said tightly.

What else was there to say? Christoph reached forward and took a sip of his tea in the silence. He had not expected sitting with a woman and revealing nothing of note to her to be this painful. He had thought it might be awkward, yes, but this guilt, rushing through him? That he had not predicted.

'Are your siblings married?'

He blinked. Miss Smith swam into view, a nervous smile on her lips. 'My brother was married,' he said curtly. 'Tell me, will you miss the Wallflower Academy?'

'Miss it?' Miss Smith repeated. 'No. What happened to your sister-in—'

'She died,' Christoph said, his stomach churning. 'Why won't you miss the Wallflower Academy?'

'Do you think it more likely that you will answer my questions,' asked Miss Smith slowly, 'if I answer yours?'

Now it was his turn to flush. It was not a bold question. At least, it was not said boldly, or to offend or provoke. It appeared to be a genuine question, one asked lightly, with curiosity. Which made the heat in his cheeks all the more provoking. He was supposed to be the one in control of this conversation—the plan required it— not Miss Smith.

The trouble was, Christoph found himself once again distracted by her beauty. She was so beautiful, so achingly soft. His fingers longed to reach out and discover for themselves whether she truly felt as soft and inviting as she looked.

And that fire, that spark in her eyes that came in a moment then disappeared again—where did it come from? Was that the true Daphne Smith, or was this the real one?

'You are curious about my life,' he said aloud, testing the waters.

'I am to be your wife,' Miss Smith said quietly. 'And—'

'In name only,' Christoph cut across her. She must understand. This was not a fairy tale. 'We will live very separate lives. Do you understand me, Miss Smith? I need you— to understand, I mean. I need you to understand.'

Perhaps she had not noticed the slip. She certainly did not flush, which appeared to suggest so.

Slowly, very slowly, Miss Smith inclined her head. 'I see. Yes, I understand. I understand perfectly.'

Chapter Five

'Ready?' trilled Lady Staromchor.

Lady Norbury, Daphne corrected silently as she sat before the looking glass and avoided her own eye. It had been a year now, and still she found it a challenge to remember that her father's new wife—his only wife—had to be addressed as such.

Daphne met her stepmother's eye. 'Y-yes.'

No. No! she wanted to cry out. *No, I am not ready. I thought this day would never come, and yet time has raced by, and I don't know how to slow this day down. I need it to slow down.*

'Are you...nervous? Excited? Can you believe it's come so fast?' Lady Norbury said a little awkwardly, dropping onto Daphne's bed without asking.

'No,' Daphne admitted, with complete honesty this time as she reached up to touch one of the delicate flowers that had been woven into her hair. 'No, I cannot.'

Four weeks had felt like an inordinate amount of time when Prince Christoph—her future husband—had suggested it. Four weeks until their wedding. Daphne had agreed. Perhaps she should have requested four months. Or four years.

'Remember my wedding day to your dear papa,' Lady Norbury was saying with misty eyes.

As though it had not been around a twelvemonth, Daphne thought with a wry smile that she quickly stifled.

'Marrying the person you love,' Lady Norbury said dreamily. 'What a wonderful day.'

Daphne swallowed.

I need your dowry.

Prince Christoph had been very clear—which was all to the good, Daphne told herself sternly as she pulled at one of the flowers in her hair, attempting to straighten it. The last thing she needed was to enter a marriage without complete understanding. It was good, was it not, that they understood each other? That she and Prince Christoph would not hope for something they could not have?

'A happy occasion indeed,' Lady Norbury said with a sigh.

Daphne remembered to reply just in time to prevent awkwardness. 'Oh, yes. Yes, very happy.'

She would have been happier, she wanted to say, her tongue biting down on her lip to prevent her from saying it, if she had been permitted to have her friends help her prepare. She was not one for company, not as a general rule, but the absence of Gwen, Rilla and Sylvia felt like a weight upon her shoulders.

Having them here, laughing and jesting, teasing her about the wedding night and squabbling over which necklace the bride should wear? That at least would have revived her spirits somewhat.

'I imagine you wish to be alone,' said Lady Norbury quietly.

Daphne started, turning on her seat to look at her stepmother. Had she offended? Had her silence been taken as rudeness? Should she have said…?

'I will leave you to your thoughts for a few minutes before the carriages are ready,' said Lady Norbury, rising from Daphne's bed and smiling. 'It won't be long.'

The door shut behind her before Daphne could say anything. Not that there was much to say. Her wedding day was here. Within a few hours, she would be…

Oh, goodness. *Princess Daphne?* Surely not? But then Daphne had not considered her future title; that had seemed the least interesting part of marrying Prince Christoph, a man she had seen but once a week since the engagement. So, thrice only.

Would he be kind? Would he be gentle? Would he really hold her to that pronouncement made when they had shared afternoon tea? *We will live very separate lives. Do you understand me, Miss Smith?*

Daphne did not need to look into the looking glass to know her cheeks would be a brilliant scarlet-red. The burn upon them felt akin to the time she had fallen asleep on the Wallflower Academy lawn while reading a book. Her forearms and nose had peeled in the end, the angry, burned skin leaving behind a pale delicacy which Miss Pike had labelled 'porcelain', then forbidden her from ever going out into the sun again.

The Wallflower Academy. It was all she knew of the world, really. Oh, it was not that the world frightened her—one could not be afraid of something one did not know or understand. This was supposed to be a happy time, the moments just before her wedding. But she sat here alone, in the Wallflower Academy. Her father had apparently not thought it fit to have her married from his own house. That, or he had not thought about it at all.

Barely moving an inch, Daphne carefully removed half of the ostentatious flowers her stepmother had placed in her hair. They were not her. They would attract attention, the very last thing she wanted. Her stomach contracted painfully. Though, today, of all days…

'Daphne Smith, are you ready?' barked Miss Pike from the doorway.

Daphne started so violently, she almost fell off her chair. 'Y-yes, I'm…'

'The carriage is waiting, and presumably your groom is too,' said the Pike with a raised eyebrow. 'I thought you wished to be married.'

Swallowing hard, Daphne managed to prevent the inside thought from spilling out: *I thought I did, too.*

Her father looked stern when she and the Pike descended the staircase. 'We're late.'

'Being late is part of being a bride,' soothed Miss Pike in a conciliatory tone. 'It is to be expected.'

'Will he expect it, though? Being from Niedernlein, I mean—not being an Englishman,' snorted Lord Norbury. 'Well, we'll have to see. Ready, Daphne?'

He did not wait for a reply, stomping out of the hall

onto the drive, with his wife in his wake. Daphne stepped forward to join them but was halted by a hand on her arm.

'Do not disgrace me, Daphne Smith,' said Miss Pike sternly, something that almost looked like tears in her eyes. 'You are the greatest product of the Wallflower Academy and you are about to marry a prince. Do not disgrace me. Or yourself.'

With that, she released her.

Daphne almost stumbled, her momentum off-balance. The words from the Pike ringing in her mind, lungs constricted and pulse hammering in her ears, she walked out of the Wallflower Academy for the last time and into the carriage that was waiting for her.

'How exciting! I've never had a daughter to marry off,' Lady Norbury said into the awkward silence of the carriage. 'Is it not wonderful, William?'

'Yes, it's very nice,' said Daphne's father stiffly.

He did not meet Daphne's eye. In a way, she did not want him to. He had been a distant father all her life. Perhaps it was only right that he was a distant father on her wedding day.

By the time they arrived outside the church, bells pealing and bystanders gawping, Daphne was not entirely sure whether she would be able to stand. Standing was for people whose legs worked.

'Ready?' said her father gruffly.

What was there to say? Daphne thought, her throat drying as her inside thoughts attempted to push their way through her lungs, up her chest and out of her mouth.

No, I'm not ready. But I don't want to stay at the Wallflower Academy either. I don't want my life to remain the same. I don't know what I want, and I suppose I don't have much of a choice, but I'm not ready.

'Ready,' she whispered.

'I'll find my seat!' said her stepmother, breaking the moment as she half-stepped, half-fell from the carriage door. 'I'll see you at the altar!'

Guffawing at her own jest, she disappeared into the church. For just a moment when the doors opened, Daphne caught a glimpse inside. People; more people than she had ever seen together in one building. There were rows and rows of them, hats, bonnets, shawls, pelisses, spencers, feathers and...

'Daphne.'

She jumped. Her father had descended from the carriage and proffered his arm. Evidently he expected her to take it.

Daphne swallowed: swallowed down her panic, her fear, her dislike of attention; her frustration that she had planned not a jot of the wedding; her confusion as to why her father would own her so publicly, and about the reserve in the presence of the man she was about to marry; and her desperation quietly to be with her friends, allowing their chatter to wash over her.

I'm not ready.

She took her father's hand.

The walk up the aisle was the longest walk she had ever taken. It was a miracle, Daphne thought, as her pulse thrummed louder and louder, that she did not trip over her own feet as she went.

The whispering did not help. It rippled through the large church as she walked up the nave, following her but also spreading out and blossoming through the congregation.

Not all of it was whispering, either.

'A prince, marrying that quiet thing...'

'Huge dowry—even I'd marry her for that!'

'Never knew the Earl of Norbury had a daughter... Why did he hide her away?'

Try as she might, Daphne could not ignore them. The voices were getting louder, bolder, but that might be the echoes, or her own mind magnifying...

And there he was.

Coming to an abrupt halt, for she had not looked where they were going, Daphne's breath caught in her throat as she looked into Prince Christoph Augustus Heinrich Maximus Anton Philip von Auberheiser's dark eyes.

He was very handsome. And he was pleasant, in a way, with a calm temperament. He was also distant and untrusting, but that did not make him in turn untrustworthy. There was a great deal of pain in his expression when he did not think anyone was looking. Daphne could not stop seeing it, now she had noticed it. And there was no cruelty in him. He had made no harsh remarks about her person, her personality or her parentage. Which made him unusual in itself.

Daphne attempted to smile. Prince Christoph gave a

taut smile, accompanied with a nod. He glanced at the church doors, as though checking to see if any other prospective brides might decide to turn up. It was not a very cheering thought.

'We apologise for our lateness, Your Royal Highness,' began Lord Norbury in an undertone.

'It is of no matter,' said Prince Christoph curtly. His attention snapped back to Daphne. 'You are here. That is all that is important.'

In the mouth of another man, it could have been a delightfully romantic thing to have said. In the mouth of the man she was about to marry, it was…matter of fact. Cold, even, as though he did not particularly mind which woman stood before him, as long as she came with sixty thousand pounds.

Do not be foolish, Daphne tried to tell herself as her father handed over her palm to rest on Christoph's. *You are not being tricked into this marriage; you know full well that is what he wants. Funds. Money. That is all.*

'Dearly beloved,' said the vicar, appearing so rapidly, and seemingly from nowhere, that Daphne started, fingers tightening around Prince Christoph's arm. 'We are gathered together here, in the sight of God, and in the face of this congregation, to join this man and this woman…'

The words became a wash that soothed Daphne's mind. She had heard the words before, after all, at Gwen's wedding, at Rilla's and at Sylvia's, only about six months ago. They were what was said, there was nothing unique about them, and she knew so well the gentle rhythm.

'I said, do you take this man…?'

Daphne started. The vicar's voice had become aggrieved and apparently with good reason. Were they at the vows already? Surely not?

There was an awkward cough behind her. Someone muttered something, something she could not quite hear, and laughter rippled out from the jester.

The burning sensation was back. Daphne was certain that her face, neck and décolletage were blotching as she stood there, panicked, frozen, unsure how to unlock her jaw and say something—anything—let alone the right words that Prince Christoph needed her to say.

Prince Christoph.

Daphne forced herself to look up and meet his gaze. The intensity of his look made her lips part.

He was…just looking at her. Strange though it was, he was just looking. There was no anger at her hesitation. No exasperation. No bitterness, no rolling of the eyes or tutting.

Daphne had expected it, all of it. That was what people did around her, and it always made her want to crawl into a hole and never come out. The rare times when her inside thoughts escaped, there was shaking of heads, hands raised to astonished mouths and mutters that ladies could not say such things.

But Prince Christoph, in his very best with gold buttons, epaulettes and a few medals on his chest, now Daphne came to look, was doing none of those things.

He was looking with no judgement, no irritation, just a tenderness that she could feel as though he were the sun beaming down on her.

'Take a breath,' he murmured, his dark eyes never leaving hers.

Only then did Daphne realise her lungs had turned to stone. A desperate, long breath brought well-needed air into her lungs, and Prince Christoph squeezed her hands. Her hands… Since when had they been holding hands?

'And another breath,' Prince Christoph said quietly. 'We're not in any rush. You have to be sure.'

Be sure? Daphne desperately tried not to glance at her father, but she could not help it. There was a stony look on her father's face. Lord Norbury in fact looked… resigned.

It was not a pleasant thing to notice. Oh, God, if that was how her father looked, then what about the rest of them—the hundreds of people who had come here to stare, watch her, watch her fail…?

'Daphne, look at me.'

Almost unsure how she did it, Daphne dragged her focus from her father to Prince Christoph. He had lowered his head slightly, bringing himself closer to her eye level, and there was a lilt of a smile at the corner of his mouth. As though…as though he was not angry. As though he did not care that she was shaming him.

'These are your vows, because you and no one else is making them,' Prince Christoph said quietly. 'Ignore them. Ignore all of them. Look at me. Do you trust me?'

She did. He was handsome. He was also kind. That

was what Daphne latched onto in this moment of panic: that this man was kind. He saw the very best in her when perhaps she could see none of that herself. He saw the truth in her, as well as the fear. Warmth spread from her chest through to her fingers and toes, but it was not the scalding, unwelcome warmth of shyness or embarrassment. It was something else. Something that strengthened, rather than pointed out her weaknesses.

Do you trust me?

Daphne did not waver in her focus, looking straight into Prince Christoph's eyes. 'I do.'

'Finally,' muttered the vicar, making her start.

She had almost forgotten he was there.

'And do you, Christoph Augustus Heinrich Maximus Anton Philip von Auberheiser, take Daphne…?'

Of course her father had never given her a middle name. That would have made her more like his daughter, and he had never wanted to accept her when a child.

'To be your wedded wife, to live together after God's ordinance in the holy covenant of matrimony? To have and to hold from his day forward, for better for worse, for richer for poorer, in sickness and in health, to love and to cherish and, forsaking all others, keep yourself only unto her, for so long as you both shall live?'

Daphne blinked, momentarily breaking the connection between Prince Christoph and her, but he did not waver nor hesitate.

'I do.'

What was it about him that did it? she wondered, as they somehow managed to get through the rest of the vows. That stabilised her, gave her a solid ground to stand on that did not shift under her fluttering panic?

Perhaps it was his firm hold of her. Her hands were in his, the grip of his fingers entwined and tight, but not possessive. Perhaps it was his gaze, without judgement and without censure, that never let her go. Perhaps it was his calm, the way his breathing never shortened as she shamed him.

All she knew was that, for a few moments, it was just them. Just Prince Christoph, her and no one else. And it was wonderful. Nothing could interrupt this moment, as a rushing tingling swept over her skin.

'I pronounce that you be husband and wife.'

Every muscle in Daphne's body stiffened and her instincts overcame her, her hand flinching away from Prince Christoph's touch to return to the safety of her side.

Except it didn't. His grip was soft, but firm. She was unable to withdraw her hand from his, and for a moment, just a moment, he smiled.

Daphne's pulse skipped a beat. The tingling sensation suddenly heightened, as though a gentle breeze was blowing over every inch of her skin, and she wanted to lean forward—why, she did not know—to be closer to him, so much closer so that she could…

Prince Christoph looked away and nodded curtly at someone behind her. Turning round, Daphne saw with no surprise that it was her father who returned the nod. Because this was a transaction, she reminded herself. This was a bargain, an agreement made between men.

She was an asset, handed from one man to another. That was all. This was not a love match. This was something far more clinical, far colder. Her friends might have had the love stories, but that was not going to be Daphne's tale.

When she looked up at Prince Christoph, it was to see the shutters come down on his eyes and the distance somehow appear behind them once again.

'Shall we depart?' he said quietly.

Daphne blinked. There was usually a sermon after a wedding…

'Princess Daphne,' her husband said in a low, proud voice. 'Are you ready to depart?'

Her mouth was dry when she spoke, and her voice was but a whisper, but she managed it. 'If you wish it, my lord.'

Chapter Six

'So fascinating. I have never met a person from Niedernlein before…'

'Yes, thank you,' Christoph said quietly with his hand on the door, tiredness tugging at his eyes.

The woman, whoever she was—too many names today—did not take the hint. 'And I suppose you and your new bride will be hosting a great many—?'

'Yes,' Christoph said wearily. 'Yes, we will.'

He would have to write formally to the royal court at Niedernlein. He could not prevent the news of his marriage from reaching his home country for ever.

How would his people feel about the news? The thought twisted his gut. He had vowed to serve his nation, when he had come of age. And now he was here, hundreds of miles away. Had he broken that vow? Would he ever be able to serve his people again?

The woman's face fell slightly as she stood on the doorstep. 'But Your Highness—'

'"My lord" will do,' Christoph said, the phrase one he had trotted out continually all day.

'You were married this morning! You and your bride are the talk of the town!'

Christoph winced. He might have been Daphne's husband for a matter of mere hours, but he already knew just how much she would enjoy knowing that. 'Be that as it may...'

'And besides, people will expect it,' persisted the woman, the very last guest from their wedding breakfast and the most difficult to send away. 'You are now a part of the *ton*. People will expect—'

'I expect you must be very tired,' Christoph said with a smile. 'Good evening.'

Even with the woman's fingers on the door, he slowly pushed it forward, his strength far greater than hers. It did not, however, prevent her from continuing to speak until the very last moment.

'But everyone will want to look at your bride. We've hardly seen the daughter of the Earl of Norbury; everyone wants to know...'

The door closed.

Christoph rested his forehead on the comfortingly solid wood.

Everyone wants to know...

Yes, he was certain they would. The gossip and murmurs about the marriage of the illegitimate daughter of Lord Norbury and a prince from a land that most of London had never heard of was surely enticing. He had avoided the newspapers as much as he could, but that had not prevented him from noticing the pointing and stares all evening.

But he'd done it.

A spurt of relief soared through him. He'd done it. He had married her. Daphne Smith—Daphne von Auberheiser, now—was safe. She would not have to marry Anton. She would be safe.

Try as he might, Christoph could not prevent himself from imagining his brother's response once the news of his marriage to Daphne arrived in Niedernlein. A shiver scraped down his spine.

Christoph knew he would have to move quickly if he was to get Laura out of there before the tidings of the happy couple reached the Winter Palace. Now she had somewhere to come, now he had a wife to be her chaperone, he could invite her to England without suspicion. To this large house in London, for a start…

Christoph straightened and looked around him, hardly able to believe it.

'A wedding gift,' Lord Norbury had said gruffly, just before he and Lady Norbury had left the wedding breakfast. 'A small place for you and Daphne to call home while you stay in London.'

Small? Yes, Christoph supposed it was small, compared to a palace. But he would have called the double-fronted, five-bed-chamber townhouse with a library and small study that overlooked the long garden rather more than a 'small place'.

And this was what he had come for, wasn't it? A home, an income…and a wife.

Christoph blew out slowly as the tension of what was to come this evening started to creep through his bones.

Everything had gone to plan. Except it hadn't, because he had not expected someone like Daphne. Someone with her beauty. Someone with her softness and her delicacy—born not from an inflated sense of importance, but a deflated one. Someone who smiled as she did and, at times, spoke like a woman with far more intelligence than anyone had any right to.

Christoph swallowed hard. It had been easy—perhaps too easy—to put together the plan in Niedernlein when he had discovered his brother's plans to marry an English heiress. When the woman he would be saving from such a dangerous man had been a faceless, nameless someone, it had been easy to think coldly, objectively, about how he would marry her then have little to do with her.

And now...now he wanted the opposite. He wanted to sit by her feet and encourage her to talk, really talk. He wanted to discover the Daphne underneath...

Hot, aching desire shot through him. The woman underneath all those clothes...

'Keep it together, man,' Christoph muttered to himself in the empty hallway. 'Focus on the plan.'

Because, though Daphne was most definitely not what he had expected, that could not permit him to deviate from his intentions. He had to follow through. The plan had to remain his focus, not the woman he wanted to know, not the hands he wanted to hold, not the...

'And will Your Highness be requiring anything else?' came a quiet question.

Christoph started. Lost as he had become in his thoughts, he had not realised there was someone else in the hall. Clearing his throat and pushing aside all thoughts of the brother he was determined to forget, Christoph shook his head. 'No, nothing else, thank you, Henderson.'

The butler inclined his head. From anyone else it would have been a gracious movement, a respectful one. Somehow this man, who was perhaps a decade older than Christoph, managed to make it slightly disdainful.

'And I suppose my lady needs nothing else either?' said Henderson. 'The maids are tired and wish to retire.'

The maids were tired? Had they just spent the last few hours attempting to remember six-and-forty family names, and how precisely they interacted with each other?

Of course, it was possible that the man spoke out of turn—perhaps even unwittingly. Perhaps the maids had no idea that the butler would say such a thing. Perhaps he should have chosen his own servants, but his father-in-law had been so obliging, and the butler apparently came highly recommended. It was easier to acquiesce, particularly when Christoph was so conscious that it was his father-in-law's money that would be paying the servants' wages. Why not let him select his household?

Tiredness tugged at Christoph's eyes. There was still one thing he had to do this evening, exhausted as he was, difficult as it would be. He had to bed his wife.

'The servants, including *yourself*, may retire for the evening,' Christoph said aloud, a small emphasis on the last word just to make sure that the man knew his place.

'Princess Daphne and I will be retiring ourselves before too long.'

Henderson grinned. 'I bet you are.'

At least, that was what Christoph thought he said. 'I beg your pardon?'

'I said, you have come far, my lord,' the butler said smoothly, his bow obsequious but at least more akin to what was expected from a servant. 'And we are glad to have you here in London.'

'Yes. Good,' said Christoph sharply, hating the arrogance in his voice, hating how he could turn it on so easily.

God, that was something Anton would say.

'Thank you for your hard work today. Please share my gratitude with the others.'

Again the butler inclined his head. 'I will, Your Highness.'

'Good evening, Henderson,' he said lightly, as though this entire conversation had gone entirely as he wanted.

Christoph stepped past the butler and into the drawing room. The place was worse for wear: several wine glasses and a few brandy glasses were still dotted about the place, and a platter of drying food had been left on the pianoforte.

And there, by a crackling fire, her face drawn with exhaustion but still remarkably beautiful, was Daphne. Ignoring the skip of his heart, and the way she made him want to puff out his chest, Christoph shut the door behind him.

The click made Daphne start, her eyes lurching to the door. When she met his eye, she flushed. 'Oh. Hello.'

Hello.

Christoph tried to smile. Well, he was married now. This was his wife. He would have to start acting as if she was.

'I hope you are not too tired,' he began as he walked forward.

The cringe tensed through his body almost as soon as the words were out of his mouth. Oh, God, did she think he was checking to see if she was too tired for...? She must do. That would explain the scarlet in her cheeks.

'Not too tired.'

Daphne was seated at one end of a sofa and for a moment Christoph considered sitting beside her. The temptation was strong to take the opportunity to feel the movement of her skirts against his breeches, to lean over and take her hand in his, perhaps to feel her breath on his cheek as he pressed a kiss on her...

Christoph dropped onto the armchair opposite her and crossed his legs.

Blast it all to hell.

'There were a great many people at the wedding,' he said aloud. That was it—conversation. He could make conversation. How hard could it be?

Very hard, as it turned out. 'Yes,' said Daphne quietly.

He waited for a moment, expecting her to say more, but it appeared that she had little interest in maintaining a conversation.

Excellent. That wasn't going to make this evening difficult in any way...

'Your father seemed pleased,' Christoph attempted.

She gave a nod. That was all.

Hell's bells, was it truly going to be this challenging?

'And your stepmother,' he tried, slightly unsure whether this was a good direction to take. How well did they know each other? He had never thought to ask. 'She appeared happy.'

She gave a smile—a slight one. 'Yes, she did.'

Despite the slightly longer reply, Daphne's response was stilted, her nerves clearly getting the better of her.

Christoph shifted in his armchair. Her lack of interest was palpable, not only in himself, but in any sort of discussion.

Okay. Well, there was only one other route he could think to take at this late hour... Goodness, was it truly past eleven? Flattery.

'Your father did an excellent job, hosting this wedding. His taste, truly, is impeccable,' Christoph said with a sweep of his arm around the room. 'He must care about you very deeply.'

His declaration had everything: a familial connection, flattery of her father, praise for the day itself, with a reminder that it was their wedding day, and a nod to the close connection between father and daughter. If Christoph had been a betting man—and he never had been—he would have wagered that Daphne would be eager to continue the conversation on at least one of those lines.

He watched, however, as Daphne's cheeks flushed, her

legs crossed and uncrossed with seeming unconscious discomfort and her gaze dropped to her hands.

'It's the only thing he's ever done for me,' came her quiet words. There was no malice, but no affection either. 'Other than send me away to the Wallflower Academy when I was a child, pretend he had no daughter, then offer that daughter to another man for money.'

Christoph swallowed hard, his mouth dry. 'I see.'

And he did, almost. It did not appear, then, that Lord Norbury had the close relationship with his daughter Christoph had assumed. This Wallflower Academy was a finishing school of sorts.

'Love, I suppose, comes in many forms,' he attempted. 'Your father, I am sure—'

'Do not speak of what you do not know.'

The words were spoken calmly yet forcefully, and Daphne clasped a hand over her mouth once the statement was out. Apparently she was horrified at what she had said.

Christoph was hardly offended. No, it was a glimpse of the woman who just as suddenly was lost as her expression darkened and she pursed her lips, as though determined not to allow another single word to come out.

It was almost…frustrating. There was a tension in his loins that he knew had to be released, and could only be released in one way, to make this day mean something.

It was also frustrating in a different way. Her father might not love her, true, but he had done what was best, as far as Christoph could see. If Daphne had had any idea what it would be like to be part of a family that had no interest in her at all... True, her father might show his regard in unfortunate or stilted ways, but still—he cared.

But that did not absolve him, Christoph, from the task he faced this evening. Taking a deep breath, he reminded himself that he had to do this. It had to happen. Yes, it would be awkward, and yes, he was certain that both he and Daphne would find it most awkward to discuss.

It helped, of course, that he was attracted to his new wife. More than attracted—intrigued; there was something about her that he could not quite understand. Something that suggested there was far more going on with Miss Daphne Smith—Princess Daphne, now—than most people ever saw.

If he was careful, the encounter would be pleasurable for both of them. That was what Christoph needed to remember: that, though this was a formality, a necessity, it was also a chance to...well...woo his wife.

And he would never force her. That was why he had to do what felt like the impossible and ask her.

'Daphne,' Christoph said curtly. She looked up, and he took another deep breath. 'I must bed you this evening.'

If Daphne had not been so ensconced on the sofa, he thought she would have fallen to the floor. The look of shock was certainly enough to startle *him*. Her hand fell from her mouth as she parted her lips, then appeared to think better of it as a dark-red flush moved up the décolletage that Christoph was desperately trying not to look at, and closed her mouth.

Well. That was the worst of it out of the way...wasn't it?

'You know as well as I that this marriage is not entirely legal unless we... Unless it is consummated,' Christoph said, as matter-of-factly as he could manage. 'I cannot risk... It would be inadvisable to wait. If you are ready.'

'Ready?' whispered his new wife.

The self-loathing was back. Try as he might, Christoph could not completely push it aside. He was using her: using her as a tool in his plan, a mere pawn in his design.

'Yes, ready,' Christoph forced himself to say, not quite sure what he was supposed to do with his hands. Perhaps clasp them in his lap?

Daphne looked down at the floor for a moment, as though steeling herself for something truly unpleasant. Then she looked up. 'If you insist.'

'I don't—' Christoph caught himself before he said something truly unforgivable. 'I do not insist, Daphne. I am your husband. I am not a monster.'

That gained a small smile, at least. 'But you wish to... to consummate the marriage. Tonight.'

'It would prevent any chance of the marriage being annulled.' That was it, focus on the legalities. Nothing else. 'It would prevent you from being sent back to the Wallflower Academy.'

He did not know what had made him say it. Divine inspiration, perhaps. Perhaps he had read her better than he had thought, for at his words Daphne looked up at Christoph with a sharp look.

'I do not want to go back.'

'And I do not want to lose...' *You.* 'Your hand. So... shall we?'

Christoph rose. Better to get it over with. Better to get her upstairs, sink himself into her, sob with joy, and... *Wait, no.* He couldn't think about it like that.

Daphne did not mirror him. 'B-before we go upstairs, I... I think we should talk about it. Some rules, if...if you will.'

Christoph sank back into the armchair. 'You wish to negotiate?'

That gained a smile, a real one, and the vision of Daphne smiling with genuine delight warmed him. 'Yes, I suppose so. Are...are there any rules you wish to propose?'

She really was a mystery. There was a no-nonsense demeanour about the woman now, almost businesslike. She made it rather hard to concentrate.

Yes. Keep it simple.

'Well, we only need to make love once. To make sure. After that, there are no expectations.'

Daphne nodded, as though she approved of his suggestion. Christoph fought hard not to glow with pride. 'Agreed. No...no cuddling. I will depart from your bed chamber the moment it...it is over. I presume we have separate bedchambers?'

Christoph had no idea, but there appeared to be plenty of room. 'To be sure, I can agree to that. Any other stipulations?'

He watched as she considered. There was an intelligence there, a raw one—one hardly tried, from what he could see. Her eyes flickered as she considered, evidently looking for ways to reduce the experience as much as possible.

Despite himself, Christoph found he was a tad piqued. He might not be the most experienced man in Christendom—fine. He was not experienced at all. But he had read books. Heard other men talk about it. Had a vague idea of what a woman wanted.

He certainly knew what he wanted.

The fire crackled between them as Daphne finally said slowly, 'And no…no kissing.'

That was a surprise. 'No kissing?'

He had not intended to repeat her words so baldly, so he was not astonished when Daphne flushed a dark red. 'No kissing my lips. This is not a love match, as you have made perfectly clear. When I kiss a man, I wish to kiss him because of the affection between us. We are married, so now I will never kiss a man who loves me.'

Her words became weak at the end, and Christoph's heart broke for her. He had done this. He had forced her, manoeuvred her father and her into a marriage to the royal line of Niedernlein, all for their wealth and position in Society.

And to protect Daphne, in a way. And give himself a future. But still; it was his desires, his intentions, which had brought her here, into a marriage where she would never be loved.

He owed her this.

'One time only,' Christoph said, ticking off their

agreements on his fingers. 'No cuddling. Immediate departure. No kissing on the lips.'

Daphne nodded, gaze averted. 'Yes. Agreed.'

A strange sort of silence fell between them, muffling out all other sounds. So, they had reached an agreement. Now all they had to do was…follow the rules.

Christoph rose slowly and held out his hand. 'Shall we?'

This time Daphne did not shrink from him, but neither did she speak. She rose in complete silence, took his hand and walked willingly with him out of the drawing room to the hall.

Christoph had not expected his heart to beat so rapidly, nor his nerves to return with such ferocity.

She doesn't know it's your first time, he tried to remind himself. *And she hasn't… She certainly won't know what to do. She won't have any expectations.*

It did not seem to matter. His pulse was thundering, making it difficult to think. To breathe. By the time they reached the bedchamber door, however, Christoph had regained the tight control over himself which he had practised all his adult life. This was an agreement, an arrangement—with limitations carefully negotiated. He just had to get through it.

'After you,' he said, his voice somehow hoarse.

There was a momentary flash of a smile on Daphne's face—why, he did not know. She reached out and opened the door to reveal…the largest four-poster bed Christoph had ever seen.

'Good,' he said aloud, as though that would be helpful. 'So... I suppose we should undress.'

Just for a moment, there was a teasing smile on Daphne's face. 'You suppose?'

It was gone in an instant, her horror clear that she had said such a thing. Been so forward. So attractive.

Christoph tried to keep his face impassive. 'Yes. Clothes off. I'll... I'll let you sort yourself out.'

Sort herself out? Come on, man! That had been the perfect opportunity to step closer, to inhale her, to touch her...

'I'll need your help,' Daphne said quietly, turning round to show him her back and the complex knots of her gown.

A knot also tied itself in Christoph's throat. Voice incapable of sound, he grunted as he strode forward and started to undo the gown. His fingers fumbled as he breathed in, his view over her shoulder of her rising and falling breasts. Was she...was her breath quickening? Was that a reaction to him?

Don't be a fool, he tried to tell himself as the gown came apart in his hands, slipping to the floor in a rush of silks and satins, leaving Daphne in naught but her stays and chemise. *She wasn't reacting to you.*

She was probably terrified. The thought was unpleasant. Christoph stepped away hurriedly. 'You...you can do the rest yourself?'

Daphne nodded, not turning to face him as she started to pull apart her stays. Try as he might, he could not help but feel despondent at the lack of intimacy. When he had thought about his wedding night—though in truth he had not given much thought to it—it had not been like this. Not cold, clinical and…and lonely.

It did not take Christoph long to strip off his clothes. When he straightened, standing in the room completely naked, he looked over at Daphne and saw…

Thinking ceased to be possible.

Oh, hell.

She was stunning. Far more radiant than he could have imagined, with soft, swelling curves and flat planes, angles and arches, softness everywhere he looked…

'I'll get on the bed,' Daphne said, cheeks red, turning away from him as soon as she could.

Christoph might have nodded. He might even have opened his mouth and said something, not that he was aware of it. He could only watch in awe as the most delicious woman he had ever seen scrambled onto the large bed and lay back, staring up at the ceiling.

To be certain, she was nervous. He could see it in the tension in her fingers, held rigidly straight by her sides. Could see it in her breathiness, her breasts rising and falling in quick succession. Distracting as their magnificence was, he could not ignore the increasing shallowness of her breathing.

Christoph bit his lip. He wanted a willing participant, and she was willing—but frightened. Did she not know what was to come? Perhaps it was not lack of interest he had detected downstairs, after their guests had departed, but shyness.

'I'm… I'm ready.'

He wasn't. He wasn't quite sure how he was still able to stand. He certainly didn't know how he managed to get over to the bed.

Daphne did not look at him as Christoph pulled himself alongside her. 'Do it.'

His heart broke. 'You are very beautiful.'

'You don't have to say that.' Her words were clipped.

Christoph swallowed. 'I know I don't. But it's true.'

She looked at him then, eyes wide and cheeks pink. 'I don't know what I'm doing.'

'You don't have to do anything. I'll... I'll try to make it good for you,' Christoph said, his voice low, almost trembling. 'Just...just lie there. If you want me to stop...'

'I'll tell you,' said Daphne solemnly, her focus resolutely on the ceiling. 'Just...just make it good. If you can.'

And that was when Christoph considered a challenge to have been issued. It hadn't been. At least, not from her mouth. But it had been in the very air of her determination to suffer through something that Christoph was determined to make enjoyable.

Did she think she wouldn't feel pleasure? He would see about that. No kissing on the lips. Okay. But that did not discount everything else. He could do...other things.

Propping himself up alongside her on his elbow, Christoph blew out a long exhale and tried to calm his rapidly thumping heart. What would bring a woman like this pleasure? It was his own nerves that made his hand shake as he raised it, but Christoph forced himself to move. A fingertip trailed down Daphne's beautiful neck, slowly along a collarbone and then gently over the rise of her breast.

Her inhale faltered.

Christoph's mouth went dry as he allowed his finger to trail to one of her nipples. He circled, slowly, and saw how it tightened, saw the flutter of Daphne's pulse quiver in her throat. Her breathing halted, then returned.

He was acting restrained, and he wasn't sure he could do so for much longer. Allowing his hand to wander down the plane of her stomach and across to her hip, caressing her skin along the way, Christoph slowly lowered his mouth, slowly, slowly…until he brushed a kiss across her nipple.

It was not his imagination. For a moment, just a moment, Daphne's back arched into him. Then she was flat on the bed again, saying nothing.

It did not matter. Christoph had felt such a jolt of desire thrum through him at the taste of the supple flesh that he returned to her nipple again, this time sucking as his hand moved slowly from her hip, clasping it, caressing it, slowly, slowly, slowly, moving it to her curls.

Daphne stiffened. He halted. She relaxed. Christoph circled his tongue around her nipple, revelling in the quivering her whole body now displayed, and slipped a finger into her soft, wet quim.

He could have wept in that moment.

Oh, God, she felt wonderful.

His manhood had begun stiffening from the moment they had been alone together in the drawing room but it was nothing compared to this. Nothing to tasting her, his mouth moving to her other breast, her other nipple, as his finger slowly explored the quaking dampness of her desire.

'I...you... You don't have to...'

'I want to.' Christoph had not intended it to be a growl, but there did not seem to be any other calibre of intonation in his throat. 'Our only time—your only time. You will enjoy it.'

He had not intended to issue it as an order, and when he looked up Daphne was still looking resolutely at the ceiling. But she nodded, and some of the tension left her face as she whimpered, a whimper of pleasure that occurred just as his finger brushed past a small, circular nub within her secret place.

That was interesting. Christoph returned his lips to her body, moving across her décolletage, pressing kisses against her collarbone, fluttering kisses up her neck and behind her ear, all while his fingers gently stroked her quim.

When he reached her ear, he didn't know what made him do it. But he couldn't help himself. 'You're beautiful, Daphne,' Christoph groaned, his thumb circling around that delicate nub. She gasped, she shivered, and he continued, both his words and his fingers unrelenting. 'You are clever, and beautiful, and wise, and brave, and I've never wanted anyone like I've wanted you...'

Daphne was panting now, whimpering, her hips rocking into his fingers as though she could no longer restrain herself.

Christoph buried his face into her hair, breathing her

in, desperate not to lose himself. 'I wanted to do this to you the moment I first met you. I wanted to know how you felt, the depth of you…'

'Please.' The word seemed first dragged out of her, as though Daphne could hardly believe she could say such a thing, but then said, 'Please, please, yes…'

It was almost too much. He had to get her there, had to bring her to a peak, because soon he would reach his own.

Christoph pressed a desperate, urgent kiss to Daphne's soft skin, just below her ear, and whispered, 'Let go.'

And she did. Daphne came apart in his arms, his fingers remorseless in the stroking and teasing, and she cried out in wonder and shock and let go, her whole body shaking, as Christoph hoped pleasure and not pain rocked through her body.

When she finally quietened, Christoph moved swiftly. It had to be now, while the afterglow of her ecstasy protected her.

Daphne's eyes widened as she took him in, nestled between her legs. 'Christoph, I…'

'This might hurt,' he warned her before slowly inching the dripping head of his manhood to her quim. When Christoph entered her, slowly, inch by inch, sheathing himself in her as though he hadn't waited his entire life for this moment, he worked hard not to let the intense sensual bliss show on his face. This wasn't about him. This wasn't about his pleasure. This was about consummating their marriage.

She looked at him in wonder, almost in confusion.

When Christoph let out a sigh, unable to help himself as he finished plunging slowly into her, she whispered, 'When is it supposed to hurt?'

Christoph breathed out a relieved sigh with a smile. 'It doesn't? Good.'

'It feels…'

'And I will be careful not to…'

'It feels good.'

It was all Christoph could do not to moan aloud—partly because he did not wish to frighten her, partly because the lack of control might mean he'd pour straight into her. 'It—it does?'

She looked up at him, nerves still visible in her eyes, but something else too. Something warm. Something trusting. 'You feel good.'

He was almost ready to spill into her immediately, the tension working on him, the exquisite decadence of feeling her come around his fingers more than he could take. She felt so good, so tight, so welcoming, so ready for him.

Daphne nodded, lying back without saying another word.

Well, it wasn't what he had hoped for his wedding night. But he could not have imagined a woman like this.

Gritting his teeth, and hoping to goodness he could give her additional pleasure, but knowing that she was getting him to a peak just by him resting within her, Christoph drew himself back almost until his manhood was free, then sank into her again, faster this time.

He groaned with the pleasure…and was that something from Daphne? No. No, he had been dreaming it, surely?

'Not long now,' he said with terrible accuracy. God, he hoped he'd be longer next time.

But there wouldn't be a next time, would there? No, this was it. The thought further stiffened his manhood and, before Christoph could stop himself, he was thrusting in and out, in and out, glorifying in the tight clenching of her body that welcomed him in, tightening around him, and it felt wonderful and…

And it did not appear to be only he who was enjoying this. Daphne was breathing heavily, her hips twisting to take him deeper, and there was a look on her face that he recognised. It had, after all, only been visible a few minutes ago.

A rush of delight soared through Christoph as he realised he was bringing Daphne to another crest, and it focused him as he built the rhythm, driving harder and harder into the welcoming wetness, and he groaned with the tension of withholding his own pleasure.

'Christoph!'

Daphne shouting his name did it. That, or how the sudden cascade of sensuality that was rushing through her tightened her quim in a desperate spasm of agonising rigidity.

Unbelievable ecstasy roared through Christoph as he pumped into her, once, twice, a third time, a fourth, pouring all that he was, all that he wanted to be, into the woman who was his wife.

His body spent, his shoulders aching from holding

himself up, Christoph almost fell into Daphne's arms but managed to catch himself. He rolled to her side, his body still spasming with the glow of his peak, not knowing where he was, what he was doing, or even his own name.

Time passed. Christoph lay back, hardly able to think, his chest heaving.

That...that was...

'Daphne,' he murmured. He needed her. He needed to touch her, clasp her into his arms.

His questing fingers found nothing but empty air. The bed was empty. So was the room.

Sitting up so suddenly that his head spun, Christoph looked around himself in confusion until the memory of their agreement returned.

No...no cuddling. I will depart from your bedchamber the moment it...it is over.

Of course. She was gone. The deed was done, and they would never have to do it again.

Christoph fell back onto the bed and closed his eyes in horror at what he had agreed to.

Chapter Seven

It was most disconcerting to wake up and not know where she was.

Daphne dived deeper into the sheets. They were soft, warm, comforting, yet somehow wrong. They didn't have the scratchy quality that her sheets had always had. And the blankets above her; they were softer, too.

She clung to the pillow but discovered it plumper than her own. Something was wrong.

Opening a bleary eye, Daphne looked around her room at the Wallflower Academy where she had awoken every day for the last fifteen years...

She sat up abruptly in the large four-poster bed. This was not the Wallflower Academy. Her heart was hammering, her thighs sore... Thighs sore?

Daphne looked down. Her nightgown was the same but, other than it and herself, everything else was different. Her mind spun, her thoughts hurriedly attempting to recall...

The wedding. The wedding reception. The wedding night.

'You wish to negotiate?'

'Yes, I suppose so. Are...are there any rules you wish to propose?'

'Oh,' Daphne whispered, wrapping her arms around her and holding tightly round her waist. So, it was done. She had married Prince Christoph, just as her father had wanted. In doing so, she had handed him a great fortune. She had been bedded by him, too, so there was no possibility of annulment.

Not that she particularly wanted one, that was.

You are clever, and beautiful, and wise, and brave, and I've never wanted anyone like I've wanted you.

Daphne swallowed, her mouth dry. It had been...more than she had expected. More intimate. More enjoyable, certainly.

Looking around, she saw that the bedchamber she had crept to—the one next door to the one where they had been fully married, for want of a better term—was rather lovely. There were tall, high windows with wide curtains, undrawn, because it had been midnight-black when she had slipped in here. There was also a beautiful dresser, with a matching toilette table and stool, a longcase clock and several elegant paintings of landscapes.

Daphne swallowed hard and brought her knees to her chest, transferring her embrace from her waist to her legs.

Well, she had done it. She was a wife. And, despite all her negotiations, despite the limitations she had attempted to put on the encounter, something...something had happened.

Something she had not expected.

Please, please, yes...

Daphne closed her eyes, just for a moment, and she was back there, in that bed, with Christoph nestled between her thighs. He had felt right there—there was no other word for it, scandalous as it may be—as though he belonged there. As though she had been waiting for him, and now that he was here...

Her eyes snapped open. No. He would not want that, would he?

Well, we only need to make love once. To make sure. After that, there are no expectations.

Still. As Daphne rose and began to dress, tugging at the bellpull by the fireplace for some assistance, and flushing as a maid she did not know arrived, she wondered just where Christoph was that morning.

'Anything else, miss? I mean... Your Highness?' the maid asked quietly a little while later, when she had helped Daphne to dress.

The maid flushed and so did Daphne, hardly aware that she was now dressed. Your Highness? She, a princess? That was the sort of game one played when one was a child. One dreamt of crowns as an escape from the Wallflower Academy.

'N-no. No, thank you.'

The maid dipped a low curtsey, something Daphne was most unaccustomed to, and slipped out of the room. Daphne remained, staring at something most odd in the looking glass: her own reflection.

Something had changed. Daphne did not know if it

was sleeping in a different bed, or now having a different name, a different title or being married…fully married.

But something was altered in her expression. Was there a sharpness in her eye where there had been naught but obedience?

'Right,' she said aloud. 'Breakfast.'

Precisely what hours they would keep—and her stomach gave a twist every time she thought of 'they', 'we' and 'us'—she was not sure. Daphne did not pass anyone as she walked down the sweeping staircase and it took her two attempts to find the breakfast room. It was elegantly decorated, with a round table in the centre covered in a white linen tablecloth.

One place contained a dirty plate. Daphne had not expected the sudden disappointment that rushed through her.

'His lordship has eaten and departed,' murmured a footman who appeared out of nowhere.

'Departed?' she echoed, her lungs tightening.

Why was she filled with such despondency at the thought of Christoph gone? Gone where? For how long?

'He had some urgent business come through the post, I am given to understand,' the footman said quietly. 'He will be returning for dinner.'

'Oh.' Well, what had she been expecting? This was not a love match, after all, Daphne tried to remind herself. Separate lives, that was what he had said. She smiled at the footman, wishing he were Matthews, the footman who had served at the Wallflower Academy the last ten years. 'Thank you.'

The footman bowed and left the room.

Why was she so surprised? Why had she permitted such hope to rise, when she knew it was almost ridiculous to aspire to it?

Daphne tried to conquer the shifting tides of disappointment within her. Yes, she was always ignored, always set aside, always overlooked. That had been her life, and over the years she had learned to expect nothing more.

Until a prince had turned up at the Wallflower Academy and requested her as his bride. This could have been different. This could have been something more, and yet within four and twenty hours Daphne had once again been ignored. Once again set aside. Once again overlooked.

Daphne did her best to blink back the tears of confusion and swirling emotions as she helped herself to her favourites: scrambled eggs, potatoes and tea from the sideboard. There was a great deal of choice for breakfast, it appeared, but at the Wallflower Academy the girls had only been permitted healthy, plain food, and her habits required her to do the same. Not everything could change.

She sat at the breakfast table and ate, her mind working rapidly.

So...she was free. Free from the Wallflower Academy, from its routines, from Miss Pike's expectations...and she had absolutely no idea what to do. She had never lived with such freedom. She'd never been permitted to choose her own activities, eat what she wanted or go where she wanted.

What was she supposed to do?

The day passed slowly. Daphne drifted from room to room. The house was elegant, well-apportioned, but nothing in size compared to the Wallflower Academy. The pianoforte was out of tune. The books were primarily scientific treatises. There was no blanket on which to sit in the garden.

By the time the dinner hour arrived, Daphne had spoken to no one and not seen her husband all day.

'I suppose I dress for dinner,' she said helplessly to a maid who appeared at her side when a gong rang out from somewhere in the house.

The maid bobbed a curtsey. 'It is the Prince's wish.'

Daphne perked up. 'Is he back?'

It was a foolish thing to say and her cheeks burned the moment the words were out of her mouth. Christoph lived here, she reminded herself as the maid peered curiously. Of course he had come back.

'Come, let us select a gown,' Daphne said as imperiously as she could to hide her momentary confusion.

Her stepmother had promised her a trousseau and Daphne had not bothered to look in the wardrobe or trunks at precisely what Lady Norbury had selected. When she did so, her heart sank. Perhaps she should have spoken to her first.

'What an elegant gown, Your Highness,' said the maid cheerfully.

Daphne tried to smile. 'Yes. Elegant.'

It had more ruffles and layers than a wedding cake, and even more lace. It was extravagant, ostentatious, and swallowed Daphne once she had stepped into it.

'I... I imagine you prefer your gowns a little simpler,' hazarded the maid, her pink cheeks pink.

Her own must be scarlet, the temperature they were, thought Daphne. 'Yes.'

'Well, I'll make some adjustments for you, and have the others sent to the modiste's for alterations,' said the maid, tying the last knot of the bodice.

It was impossible not to stare. 'I... I beg your pardon?'

Now it was the maid's turn to look confused. 'Well, they're your gowns, Your Highness. You can have them altered, or changed, or buy others....can't you?'

Could she?

Daphne considered this as she walked downstairs, the second gong still echoing in the hall. She supposed she could. She had never had any control over her gowns before. Miss Pike had been given a clothing allowance for her, and Miss Pike spent it as she wished.

It was most odd. Perhaps she should...

'Goodness,' said Christoph as she came into the dining room. 'What a gown.'

Daphne briefly considered running and never being seen again, but that felt like an overreaction—even for her. 'It is a...a bit much. I'm going to have it altered.'

'Good,' said her husband fervently. 'Shall we?'

It was not, perhaps, the conversation she had expected after...well...after the last time she had seen him. After he'd been thrusting between her legs, bringing her to ecstasy, pouring himself into her.

Daphne swallowed. Her throat was dry, a knot in the middle making speech almost impossible.

Say something. Say something!

'I… I hope your day was a successful one,' she managed as a footman pulled out a chair. 'Thank you.'

'Successful?' said Christoph vaguely as he sat opposite her.

'A footman mentioned something about the post,' Daphne said, trying to inject a little earnestness into her tone.

It did not appear to matter. Her husband nodded. 'Yes. I had a letter to post.'

Daphne waited as they were served their opening course, a pea soup that smelled delicious, but apparently there was no more to be said. Christoph started to consume his soup, his focus fixed on the soup plate. What should she say? And how could she say it, with two footmen in the room, standing by the walls and staring fixedly before them as though they were pieces of furniture?

'You will have to excuse me.'

She looked up. 'Excuse you?'

'I…my English…it is good, but I do not always get it right,' Christoph said quietly, a wry smile on his lips. 'You will have to excuse me if I sound abrupt. I mean no disrespect.'

Sympathy washed through Daphne. Of course—it

was easy to forget that her husband spoke in his second language.

Daphne cleared her throat and looked at the footmen. 'You...you don't need to remain here. Thank you. I mean, bring in food, yes, good, but...but you don't have to...'

Her voice trailed away. She had never ordered servants. She'd never had to. That was what Miss Pike did. Miss Pike would have come down very hard on one of the wallflowers at the very idea of one of them ordering around a servant. So how was she supposed to manage it?

Christoph glanced up and Daphne's face burnt as he sighed. 'That will be all, thank you.'

The two footmen bowed and stepped out of the dining room. The silence that fell after the door clicked felt friendlier, somehow.

Daphne let out a long exhale. *Good. Well, that was half the battle.*

'I...last night...' she began awkwardly.

Christoph did not look up from his soup. 'Yes, very satisfactory.'

Satisfactory? *Satisfactory?* For a moment, she was in half a mind to throw her spoon at him. Perhaps the soup too. Satisfactory? Was that truly all he could say about an evening during which she had laid herself bare, he had brought her to ecstasy twice and poured into her what could make a child?

Daphne wet her lips. For a heartbeat she thought Christoph's gaze flickered to her mouth, but she must have imagined it, for he was still staring resolutely at his soup. 'I thought we could...we could talk about...'

'There is nothing to talk about in...in that regard,' Christoph said shortly. 'We knew what we needed to do. We did it. As agreed, there is no further requirement in that...direction.'

Daphne's fingers knotted together in her lap, her soup forgotten.

But I want more, she wanted to say, her rigid control over her inside thoughts preventing them from being spoken. *I want further requirements in that direction. I want to understand how you made me feel so...so good. So desired. So beautiful. I've never felt that way before and I don't want to go through my life never feeling it again. Tell me. Talk to me. Show me.*

But she couldn't say that. Instead, she said, 'It was just, I thought—and I might have been wrong, obviously—but I thought... I wondered if there was something.'

Christoph looked up. His expression was uninterested. 'Something?'

Something between us. 'Something different.'

'Different? Yes, we are man and wife now. That is the difference, I suppose,' said Christoph vaguely. 'Are you finished?'

She had barely started, but Daphne could not summon the strength to point this out. She nodded.

Christoph rang a silver bell on the end of the dining table that she had not noticed before. The footmen returned, removed their soup plates—hers almost full—and returned with platters of roast pheasant and vegetables. They served the couple, then departed. All this was conducted in silence.

Daphne watched as her husband began to eat. This was the first meal they had ever shared, just the two of them. It should be…well…filled with conversation. A growing understanding between each other. *Something.* Instead it was emptiness.

'You're not hungry?'

Daphne started. Christoph was looking up at her, his plate half-empty. Hers had not been touched. 'Oh. Oh, yes.'

She picked up her fork and for a moment, a mere heartbeat, she saw something on Christoph's face: a smile, a look, warmth, something that had not been there before, and she looked up. It was gone. Christoph was looking blandly down at his plate as he cut his food, though his cheeks were pinking.

Daphne's stomach twisted as she returned to her own food. A spark had perhaps been there, but it was just as possible that she had dreamt it. Or wished it to be there.

So, conversation… Miss Pike had given her over a decade of lessons on conversation. Surely she could think of something? 'What splendid weather we've been having,' Daphne said quietly.

Christoph did not look up. 'It rained all day.'

Had it? Bother.

'In that case, I hope you did not get too damp on your errands, Your Highness.'

She had not intended to call him that. The honorific

was one that Christoph disliked, and had asked her not to use. Daphne was not quite sure why she had used it.

It garnered absolutely no reaction. Apparently, he wanted the distance, the distinction, of rank. 'I did not.'

'I'm glad,' said Daphne quietly, pushing her food around her plate without really looking at it. 'That's good. Good.'

Why was this so difficult? The man had seen her naked, after all—the thought burned the back of her neck—and she had seen him just as naked. She'd felt him naked. Yet the closeness she had presumed would come from such an encounter was entirely absent.

And the secret place between her thighs was aching for him. Try as she might, Daphne could not completely ignore it. Having him so close, the scent of him filling the small dining room, was…distracting. It made her think of those delicate caresses, those wonderful words he'd whispered and the way that he'd seemed to know exactly how she liked to be touched. How she wanted to be loved.

'You look very pretty.'

Daphne almost dropped her fork. 'Do I?'

'I mean—yes, very pretty.' Christoph's face was red now, and there was a look in his eye which could have been embarrassment or could have been… Did he desire her? 'Your gown. Your eyes.'

Her eyes? Heat blossomed through Daphne's chest at the moment, a frisson, something in the air between them that spoke of promise, the future and…

'By the way,' said Christoph quietly, 'I have invited someone to come and stay with us.'

Daphne blinked. 'Stay?'

'Yes. Her name is Laura.'

Daphne had never felt heartbreak before. When one had not had any opportunities for love, one had no opportunities to be betrayed. And she did not love Christoph—certainly not—but they had shared all that a husband and wife could share. He had bedded her, and most thoroughly.

And now...now another woman would be coming to live with them?

'Laura,' she repeated, her voice hoarse.

Christoph nodded. 'Make her welcome, will you? She'll be staying with us indefinitely. Now, if you do not mind, I have some business to attend to.'

'I...'

It apparently did not matter whether she minded or not.

Swallowing hard, Daphne attempted to regain her equilibrium, but her world was rocking so completely that it was impossible to think.

Another woman—Laura—coming to stay. Indefinitely.

Perhaps she should have tried harder. Daphne could almost hear Miss Pike in her ear, criticising her for her insufferably bad conversational skills.

You'll never get a husband like that!

Well, she'd managed to get a husband, but her skills had still not improved. Daphne picked at her food, abandoning her knife and fork, for the food was lukewarm now, taking small mouthfuls of the roast pheasant smothered in gravy.

Was this how it was going to be with Christoph for the rest of her life? Would he remain distant, cold, uncommunicative? Inviting his mistress to live with them the day after their wedding!

So, Laura was his mistress.

The thought had barraged through her mind before Daphne could stop it and, now that she had thought it, she could not unthink it.

Laura. As a name it did not give much away. Yet she was to come and live with them. Surely Christoph would not… Surely no man would move his mistress into his home mere days after his marriage?

Daphne picked up a roast potato, examined it and put it down. She would have thought not, but what did she know about married men? The only married men she knew were her father—not a paragon of virtue—and her friends' husbands, and she barely knew them at all.

You are the Prince's wallflower wife, she reminded herself. *You have a fortune. You have freedom. What else could a woman want?*

This time yesterday, she would have wanted absolutely nothing else. Now, after sharing such an encounter with Christoph, she wanted…more.

A chair moved—it was Christoph. He was…leaving?

'Well I… I hope you sleep well.'

She started. Christoph had stridden over to the door and gone right through it, before poking his head round the door as though waiting for an answer. It was a face that was…well…perhaps 'anguished' was too strong a word.

His smile was awkward. 'I… I do not pretend to be an expert in the matter of husbands, Daphne. It is all new to me. I do not know how to… I want to be a good husband to you.'

It could not be clearer that the man wished to say more, but perhaps did not have the words. His hand was clasped round the side of the door so tightly that she could see the white of his bones.

Was he nervous? What did a man like him have to be nervous about?

Daphne swallowed. 'And I wish to be a good wife to you.'

'We will find a way to get along, I am sure.' Christoph did not sound sure.

Was he attempting to convince her, or himself?

She nodded. 'Y-yes. Yes, we will.' And, with that, he disappeared back behind the door.

Daphne barely slept that night. When she awoke, it was with a fresh purpose.

She was going to make an effort with Christoph. Precisely how, she did not know, but she would be pleasant, entertaining. They were not in love with each other, to be sure, but she could make their life together enjoyable. Perhaps, she could not help but think, then invitations to Lauras would not be necessary.

The breakfast table only had one place laid. Clearly no one was to join her.

'Erm…excuse me,' Daphne said to a man who had to be the butler.

He turned. 'Yes?'

Daphne almost took a step back, but she managed to hold herself in position. It was not the sort of reaction she had expected. 'I… Where is Prince Christoph?'

'Gone.'

She sat rather hurriedly on a chair at the breakfast table. 'Gone?'

'Gone for a few nights, he said,' the butler replied coldly. 'Didn't tell me where, and didn't tell you, by the look of it.'

Daphne swallowed, her hopes deflating. 'I… I see.'

And she did. This was to be her life, and she had been a fool to hope for anything else. There was no romance in this marriage and no hope of any.

The sooner she accepted that, the better.

Chapter Eight

The carriage was far too small.

Christoph attempted to push himself right to the edge of it, but it wasn't far enough. He would never be far enough away from Daphne to stop himself thinking of her. Wanting her. Wanting to reach out...

'I have never attended Almack's before,' Daphne said softly, her eyes downcast, her attention on her twisting fingers. 'I... I admit I am attempting to recall all Miss Pike has ever taught me, terrified that I will forget some crucial element of courtesy. Have...have you ever attended?'

'No,' said Christoph quietly, attempting not to let his excitement overflow.

He wanted to say more. He wanted to tell her again how beautiful she looked; how the restyled gowns suited her so much better than the monstrosity she had worn on their second evening together. How he missed her. How something had changed between them, the gentle companionship they had somehow found in the lead up to their wedding broken because of his own foolishness, his own stupidity.

What had he done, agreeing never to touch her again?

'I hope it is diverting,' came Daphne's soft words.

Christoph swallowed as the carriage rattled along the London streets and forced himself not to allow her to draw him into conversation. Even if he wanted her to.

You cannot deviate from the plan, he told himself sternly. *The last thing you need is your heart getting entangled. This woman is a means to an end, and you're almost there.*

It had been bad enough just how…how connected he had felt to his wife when they had made love. Because it had been making love, and Christoph could not deny it. The vulnerability, the openness they had shared, even in the awkwardness… He had never felt so seen, so understood, by another person. Had he lowered himself in her eyes—had he showed too much emotion? It had been a moment of weakness. He could not, would not, permit that moment to define his character.

'I suppose we shall have to dance together.'

Christoph smiled, despite his attempt at focus. 'I suppose so.'

It was painful to see the hope in her—hope he could not allow to flourish. This was not a love match, and emotions would only make him weak, give him a vulnerability he could little afford. He still did not know whether Anton yet knew what his brother had done. That he had reported Katalina's death to the authorities, only to discover that their hands were tied—no one could not arrest the King of Niedernlein. He'd realised he had no choice but to leave the country. He'd stolen out of Niedernlein. Crept across Europe. Lied to the Earl of Norbury. Married the bride intended for the older brother.

Still, excitement was thrumming through his veins. The famous Almack's; tales of its gatherings had reached across Europe to Niedernlein and it was a sight he had always wanted to see. And here they were, moments from it.

Christoph cleared his throat. 'You…you enjoy dancing?'

Daphne looked up at him and his pulse skipped a beat. Such beauty. Such uncertainty. Did she not know how beautiful she was, how his whole body responded to her?

'I don't know if I enjoy dancing,' she said quietly. 'I have never danced with a man before.'

'Never danced with…? But then, how do you know how to…?'

'We practised at the Wallflower Academy, and there weren't any men to practise with,' Daphne said lightly. 'I…you will be my first.'

It was all Christoph could do not to launch himself the few feet across the carriage, pull the woman into his arms and claim their first kiss. Yes, he was her first. In everything. The strange possessiveness which encircled his heart made him captive to her. Christoph had been entirely caught by this woman the moment she'd quivered under his touch.

He swallowed. 'Well. I hope my skills are sufficient.'

What had possessed him to say such a thing?

Daphne smiled, and the carriage warmed by several degrees. 'I have not been disappointed so far.'

Despite himself, despite all his finer feelings and grand plans, Christoph returned her smile. Why, this was almost akin to flirting—and he was enjoying it. Flirting, with his wife.

Christoph's breath caught in his throat and he forced himself to look away from the woman seated opposite him.

'I suppose Laura is a good dancer.'

'I... Yes. Yes, I suppose she is.'

His sister had always been a good dancer. God, he hoped she had managed to get out. He hoped she was somewhere in France by now, getting closer every day to the safety that England, that his new wife's money, could provide.

But it wasn't about the money. If he were to tell the truth, Christoph was not certain when the money had ceased to be his greatest concern, but it felt long ago. No, it was the connections, the position in Society. Son-in-law to the Earl of Norbury was a powerful position to hold indeed. Yes, the ability to gain acceptance into English Society had become far more important. Daphne, he was certain, would act as his key to unlock his new position here in England.

And now...now it was diffcrent again. The drive that spurred him on was not wealth, or position, but...family. Was it possible? Could he and Daphne build a life, build a home that would welcome others and form the very foundation of his life? A place of laughter and joy, of opportunity, of prosperity?

Christoph caught movement out of the corner of his eye. He blinked, and saw Daphne twist her hands together in her lap, her nerves palpable.

'You do not have to be anxious.'

The words had slipped from him before Christoph could stop them, but he did not regret them, as he saw his wife smile apprehensively.

'I... I do not think I have much choice,' she admitted quietly.

Christoph nodded. He should have expected this. True, it was their first Society event as man and wife, but as far as he could tell this was also Daphne's first Society event without the security of the Wallflower Academy around her. Miss Pike might be formidable, but she surely gave her charges comfort that she was for them, not against them. Now Daphne would have to stand without the shield of Miss Pike.

He leaned forward and captured her hands with his own. Her sudden gasp did something strange to his stomach, twisting it in a most pleasant way.

'I am here,' he said quietly. 'And we are going to have a wonderful time.'

Daphne's nervous eyes widened. 'Are we?'

'We are,' Christoph repeated, squeezing her hand and wishing to goodness it did not feel so right to sit here with her hands in his own. 'And we—'

The carriage jolted and he smiled. 'We are here.'

One of their footmen—he really would have to remember their names—opened the carriage door. Christoph stepped out and turned instinctively to offer his hand to Daphne. She emerged from the carriage flushing a deep red that he was starting to grow accustomed to. It was... Daphne. And he liked it. He liked her.

Focus, man!

Wordlessly, Christoph offered his arm to his wife and she took it just as silently. They entered the atrium at Almack's, were relieved of their outer garments and had just stepped into the large ballroom when a whirlwind most disobligingly attacked them.

Well, it felt like a whirlwind...

'There you are! Didn't I tell you they'd be here? Daphne! Daphne, it's been a week since we've seen you!'

'Don't shout, Sylvia, you know how she feels about that!'

'What are you doing here? I thought you'd be enjoying wedded bliss!'

Three women descended on them, chattering away over each other as though it did not truly matter whether anyone was listening, as long as they were talking. Somehow they had managed to detach Daphne from him, pulling her a few feet away and embracing her heartily while they continued to talk.

'Oh, this gown is exquisite. I don't remember it being in your trousseau.'

'How sore are you? I couldn't walk for a week after!'

'Sylvia!'

'Well, a friend can ask, can't she?'

Try as he might, Christoph could not prevent his

cheeks from burning much as his wife's often did. It was hardly an appropriate conversation to be had in public! Evidently, though, Daphne did not mind.

It was most odd. In the presence of her friends, he clearly momentarily forgotten, his wife seemed to blossom. Her cheeks were still pink, true, but she was attempting to reply to a great deal of the conversation around her, placing her hands on the black woman's stomach, which was clearly with child, and laughing at their nonsense.

'I can walk perfectly well, I assure you... The gown was altered; so many ruffles! We thought we'd dance; you know I've never danced with a gentleman before... Where are your husbands?'

'Oh, we left them somewhere over there,' the woman whose eyes were clouded said vaguely, gesturing a hand to their left. 'They'll find us again, they always do.'

'They don't dare not,' said the third woman with a laugh. 'And speaking of husbands... Ah, there he is! Prince Christian!'

'Christoph,' said Daphne with a laugh, rolling her eyes. She turned to him, and Christoph's heart skipped a beat as she gestured for him to approach. 'Christoph?'

He shouldn't do it. Starting an acquaintance with Daphne's friends was the last thing he should concern himself with, after all. He needed to review his new servants' backgrounds and ascertain that none were spies, gain access to a full account of his wife's means and write another letter to where Laura should be in a week's time. He should keep his distance from his wife, keep his father-in-law happy. Not…not befriend people.

But he had never seen her laugh like that. Oh, it opened a wound he had not even known had begun to heal; there had been so little laughter in his life, and it was difficult indeed to make his wife laugh. Now Daphne was laughing, and it was a connection from which Christoph flinched as much as he was desperate to step closer to it.

But, no: he could not be weak. He could not allow himself to laugh with them. Charm them, yes, but he had to retain distance between them. He could not allow himself truly to care for her.

Daphne's smile was eager, but it faltered as she saw he had not moved.

It was the disappointment in her eyes that made Christoph step forward and bow low to the three women who had so eagerly embraced his wife. 'Ladies.'

'Don't worry if you have forgotten our names, it's easy enough,' said the third woman with a laugh. 'Sylvia is the one who is always getting into mischief…'

'Outrageous slander, and completely true,' grinned the dark-skinned woman.

'Rilla is the one who sees through any nonsense.'

'And little else, but that's all that matters, isn't it?' said the woman with cloudy eyes with a wink. *A wink?*

'And I'm the one that's Gwen,' said the third woman. 'We have husbands, I assure you, but we've put them down somewhere and momentarily lost them.'

'They always come back,' said Daphne with a giggle, her cheeks pink but her expression joyful.

Christoph could not help but stare. The change in her... It was not a change, as such, but an opening up, a relaxation that revealed the depth of her character. She was still shy, still quiet, but when she stood here with friends, with those she so clearly trusted and was adored by in turn, she glowed.

'I must say, it is delightful to see you all again,' he said with a broad smile, inclining his head to all three of them. 'And, though I did not think it possible, you have all gained in beauty.'

Sylvia snorted. 'Where on earth did you find such a charmer, Daphne?'

'Oh, I think you will find that I am the one who is charmed, ladies,' Christoph countered, slipping more easily into the mesmerising skills he had always depended on. 'Your husbands are brave indeed to risk other gentlemen fall in love with you.'

'Half the *ton* has already fallen in love with Gwen,' Rilla said with a laugh. 'And the other half—'

'Are trying to fall out of love with me,' Sylvia interjected.

'Now, that I can well believe,' Christoph said gallantly, though he could not prevent his eye from being drawn to his wife beside him. 'I admit myself, I am afraid, far too interested in my own wife to fall in love with anyone.'

Daphne's eyes met his and a ripple of heat cascaded through him. Now, where on earth had that particular piece of vulnerability come from?

'That's the Wallflower Academy girl, old Norbury's shame...'

Christoph stiffened. A lady and gentleman had passed by and the woman had spoken to her companion in that discourteous tone.

And Daphne...did not defend herself. She did not speak up, or accost the woman, or anything like that. Instead she curled in on herself, somehow making herself smaller, quieter, less intrusive.

The lady who had spoken snorted, continuing, 'Wallflower, indeed. Well, that's a more pleasant way to describe Lord Norbury's...'

Christoph turned, his pulse racing as he took his wife's hand, brought it to his lips for a slow kiss while others around them gasped at the blatant display of affection and said quietly, 'Say that again.'

The lady flushed a dark crimson and the gentleman stepped between them. 'Come on now, man, everyone's thinking it.'

'Everyone is most definitely not thinking it,' Christoph countered mildly, as though confused.

'Hear, hear,' said Gwen unexpectedly, folding her arms.

'In fact, I think you'll find that Princess Daphne is greatly admired by all who have the pleasure of her acquaintance,' said Rilla, glaring in their general direction.

'And, as you so clearly do not have that pleasure, I would suggest you keep such unfounded remarks to yourself,' sniffed Sylvia, crossing her own arms, but finding it difficult to do so over her swelling belly.

Christoph's desire to protect his wife had rather astonished even him, but it had been instinctive. Pleasant as it was to have Daphne's friends do likewise, he would have defended his wife against every single one of them in this place.

The gentleman ushered the lady away, their cheeks pink, and Christoph tried to smile as though nothing had occurred.

'Daphne,' Christoph murmured, turning back to her... turning back to where she had been. His eyes widened as he looked around him, gaze desperately searching for the golden-blonde hair and the delicate beauty that was his wife.

'She does this,' said Sylvia quietly, patting him on the arm.

Christoph turned to her, brow furrowed. 'Does this?'

'Disappears,' said Gwen with a sigh. 'She always comes back, but…'

'Ah, I thought she might,' said Rilla sagely, nodding. 'Do you remember when the Pike pointed out that her singing voice was not sufficient for opera, and we lost her for a day and a half?'

Christoph blinked. 'A—a day and a half?'

'That dinner when Sir Harold laughed at her when she dropped her fork…' Sylvia sighed. 'We didn't see her for the rest of the evening, or breakfast. She missed scrambled eggs, a huge sacrifice for our Daphne.'

'She managed to go a week without being spotted when Lord Norbury invited her to afternoon tea and she did not want to go,' said Rilla, her expression set.

'Daphne is not one to be forced to do anything, and she is not one for confrontation.'

Christoph swallowed, a knot tangling in his throat and his breathing short. It was strange. Daphne had of course had a life before he had ever been introduced to her as her future husband. It was natural that her friends, those who had lived with her, knew her far better than him. And yet it rankled, that they had this knowledge of Daphne he did not.

'There cannot be that many places to hide,' he said aloud, his eyes darting around the ballroom.

Sylvia shrugged. 'It doesn't matter. Daphne can always hide.'

And her friends were correct. It took over an hour for Christoph to find her, peering into corners, looking behind curtains, opening doors that he probably wasn't supposed to look behind. He interrupted two kissing couples, one couple doing far more than kissing and a trio of gentlemen who were obviously involved in some sort of gambling ring.

But it wasn't until Christoph thought of the one place he had not looked that he found her. He opened the carriage door. 'Daphne.'

Daphne looked up at him. She had been sitting in their carriage that waited outside Almack's with her hands folded in her lap and her expression downcast. She had been crying.

Christoph attempted to ignore the tear tracks that trailed down her cheeks, the knowledge that she had been so upset and so alone saddening his own heart. 'Shall we call it a night?'

Daphne nodded, as though her throat was too raw for speech.

The carriage clattered forward almost as soon as Christoph entered. The silence continued, stretching out longer and longer until eventually he had no choice but to break it. 'You should have faced her down.'

Daphne looked up. 'I beg your pardon?'

Christoph sighed, leaning back in the seat of the carriage and shaking his head. 'You should have faced her down. The lady who spoke ill of you—why did you not confront her? Any other woman would have done so.'

He had not intended to berate her. He had spoken softly, or at least as softly as he could, with the anger at how Daphne had been spoken to still coursing through his veins.

Precisely what he had expected Daphne to say to him in response, Christoph did not know. What he had not expected was for her to snarl, 'I don't have to be like any other woman, Christoph!'

The blazing heat from her words burned across the few feet between them and Christoph's eyes widened. 'I—'

'I am shy, Christoph! Shy! That by definition means that I do not want confrontation!' Daphne said sharply, a flickering power in her eyes that he had never seen before. 'And there is nothing wrong with that!'

'I didn't say there was anything wrong with—'

'You just asked me why I had not confronted her,'

snapped Daphne, an edge in her voice that he had never heard before. 'So I repeat: I am shy. I don't want to draw attention, I don't want to argue with strangers, and I don't… I've never…'

Her voice lapsed into silence. The realisation about how she had spoken seemed to wash over her and, before he could clasp her, the Daphne who was forward, direct and spoke her mind, she was gone. She'd crept into her shell, her gaze now focused on the dark window.

Christoph stared and his jaw dropped. She was right. He had no business criticising her for something that was part of her. Part of who she was.

And yet…there was more to Daphne, was there not? This sparking fireball which had erupted over him was also Daphne. The fire and the power, the certainty with which she had spoken, was her.

She was embarrassed now. Christoph could see it clearly written across her face. But that did not mean that he did not have to say what he was about to say.

'I apologise,' he said quietly.

Daphne said nothing. She did not even look at him. Her refusal did not help with the self-loathing that now poured through Christoph's veins like ice. Just when he thought he had entirely ridden himself of all remnants of his family, just when he thought he was truly different from his father… It had been cruel, attacking Daphne's response like that. How had he managed to become everything he hated? Everything that he had seen in his father?

'I am sorry, too.'

Christoph's head jerked up. Daphne's voice was soft, almost a whisper, but loud enough to be heard over the clatter of the carriage wheels on the cobblestones.

'Why are you apologising?' he said quietly. 'I am the one who—'

'I should not have... You are my husband. I should respect your opinion.'

Christoph's stomach clenched. 'Only if it is worthy of respect.'

Daphne's eyes were wide, her confusion evident. 'It's just...the Pike—I mean, Miss Pike—always said...'

'You may not have noticed, but Miss Pike is not married and, most importantly, she is not married to me,' Christoph said, partly in an attempt to make her smile. He did not succeed. 'My point is, I know what I want from a wife. And honesty is important. I want to know what you're thinking, Daphne.'

'No, you don't.' Her words were spoken automatically, as though she could not imagine a world in which things were otherwise.

Christoph managed to restrain himself from reaching out and taking Daphne's hands. 'Yes, I do. There...there is clearly more to you than meets the eye, Daphne, and we are husband and wife. If we are to make a life together in mutual companionship, which I hope we will, then I need to know you. The real you. All of you.'

Daphne did not meet his eyes. 'I... I see.'

He was not sure she did. 'You have a sharp mind, Daphne.'

Finally, he'd managed to elicit a smile. 'I am quiet. People talk in front of me, things they would not say to anyone else, because they assume I won't repeat their nonsense. Most of the time I think people do not even notice that I am there.'

'I notice you.'

It was perhaps a foolish thing to say. It certainly wasn't completely logical. As the carriage rounded a corner and started to slow down, signalling their approach to their home, Christoph reached out for Daphne's hand. 'Daphne...'

She pulled away. His hand closed on empty air, and he swiftly returned it to his lap, his neck burning. It meant nothing. It was probably a good thing, Christoph told himself. It was good that he did not become too attached.

'This...this marriage, it is just an arrangement,' Daphne said, a coldness entering her voice. 'You don't have to worry about me, Christoph.'

'I know I don't.'

'I think I will retire. I am most tired,' said Daphne as the carriage slowed to a stop. She did not wait for the footman, instead opening the door herself and stepping down. 'Goodnight.'

'Goodnight,' Christoph called after her fruitlessly. She did not reply and she did not turn back.

He fell back against the carriage seat and exhaled slowly. Yes, he did have to worry about her. There was far more danger than Daphne could possibly know. And, even if there had not been murderous brothers to worry about, she intrigued him. Here was a woman, if he was not careful, he could truly care for.

And that was perhaps the most dangerous thing of all.

Chapter Nine

When Daphne came downstairs the next morning, it was with a fresh resolution: absolutely, positively, no matter what, do not speak her mind.

After all, where had it got her—an argument in a carriage?

I am shy, Christoph! Shy! That, by definition, means that I do not want confrontation!

Daphne winced as she walked across the hall towards the breakfast room. No, it was not worth it, speaking her mind. She had learned a long time ago that it was a bad idea, and for a moment yesterday she had allowed herself to say utter nonsense.

Well, no more. Christoph wanted a calm, quiet life with a respectable wife. And that was exactly what she would give him. No more outbursts. No more speaking her mind, despite his request that she do so. And absolutely no more speaking out of turn.

The breakfast room was empty.

Daphne's shoulders slumped. Why she had hoped, wished, thought, that he would be there, she did not know. It was foolishness itself. Christoph had made it perfectly clear that he had married her for her funds. There was no dream of romance here.

'Husband not here?'

Whirling round, Daphne saw their butler, Henderson, leaning against the doorframe with a grin. He straightened up as he met her eye, but still, there was something…something about his eyes which she did not like. It was mighty irritating that she'd had absolutely no control over the selection of their servants. Apparently her father and stepmother had conducted the interviews. That was perhaps why they were stuck with a rude man like Henderson.

Daphne castigated herself silently. *That isn't very nice.*

The trouble was, neither was he.

'I suppose you missed him, Your Highness,' murmured Henderson.

A small nibbling worm gnawed at Daphne's stomach. It was not precisely what the butler was saying, though that certainly wasn't pleasant. It was the way the man seemed to gain so much enjoyment from saying such unpleasant things.

Still, she had been raised by Miss Pike both to stand her ground and be polite to all. Daphne tried to smile. 'I imagine he had an…an errand to run.'

'Probably sending letters to that Laura of his,' suggested the butler.

Daphne tried not to show the pain she felt on her face. *Laura.* There was that name again—and, really, she should grow accustomed to it. The woman, whoever she was, would soon be living with her. Christoph and her.

'And who do you think Laura is, eh?' Henderson asked quietly.

Try as she might, Daphne could not help but gasp at the clear delight that his mistress was going to be usurped by...well...a mistress, quite evidently. What on earth had she done to offend the man? Daphne had only met him days ago. Servants should not treat their master or mistress like that, she knew, and yet...well...what was one to say? How did one dress down a servant when her tongue was tied in a knot, her hands were burning and she couldn't think about...

'Ah, there you are, Henderson,' came a voice from the hall, accompanied by footsteps. 'Where have you been? I asked you to retrieve a set of six bottles from the cellar.'

Christoph strode into the breakfast room.

Daphne had not realised just how much tension she had been carrying in her shoulders until that moment. Only then did the strain melt away, hot trickles of discomfort flowing down her back, warming her as she looked at him.

That was the difficulty, wasn't it? He was so handsome. Charming. If this had been a love match...

'I'll go right away, Your Highness,' said Henderson, inclining his head before turning and striding away.

'Breakfast,' said Christoph heartily. 'Shall we?'

Daphne was all of a flutter—which was ridiculous. It was perfectly normal for a husband and wife to eat breakfast together, after all. But it wasn't for them. They had been married but days before, and it was hardly a love match…

Daphne blinked. Christoph was waving a hand before her eyes. 'Daphne?'

'I—I am perfectly… Breakfast,' she said hastily, stepping towards the sideboard.

'Good,' said Christoph. His voice was short, though it so often was. 'What will you have?'

Her fingers hesitated as they lifted a plate from the sideboard. What would she have? She had been acting on pure instinct: eggs, potatoes, tea. That was what she always had. But was it what she wanted?

Daphne remained standing, frozen, her fingers gripped tightly round the plate, unable to move. What did she want? She had never had free rein over her breakfast choices before. What did she want? She wanted lots of things. She wanted nothing. She did not want eggs, which was most strange. Her stomach growled with hunger yet her throat rebelled at the idea of even eating.

'It was not supposed to be a difficult question,' said Christoph quietly, brushing past her to pick up his own plate.

For a moment she breathed in deeply, wanting to drink in the scent of him. And then he was moving on, loading up his plate with a great number of fried potatoes, eggs, a tomato and two slices of toast.

'You're hungry,' Daphne managed to say.

Christoph chuckled from behind her. He had already filled his plate and was now seated at the table, where she should be.

Get some food, Daphne!

Placing a random assortment of food on her plate, and trying not to trip over her own skirts, Daphne hurriedly sat opposite her husband.

He smiled awkwardly, then looked down at her plate. 'Goodness. The English have breakfast so differently.'

Daphne looked down at her plate. Upon it was a pickled herring, a tomato and a drooping green something she was half-certain was supposed to be a garnish.

'I'm not that hungry,' she said quietly.

Christoph, on the other hand, appeared to be half-starved. He was eating with gusto and Daphne found it rather enjoyable to watch—just…watch him. Be in his presence, nothing being demanded of her, no one expecting.

'Breakfast is very different in Niedernlein,' Christoph said with a smile as he looked up. 'Though I had heard of the famous English breakfast before I came here. It is one of the things I had not expected to miss—though I hope, one day, to return and assist in bringing new ideas and new cuisine to my homeland. You like it—the English breakfast?'

It was almost as bad as talking about the weather. Daphne stared, trying to understand precisely what she was supposed to say to that.

Yes, she liked breakfast…?

'And…and tea?' Christoph said, a strange sort of desperation in his eyes. 'You like tea?'

Poor man; he was at least attempting conversation.

Daphne tried to rouse herself. The least she could do was speak to him. 'Yes. Yes, I like tea.'

Could she sound any more dull? *Laura probably has excellent conversation,* Daphne could not help but think. She would probably have had Christoph in stitches, regaling him with a hilarious tale while eating a delicate and dainty breakfast without clattering her cutlery or spilling her tea.

She swallowed. Well, she would find out soon enough.

'The weather is very fine,' Christoph said quietly, sipping his tea.

Daphne tried to smile, but it might have looked like a grimace, from his expression.

Oh, this was mortifying!

Over a decade at the Wallflower Academy and she could not maintain a conversation with a man who had put his hands—the very hand that was curled around that tea cup—between her legs and made her...

Daphne knocked over the pepper pot. Black granules spread across the white and previously spotless linen tablecloth. She leapt into action, desperate to clean up the mess, but only seeming to make it worse. 'Oh... Oh, dear, I—'

'Leave it, Daphne.' The order was not barked, but it was hardly spoken softly either.

Mortification drowned Daphne in heat. She was either dull as ditch water or making a mess. 'I am sorry, Prince Christoph.'

'Do not call me that,' he said quietly, placing his tea

cup down and examining her. 'I don't like it when people call me that. Least of all you.'

Least of all you.

What did that mean? What did he mean by that—was there a meaning behind it?

Daphne swallowed, attempting to allow her inner thoughts to spill out, but years of restraint meant it was almost impossible. 'What I mean...'

He did not reply. It was not much of a question, really. *Oh, hell*, Daphne thought darkly, thinking the oath as hard as she could in the privacy of her own mind. This was excruciating!

As though he could somehow sense the thoughts with which she was punishing herself, Christoph looked up with a vague smile. 'Now, tell me. What can I do to make you feel more comfortable?'

Daphne's lips parted in astonishment.

No one—not Miss Pike, not her father, not even her friends, who meant well, even if they were a bit much—had ever asked her such a question. No one had ever truly wanted to know what would make being Daphne Smith—Daphne von Auberheiser now, she supposed—more comfortable. Comfort? She could barely recall what comfort was. Life was living on a precipice, at any moment certain that you would tip over into discomfort. There was no let-up, no respite. Life was embarrassment, and that was it.

'I... I... I don't... I don't know,' Daphne managed.

Well, she'd had to say something. Christoph had leaned back in his chair and looked at her expectantly, so she'd said something. Even if it had made little to no sense.

And yet he was nodding slowly, as though he understood. 'Well, what do you want to do today?'

Today?

Today was like any other day: empty, without the routine of the Wallflower Academy. Strange, as she still tried to learn what it was to live in this house. Lonely, as she attempted to work out whether she could visit her friends without a chaperone, without an invitation. Or should she invite them here?

Daphne could sense the panic rising. She was a princess, but what did that mean? Were they supposed to visit the royal court at St James'? Did she have duties, now she was a foreign dignitary? Should she…?

'Daphne?' Christoph said quietly. 'What shall we do together?'

It was his quietness that calmed her, probably. He did not shout, or berate, or criticise. He'd just said her name.

Daphne swallowed. 'I… This is a marriage of convenience. You do not have to spend any time with me.'

'I know that,' he said softly. 'I want to.'

When she finally managed to bring herself to look up, Daphne saw a powerful look in his eye, rather as if he were saying, *I wanted to do this to you the moment I first met you. I wanted to know how you felt, the depth of you.*

Daphne's mouth went dry. Well, she could not deny it: he had the same expression as when he had said those very words to her. Though they had both been significantly more naked at the time.

'Daphne, I... Well, I think there is no reason why we cannot decide for ourselves what a marriage of convenience should be like.' Christoph's words were quiet, soft, gentle. The import of them was belied by his casual tone. 'We can be friends. There is nothing stopping us from enjoying each other's company.'

Enjoying each other's company... Well, it would still be warmer than many marriages of the *ton,* as far as Daphne could make out from the scandal sheets. So many husbands and wives came together to create children—her stomach lurched—to host a ball or two over a year and for little else.

She had presumed that was what Christoph had wanted. Perhaps he had—but not anymore.

'Well,' she said awkwardly, looking away and flushing a deep, burning crimson. 'Well. We...we could go for a walk.'

It was a most dull suggestion, and she hated that her mind could provide her with no better idea than that. A walk. A walk? Who wanted to go on a walk?

'A walk sounds lovely,' said Christoph, rising from his chair and throwing down his napkin. 'I shall meet you in the hall in ten minutes. Prepare yourself.'

Prepare yourself.

Daphne could not help but smile as she selected a pelisse from the choice of three that her stepmother had gifted to her.

Prepare yourself.

There were times, whole stretches of hours and days,

when she quite forgot that Christoph spoke English as his second language. And then he went and said something like that.

He was waiting for her patiently in the hall when she had dressed and come down the stairs.

'I am sorry to have taken so long,' Daphne said in a rush as she hurtled down the last few stairs.

His smile was genial, warmth clear in his eyes. 'It has not quite been ten minutes. You are ready?'

Daphne nodded. A walk—fine. She knew how to walk, almost certainly. She could do some walking. Walking would be possible.

Hyde Park was not far from her father's house—*her* house, Daphne tried to remind herself. Strange; it still felt as though she were visiting a friend who had momentarily gone out. It did not feel like home, any more than the Wallflower Academy had felt like home. Had anywhere felt like home?

No sooner had the thought flickered through her mind than Christoph said quietly, 'London feels more like home than Niedernlein did in recent times.'

Daphne started, growing the distance between them from a few inches to almost a whole foot as they stepped onto a path in Hyde Park. 'I beg your pardon?'

Christoph smiled. 'I suppose it sounds strange but, well, I was not always happy there. I have found myself much happier here. In England.'

It did sound a little strange, yet it was a strangeness that Daphne quite understood. 'I… I am sorry. Do you not miss it?'

'I miss the country itself. The people. The opportunity to do good, champion justice. And Niedernlein is beautiful. I wish I could show it to you.'

He did not say, *I will show it to you*. He did not want to go back, then. Curiosity rose but it was quite clear by the expression on Christoph's face that he would not welcome any questions. Which only made her curiosity sharper.

'My father... You are fortunate, I think, in the father you have,' Christoph said with a brief smile.

Daphne swallowed. It would not be ladylike, or polite, to give her real opinion on the man who had essentially ignored her until he'd realised she would be his only offspring. 'Many others are less fortunate.'

Her husband glanced at her as they turned a corner on the path they walked along. There were laughing children playing a game with skittles on the grass, and a trio of gentlemen arguing vociferously about something that sounded like politics strode by them. And still Christoph said nothing.

Well, she would have to ask. They were married for convenience, but that did not mean they could not converse. 'Your parents—what were they like?'

Christoph blew out a long breath before replying, and Daphne was in half a mind to tell him that it did not matter, before he said, 'My father was a very harsh man. Very harsh. Cruel, even. But it did not start that way. He... When he lost my mother, when we lost her, my father changed. He was devoted to her, you understand, besotted. When she died, I think my father's purpose for living died with her. He became cold. Distant. Unfeeling. His worst was reserved for my brother, but my brother had always been cruel. My mother's death...it gave Anton an excuse to do precisely what he had always done. Love, kindness, gentleness were no longer rewarded or encouraged.'

Daphne looked at him as he spoke. There was pain there, deep pain. Agony. An estrangement, but one of his choosing, from what she could guess.

'I thought... Well, I could see that love, that marriage, was for the weak. Or it made you weak... I do not know,' Christoph continued in a low voice, a dark chuckle not quite reaching his eyes. 'Love is a weakness. To open oneself up like that, to become so vulnerable, to place all one's happiness in the life of another... I swore then I would never do it. I have kept to that promise.' He breathed a laugh that sounded pained. 'I cannot tell you how strange it is to tell you all this. I always vowed... I hate that you can see my weakness.'

'You are not weak.' Daphne's voice was measured, low, but she sounded certain. 'It takes great strength to face one's past.'

Christoph's laugh this time was dark and pained. 'It goes against everything I know, everything I believe of myself!'

It was difficult to know what to say, so Daphne kept quiet. What could she say—that love was to open oneself to pain? That grief, perhaps, was only the other side of love? That would explain his reticence to speak of his brother for weeks now.

'Soon everything was a competition between us brothers,' Christoph continued with a bark of laughter that held no mirth in it. 'And I was never good enough, always falling short.'

Never good enough? It was hard to reconcile that description with the tall, handsome, charming man beside her.

Without a thought, Daphne closed the gap between them and slipped her hand through his arm. The instant she did, she realised what she had done. She would have pulled away, her neck already burning with embarrassment, but in a smooth movement that held no self-consciousness Christoph placed a hand over her own.

'I had to become resilient,' he said quietly. 'Strong. Controlled.'

'And so…you do not miss your brother?'

'No,' came the immediate response.

Daphne started, colour darkening her cheeks momentarily.

'I am sorry for making you jump,' Christoph said with a wry smile. 'It is…difficult. Siblings are not always the people we would have chosen, you understand?'

Daphne did not understand, having no siblings at all. She nodded all the same. 'My friends are my family.'

'Yes, they treat you like a sister—as a sister should be treated,' amended Christoph, his smile softening. 'And I am here now. Being in England makes me free. Free thanks to the distance and…and thanks to the money. I can support Laura with the money.'

My money, Daphne could not help but think indignantly. *My father's money.*

And yet…distance. He had said the word with a heavy weight, but one of relief more than disappointment. This brother, he sounded unpleasant to be sure, but that was assuredly no reason to leave the country that Christoph so clearly loved.

'But enough about me,' her husband said with a heavy sigh and a plastered-on smile. 'What about you? Tell me something you have never told anyone.'

Never told anyone?

That was hardly difficult. Daphne was accustomed to being the person that others spoke to, poured their hearts out to, expecting nothing in return but sympathy. And Daphne always gave it. But then the moment moved on, the person wandered off to solve their own problems and there was no chance for Daphne to unburden her own soul.

She glanced up to see that Christoph was smiling.

'I am your husband,' he reminded her, his dark eyes so deep she could almost fall into them. 'Come on—something you've never told a soul.'

Daphne took a deep breath. 'I… When I was small—very small, before I went to the Wallflower Academy—I had a governess. She…wasn't very nice.'

It was an understatement, but it was an understatement she had always clung to. To accept what Miss Donovan had done, to admit what had happened, would be to face those fears. She did not want to do that.

Christoph squeezed her hand on his arm. 'Not very nice?'

Daphne shook her head. It was easier to talk if she just stared ahead, looking at the people of London who were out enjoying Hyde Park, not at the man by her side.

'No, not very nice,' she echoed. 'I... Whenever I spoke my mind, I was punished. Those were "inside thoughts", she said. Thoughts never to be spoken.'

His grip on her hand tightened and did not let go. 'Punished?'

'Oh, just silly things,' Daphne said lightly. 'Dousing me with water and not permitting me to get dry. Or warm. Making me stand on one leg until I fell. Pins. That sort of thing.'

Her arm jolted—she had continued walking but Christoph had halted. She finally forced herself to look at his face.

'Daphne, that is cruelty beyond the extreme,' he said slowly. 'And you were how many years of age?'

She shrugged. If she gave it no weight, it couldn't hurt her. Miss Donovan could not hurt her. 'Four, five years, perhaps?'

He pulled her closer, so close that her breasts were pressed up against his chest, and Daphne could hardly think for they were standing right in the middle of a path in Hyde Park. Surely people would be staring?

'Christoph,' she managed.

'I know I am not always so open with my thoughts, my feelings, as you deserve,' he said in a low voice. 'I know sometimes I am weak and I reveal my emotions, and then I pull back—'

'That does not make you weak,' Daphne said fiercely, hating the pain, the disappointment, in her husband's eyes directed at himself.

'But I want to hear your "inside thoughts",' Christoph continued.

'No, you don't.'

Her dismissal was roundly ignored. 'Yes, I do,' he said passionately. 'I always want to know what you are thinking, Daphne, always.'

Her laugh was a little strained. 'I—I don't know if I can.'

Christoph's eyes searched hers, and there was compassion there, the like of which she had never known before. 'I know. I know I ask a lot of you, Daphne, but I... I want you to feel free. From now on, *inside thoughts* don't have to stay inside. All thoughts can be outside thoughts.'

All thoughts can be outside thoughts? Daphne could barely breathe. She was intoxicated by his presence, his intensity, his determination to say things that could not, should not, be said.

'From now on, inside thoughts are forbidden. All thoughts are outside thoughts.'

Then he released her. Christoph said nothing but he interlocked his hand with hers, his fingers strong alongside hers, and they continued to walk in silence, holding hands.

She was holding hands. *Holding hands with a man!*

'Tell...tell me something you've never told a soul,' Daphne said aloud, the silence too much to bear after such revelations.

She had never told anyone about Miss Donovan. Ever.

Her husband had a rueful smile on his face. 'I always wanted to learn the violin.'

'The violin?' It was not the sort of thing she had expected. 'Truly? I... I also.'

It was a beautiful instrument. It sounded like angels singing and the first time she had ever heard it...

'There you go again.'

Daphne swallowed. 'I beg your pardon?'

'Inside thoughts,' Christoph said, squeezing her hand and shooting her pulse to a most riotous rate. 'Talk to me. Your thoughts are so important, so fascinating. I want to hear them.'

His statement was difficult to take in. *Her* thoughts, fascinating? And something swelled in Daphne, something she had either never felt, or had felt once so long ago that she could no longer recall it: pride. Pride in herself.

'I was just thinking—'

'Not *just*,' he said with a warm smile. 'You were thinking.'

There came a flicker of confidence. An answering smile on her lips. Daphne tried not to beam. 'I was thinking, a violin... I mean, when I first heard one played, I thought... I thought it was like angels singing.'

Christoph's eyes widened, his expression one of surprise. 'I… That is precisely what I thought as a child. My God, I… I did not think we would have that in common.'

He squeezed her hand again, heat radiating through her body from the touch of his hand, and Daphne thought, *He is mine. Laura or no Laura, Christoph is mine. I will make him mine, somehow.*

She smiled, her heart fluttering at the boldness of the words she was about to say. 'Royal or illegitimate, perhaps we are not so different.'

Chapter Ten

'Aces are high, man!'

'Yes, of course, my apologies,' said Christoph hastily, picking up the card he had just laid down and returning it to his hand.

Then he made the mistake of glancing up. Daphne was seated opposite him—it had been her request, when they had entered the card party almost an hour ago, that he not part from her. It was not a very difficult request to grant. He wanted her by his side at all times. So, when they had sat down at the whist table and she had muttered the rules under her breath, Christoph had felt confident. It was much like a game that was played in Niedernlein, after all, and he had been proficient at cards for at least a decade. Not that that mattered, with Daphne opposite him.

'Pay attention, can't you?' Percy Devereux, Duke of Knaresby, shook his head as he grinned. 'Can't think what's distracting you.'

Christoph ensured his face remained entirely passive as he shrugged nonchalantly, as though none of this mattered; as though he wasn't mortified by continually getting this wrong. 'It is different from the game we play at Niedernlein. I can assure you, if we were in the Winter Palace, I would be trouncing you all by now.'

'Now, that I can believe,' Sylvia, Duchess of Camrose, said with a laugh as she settled her hand of cards on her swelling stomach. 'Daphne, I believe it is your turn.'

Excellent. A ready-made excuse to look up at his wife.

Christoph's stomach lurched as he watched the little frown puckering between Daphne's sky-blue eyes. The concentration was intoxicating—to a lesser man, that was, he thought as he hurriedly looked away. To a man who cared for her. Not himself. Obviously.

'Very well,' Daphne said quietly, placing down a card.

Both Percy and Sylvia groaned.

'How are you this good at cards?' Sylvia said with a dramatic sigh, though she winked at Daphne, who smiled.

Christoph's heart skipped a beat. He had rarely managed to elicit such a smile from his wife. It was soft and small, but it was heartfelt. He had managed it, what, twice, perhaps? Sylvia had done so three times in the last hour.

'When you spend a great deal of time alone, it is inevitable, I think, that you become sufficiently good at cards,' Daphne said, cheeks pinking as she spoke.

His jaw tightened.

When you spend a great deal of time alone. There was so much about Daphne under the surface, wasn't there? So much he had not yet discovered—but he had discovered that she had led a very solitary life. One that made her shy. A life with cruelty near its beginning which had made her censure herself.

Whenever I spoke my mind, I was punished. Those were inside thoughts. Thoughts never to be spoken.

'Careful, there, you'll rip them in half!'

Christoph blinked. Percy had reached out a hand to jerk his cards away—not to view them, it seemed, but because he had been gripping them so tightly that there was a good chance he might destroy them.

'Ah,' he said weakly. 'My apologies. I am concentrating very hard.'

'And yet making more mistakes than the rest of us combined,' Percy said with a laugh. 'I don't know, Daphne. You'll have to take this man of yours in hand!'

He chuckled, and Sylvia joined him. Christoph tried to smile as he watched the burning scarlet he knew so well creep up Daphne's neck. A neck he had kissed. A neck he had tasted, and wanted to taste again… Probably best not to think about that at a card party.

'Well, I have to say, I will be sorry to enter my confinement,' Sylvia was saying. 'I told Teddy we simply had to throw one last party, force everyone to come to us, before I disappear from Society.'

'You'll never truly disappear, I think,' snorted Percy. 'Gwen was telling me the most ridiculous tale of when you…'

The story continued. At least, Christoph was almost certain it did. He could not tell, not with his gaze getting distracted by Daphne again. This time it was her fingers. She was shuffling her hand very slowly, almost as though she was not thinking about it. He gazed at the gentle shifting patterns of her fingers, soft and supple, the way her fingertips caressed the corners of the cards...

Christoph shifted uncomfortably in his seat. Not that he was thinking of those fingers caressing something else. Most definitely not. When he forced his attention away from her fingers, he was surprised to meet her eyes. Throat firmly knotted, Christoph hurriedly tried to rearrange his facial features into something normal. What *was* normal? How did he normally smile? Was it like this—with so many teeth?

Daphne smiled, her cheeks pinking as she looked swiftly at her cards.

It shouldn't matter this much, Christoph tried to tell himself as Percy and Sylvia bickered good-naturedly about whether or not her card play was permissible. A smile from his wife should not heat his loins, make his spine tingle and grit his jaw. And yet it did.

'They will keep bickering until we break it up, you know.'

Daphne's words were quiet, low, creeping under the growing debate of the other two at the card table.

Christoph could not help but smile. 'I... I suppose so.'

'And you have been playing quite...well...poorly,' said Daphne, evidently embarrassed at having to point out his shortcomings. 'Do you not understand the game? Would you like me to explain it to you again?'

Heat blossomed across Christoph's chest at the

thought. It was tempting to take Daphne to a quiet corner, just the two of them, and have her explain something to him in soft tones, growing closer and closer so he could hear her over the chatter of the card party...

Damn it, why was he continually being distracted by this woman?

'No, I thank you,' he said stiffly. 'I understand perfectly.'

There was a teasing look in Daphne's eye, just for a moment. And then it was gone.

An inside thought. Christoph was starting to spot the signs, though he could not always persuade this wife of his to spill her thoughts. It was starting to become a diverting challenge, though of course he never forced her. He would never force Daphne to do anything.

Still, a little prompting never hurt. 'What was that inside thought?'

Daphne's colour heightened but she met his gaze, unfaltering, as she said more in a breath than a whisper, 'I... I was thinking, if you understood perfectly, you would not be losing.'

Christoph chuckled. He couldn't help it. 'Perhaps you are right. Perhaps I am distracted.'

No, this was dangerous. This was flirting, and that was absolutely not part of the plan. He could not flirt with his wife—the very idea!

He had to remain aloof. He had to. Loving Daphne, loving any woman as his father had loved, brought nothing but pain. It would destroy him. The loss of that love, the loss of Daphne—and he would lose her, inevitably;

he would do something wrong, he'd hurt her—would transform him into a cruel man, a cold man. He had to keep her at a distance.

Easier said than done.

Daphne swallowed, then said softly, 'I can't imagine what you could be distracted by.'

Somehow his throat was dry, his voice hoarse. 'Can't you?'

It wasn't supposed to be like this. He wasn't supposed to be giddy, and his mind wasn't supposed to wander back to Daphne at all times. He wasn't supposed to be so preoccupied at a game of cards.

And there she sat, glowing in the knowledge that she was teasing him, and he could do nothing about it. Christoph wanted it. Wanted more.

'You are such a charmer.'

His gaze focused. 'I beg your pardon?'

'You. You charm people everywhere you go,' she said softly. 'I do not even think you notice you're doing it.'

'Oh, no, I am sure—'

His wife cut across his bluster. 'It is one of the things I like best about you.'

Christoph's throat became even dryer, if that were possible. How was it possible that she could do this to him—and in public too? 'Are you flirting with me, Daphne?'

She was! Her face was flushed—she was clearly unaccustomed to being so forward, so aware of her own sensuality—and yet she was doing it.

Dear God, she was magnificent.

'Perhaps,' came her quiet reply. 'You bring it out of me, Christoph.'

His stomach lurched. This woman...

A poor excuse for a woman. An illegitimate child of a lord that no one in Society even knows about? If it wasn't for her wealth, I wouldn't even consider her. Dull, I would imagine.

Anton's assessment of the Miss Daphne Smith about whom her father had written to him resounded in Christoph's head. His hands clenched into fists, the automatic response to any thought of Anton overriding his good manners. He caught the movement swiftly and forced his hands to calm.

It did not prevent the thought from echoing in his mind.

Dull, I would imagine.

God, his brother had been wrong. How wrong, Christoph had not realised perhaps until this moment. Daphne was beautiful, yes, but there was more to her, so much more. Money could perhaps have been gained another way. Christoph had married her to protect her—that was what he had told himself. The money was convenient.

But now, sitting here...

'Come on, then, why aren't we playing?' Sylvia said with a grin.

Christoph opened his mouth to reply—but Daphne was quicker.

'Because you two keep arguing,' said his wife with a docile smile that belied the mischief in her words.

Sylvia's eyes widened in shock and Percy laughed.

'You know, it does me good to hear you speak so, Princess Daphne. You have worked wonders, Your Highness.'

'Christoph, please,' Christoph said hastily, trying to keep his voice level.

Daphne was smiling in a flushed, surprised way, as though she had not expected to say such things and gain such praise. Christoph was still attempting to unpick the complex knot that was Daphne Smith—Daphne von Auberheiser—and he rather thought it would be the challenge of a lifetime. A lifetime he now had.

Daphne Smith. On paper, she was not very much. In reality, she was everything.

'I don't suppose you would want to play a game you can actually win?' his wife said, jolting Christoph from his thoughts as Percy started to deal out the next hand.

There was no suggestive tone in her voice. Christoph had to give her that; there was innocence in her question, perhaps pity too. She wanted him to feel as though he could enjoy the card party the Duke and Duchess of Camrose were hosting. The trouble was, the only answers he could think of were highly suggestive.

I know a game we could play...in the bedchamber.

My favourite game is one in which we both win.

How about I make you win again and again and again...?

Christoph managed to swallow all the answers that rose to the top of his mind. There was flirting with one's wife, something he had never considered possible in the first place, and then there was shooting lewd suggestions at one's wife at a card table at which others were seated.

Daphne's eyes sparkled. 'Now who is keeping inside thoughts?'

Almost choking, Christoph tried to grin through the tears in his eyes as he thumped his chest. 'Wh-what?'

She could not have said that. He must have dreamt it—he must have done.

When he finally caught his breath, Daphne had risen from her seat. 'I... I feel in need of movement. The game is enjoyable, but I think I would rather be on my feet. Christoph, will you—I mean, would you like to—take a turn around the room with me?'

It was, perhaps, the longest speech that she had made since entering the Camrose residence.

Christoph's legs acted on instinct, forcing him suddenly upwards, his chair falling to the ground beside him. He ignored both the fallen furniture and the murmurs that rippled around the room at such a thing. 'Yes—yes. Yes. Yes, good idea.'

Studiously avoiding Sylvia's expression, which was far too knowing, Christoph walked round the card table and proffered his arm. Daphne took it. The gentle weight of her hand on his arm felt like a seal, a promise...

No, he had to stop this.

Christoph tried to keep his head level as they slowly started to walk around the edge of the large room that the Camroses had opened up by removing the double doors dividing the drawing room and dining room. It had created a great space in which to play cards, and allowed he and his wife a long circular route.

Okay. All he had to do was return to the plan, Christoph tried to tell himself. This was an arranged marriage. Nothing more. Finding emotions here was not the plan. Falling in love? Absolutely not.

Miss Smith, I would like to make it very clear that this marriage is one of convenience, and convenience alone.

They had agreed to that before they had even been married. He was not about to break that agreement.

'Everyone is watching.'

The whisper was low and soft, for his ears only, and for a heartbeat Christoph revelled in the fact that Daphne was on his arm, whispering her thoughts for his hearing only.

Then his mind caught up with his loins.

Damn it, man!

'Everyone is admiring,' Christoph countered quietly as they slowly walked past a quartet at another card table. 'You must be used to it.'

The gentle nudge into his side was more than enough to inflame him. 'You know I am not.'

'You are beautiful, Daphne. I've told you that before.' All too late, Christoph recalled precisely when he had said it. Damnation—it was while he'd made love to her. A moment that would remain in his memory for ever, yes, but probably not something he should reference while in public. It might explain the burning patches on her décolletage. Blast, now he was looking at her…

'You have, but that does not make it true, nor habitual for me to hear. I... I am more accustomed to being a wallflower, standing there and watching life go by,' said Daphne in an undertone.

They passed another card table and Gwen smiled up at them. 'Enjoying yourself, Daphne?'

Precisely why Christoph took his wife's response as a verdict on his company, he did not know. It had not been the question. Why did he care so much?

'Oh, yes, I am having a wonderful time,' said Daphne brightly, though her fingers tightened on Christoph's arm and she did not pause to converse with her friend.

Christoph took the silent cue, keeping them moving forward, preventing any further conversation. They walked in silence for a few feet, then he said, 'You may have been a wallflower, but that does not prevent you from being beautiful. It does not prevent men from having eyes to see your beauty—eyes to see and admire. Admire you.'

He had not intended to speak so openly. Daphne glanced at him with a nervous smile. 'You speak as though you are jealous.'

Jealous? He wasn't jealous. Not jealous at all. *No*, Christoph thought darkly. All he wanted to do was rip out the eyes of any man who deigned to look at his beautiful wife, as though it were a slur against him, against her, against who they were to each other.

By Jove, he needed to get a better handle on himself. Who they were to each other? They were nothing to each other. Nothing, save husband and wife. Why was that becoming so difficult to remember?

'I am proud to have you as my wife,' he said shortly.

Yes, that was it. Much safer to keep his thoughts short and to the point. The likelihood of him saying something ridiculous would then be much reduced.

'Because you think I am beautiful.'

The words were not said with despondency—not exactly. But there was something sad about the way Daphne had spoken. Prickles of discomfort speared through Christoph. What had he said wrong? How had he caused such pain when he had only sought to flatter?

'I know you are beautiful,' Christoph said softly as they passed by the fireplace, the fire crackling and sparking. 'But I am proud to have you as my wife because you are kind, and you are thoughtful, and you are clever. There is no artifice in you, Daphne, nor misplaced pride. In fact, you could do with a tad more pride.'

That was what he had intended only to think. The fact that the words pushed themselves out was just as much a surprise to Christoph as to Daphne. Her deep-red flush could not be explained purely by the heat of the fire. No, Daphne did not hear such words very often. In fact, he wondered whether she had heard such words before at all.

'I…thank you,' she whispered.

Christoph exhaled slowly. 'You don't have to thank me. I… I suppose I should be the one thanking you. You could have been anyone. You could have been anything. I am fortunate indeed to have an arranged match with such a woman.'

He had meant the words in praise—but perhaps it was the reminder that their match was an arranged one that caused Daphne's expression to falter.

'I wish to go home,' she confessed quietly.

Christoph's stomach tightened. 'It is a long way to the Wallflower Academy, but I suppose—'

'Not... Our home, I mean,' Daphne said, her cheeks now very definitely pink.

How was it that such a small confidence could cause such joy? 'Oh, I see. Well, I'll request our carriage.'

A simple catching of the butler's eye was sufficient.

Well, this evening hadn't gone entirely to plan. But still, the overall plan was still working. Laura would be here any day.

'What are you thinking about?'

Christoph started. They were still walking slowly around the room, not yet having completed a single turn. 'I beg your pardon?'

There was a knowing smile on Daphne's face. 'You just looked very happy. What were you thinking of?'

The answer fell from his tongue before he could think. 'Laura.'

The knowing smile on Daphne's face disappeared. 'I see.'

Christoph did not understand it. Why a mention of his sister should dampen her spirits, he did not know. 'It was just—we were speaking of home, and I was recalling a wonderful summer with Laura in Niedernlein when we—'

'I don't actually want to hear it,' Daphne said

sharply—far more sharply than he had ever heard her speak.

Christoph's shoulders slumped—not enough for an onlooker to tell, but still, enough. 'We shared quiet moments in a house of chaos. In fact, one of my favourite memories is—'

'I said, I don't want to hear it.' Daphne's voice had never been so blunt. 'I don't want to hear about the woman you've invited to live with us.'

Something was wrong here. There was a tautness in her expression, a pain in her eye...

The woman you've invited to live with us.

Christoph halted. 'Daphne. Daphne, please tell me that I told you that Laura is my sister?'

Daphne blinked. 'Your...your sister?'

He could have laughed, only that would have drawn the entire card party's attention, and he knew his wife would hate that. 'Yes, she is my sister—my little sister, five years younger than I. I wanted to... She's my sister. I did not mention that?'

For a moment, Daphne just stared up at him in wonder. Then she laughed, a gentle chuckle that warmed him to no end. 'No! No, you didn't. Oh, Christoph.'

Her smile would have been enough to make Christoph march into the Russian winter. How was it possible to feel so close, so intimate, with a woman—his own wife!—while standing in the middle of a card party?

He was in danger here—a kind of danger he had never known before. Guarding himself against assassins, against his brother's machinations, he was accustomed to. Guarding his heart, when despite his best efforts he found himself falling in love with this woman, was infinitely more difficult.

'Laura. Your sister,' Daphne said, exhaling slowly, her smile remaining. 'Your sister. Let's go home, Christoph.'

Chapter Eleven

Something was wrong. Something was different. Daphne knew it the moment she opened her eyes, but precisely what was wrong, she did not know.

She blinked. The ceiling looked the same. The four-poster bed appeared the same. The curtains were still drawn, autumn sunlight weakly attempting to make its way around the edges of the fabric. The flowers…

Daphne sat up. There were flowers beside her bed. A smile drifted across her lips. Flowers… Beautiful ones, too—dahlias. They were arranged delicately in a pretty vase, and they had not been there when she had gone to sleep.

Where had he found them?

The moment Daphne reached out and touched a petal, she realised the truth. Christoph would not have placed them here. He was a prince—he had servants to do that. It probably hadn't even been his idea.

Daphne lowered her hand to the bed and tried to fight the disappointment.

Perhaps she was falling in love with her husband.

Drawing her knees up, Daphne sighed as she tried to put the thought from her mind, but it was impossible. Foolish woman that she was, she was making the ultimate mistake when it came to an arranged marriage: she was starting truly to like her husband. Not that she was forced to dislike him. Not at all. But this was nothing but a convenience for him. A means to an end, the end being money. A chance for him to live with his sister again.

Daphne, please tell me that I told you that Laura is my sister?

Daphne chuckled into the emptiness of her room. The weight that had been lifted in that moment was extreme. How could she have thought even for a moment that Christoph would move a mistress into their home?

Her fingers tingled and her stomach swooped most strangely. Christoph: she wanted to see him.

It did not take long for Daphne's maid, with whom she was starting to grow an awkward friendship, to dress her. Within twenty minutes Daphne was trotting down the staircase, her spirits high and her hope to spend some time with Christoph undiminished.

He was often very busy, it was true. Now she knew the preparations were for her sister-in-law, not a rival, Daphne felt a little better about them. But, still. Time with Christoph was precious, somehow. Rare, but desirable, because it was so…enjoyable.

Daphne swallowed as she hesitated outside the breakfast room. She had never enjoyed time spent with another person as she enjoyed time spent with Christoph. Which was ridiculous. She could not go round falling in love with her own husband!

Turning the handle, she entered…the empty room.

Henderson was grinning. 'Morning, miss.'

Daphne bit back the retort which would have been most unladylike, though she desperately wished she had the boldness to say it.

How dare you speak to me in that manner? If you cannot be civil, then you should leave this house. I am Princess Daphne, and if...

'There you are!'

Daphne twirled on her heels and beamed at the incoming Christoph. 'Good morning.'

'A splendid morning it is about to be,' said the grinning Christoph, almost bursting with visible excitement. 'We are going on an adventure! Oh—after you have breakfasted, of course.'

'I don't actually want breakfast,' Daphne said honestly, her stomach twisting at the thought of eating this early in the morning. *I want you.*

The last three words were not spoken aloud. They were merely thought, very loudly, in the privacy of her own mind. Still, she rather thought that Christoph could hear them, for his grin softened and became a truly attractive smile.

'An adventure?' Daphne repeated as her husband stepped into the hall and she followed him. 'I… I am not sure what you mean, but—'

'Oh, it's an adventure, all right,' Christoph said brightly, grabbing a pelisse and holding it out. 'Come on!'

A fluttering of excitement percolated through Daphne's whole body. This was…different. And, at the same time, completely expected. Christoph had these moments, these exuberant moods in which he wanted to do nothing more than sing from the rooftops and dance through the streets.

He had his melancholy moments too. Daphne was starting to spot them from a distance, see them creeping up on her husband. Soon, she hoped, she would know how to ward them off. How to comfort him.

It is merely a case of spending time together, she told herself sternly. *Nothing more.*

'Right, last thing…' Christoph said cheerfully as Daphne adjusted her bonnet. 'You'll need to put this on.'

For a moment, she had no idea what he was talking about. He was holding out a ribbon, of sorts, though it was much thicker than anything she had seen before. A…cravat?

'It's a blindfold,' said her husband with a grin.

Daphne took a hasty step back. 'N-no.'

His expression faded almost at once. 'No?'

'Absolutely not,' she said firmly, pulse thundering, palms sweating.

The very idea of… No. No, she would not blind herself in the presence of anyone. She would not restrict her vision, allow herself to become vulnerable, just as when she had been forced into that cupboard all day, in the dark, no light, no sense of time.

'Daphne… Daphne, whoa, there.'

There was pain…pain in her chest, and Daphne was scrabbling at her bodice in an attempt to loosen it. She couldn't get air, and there was a hand on her décolletage. A hand pressed gently between her breasts. A hand… and a voice accompanied it.

'Daphne, I'm here…'

The voice was coming from a long way away but it was strength, an anchor in the storm in which Daphne had found herself. Vision started to blink back into existence. The darkness started to fade and before her was the concerned expression of Christoph von Auberheiser.

Daphne took in a jagged breath. 'I won't—I won't wear—'

'It is forgotten; we never have to mention it again,' Christoph said in a rush. 'I am sorry, I did not… My intention was not to…'

'I know.'

Oh, she must look the complete fool. What woman started to lose consciousness because of the mere suggestion of a blindfold?

Yet the memory was potent, stark, in her head. Daphne could not force it away but it faded, slowly, Christoph's hand on her bodice slowly encouraging her back to steady breathing. She had never felt more vulnerable in her life. But he had not laughed. He had stayed. He had helped.

Daphne blinked. Her vision had returned.

Taking a step back, and ceasing the physical connection between them with some regret, she blinked again. She would not let tears fall. 'I am sorry. You will not want to… The adventure: you won't want to—'

'The adventure was not about the blindfold, it was about taking you somewhere, showing you something and…and spending time with you.'

For some reason Christoph looked most miffed—though not with her. *With himself?*

'I am sorry. I did not mean to tease.'

Daphne swallowed. It was not his teasing that was the trouble. 'I…the governess, Miss Donovan… A cupboard—I was there all—all day.'

And she could say no more because Christoph had pulled her into such a tight embrace that speech became impossible, her face flush against him.

But communication was not impossible. His arms around her, strong and protective; his warmth; the very solidity of his body: it all spoke of a shield Daphne had never felt before.

She clung to him, her palms splayed against his chest and her eyes closed as she inhaled him. Was that a kiss pressed against her hair? She could not tell.

Within another heartbeat, Christoph had released her, looking mightily apologetic. 'If you do not want to go…'

'On an adventure?' Daphne tried to laugh. 'I think I have earned it.'

His smile was tender, his hand outstretched—not his arm, but his hand. 'Then come with me.'

She tried not to think too much about the way his fingers interlocked with hers.

They remained holding hands in the carriage, as it rattled along the London streets, taking a route she did not recognise. Why should she? She hardly knew London, and besides, almost all her concentration was focused on the gentle pulse that could be hers, or could be his; she did not know.

When the carriage finally drew to a stop, Daphne peered out of the window expectantly. 'Where are we?'

'We have arrived at the Regent's art gallery,' said Christoph, stepping down from the carriage without letting go of her hand after the door had been opened by a footman. 'It is newly opened. I thought we could explore it together.'

Daphne smiled as she stepped onto the street and looked up at the tall redbrick building. 'An adventure indeed. I have never been to an art gallery.'

'Never—never been to an art gallery?' Christoph sounded incredulous as they walked forward into the building. 'Truly?'

He didn't have to sound so astonished. Had she not been clear enough? The Wallflower Academy hardly existed to allow its inhabitants to live. It was…a waiting room. A waiting home. She had waited and waited… and now she had him.

'I have no idea, truly, just what we will find in here,' Christoph said quietly as they stepped into the first room. 'Oh, my.'

Oh, my, indeed. Daphne could not help but gasp as she stared up at the lantern light in the centre of the roof that allowed warming sunlight to soar through the room. The paintings in this room were huge—several feet across, perhaps more, all showing elegant landscapes that did not look English.

At least, they did not look like the route between the Wallflower Academy and London, which was all Daphne had seen of the country.

'This one looks like Niedernlein.' Christoph stepped towards one with a shining smile. 'Look at the mountains!'

Daphne followed him, staring. 'I've never seen mountains before.'

He turned to her with some surprise. 'What, never?'

'When would I have seen mountains?' she said with a smile, staring up at the painting. The mountains looked beautiful—snow-capped, with either a sunrise or sunset pouring gold upon them. Trees were scattered on the mountain sides, but not trees she knew. Was that what a pine looked like?

'I would like to take you to Niedernlein one day,' Christoph said quietly.

Daphne squeezed his hand. 'We could go in the new year, see the mountains covered with—'

'No, we can't.' His words were curt—not cruel, but inviting no further conversation.

She swallowed. 'Oh. Well. We don't have to.'

Christoph continued to look at the painting for a few minutes, a wistful expression on his face that Daphne wished she could capture in a painting of her own. Then he shook his head, as though to rid his mind of thoughts that were unpleasant, and smiled. 'Shall we continue?'

They spent a few more minutes in the room before stepping through a doorway into another. This room was filled with portraits.

Daphne giggled as they approached the first on their left. 'Rascals, the pair of them.'

The painting, framed in gold gilt, was of two young boys, perhaps brothers. They were laughing together, as though one of them had told a hilarious joke.

When she looked at Christoph, however, he was not smiling. 'Brothers, I suppose.'

Daphne's stomach contracted painfully. 'I suppose.' *She should have remembered.* 'Come, let's look at another one.'

She tugged his hand to lead him further along the wall but, when they halted by a portrait of a woman looking imperiously down at them, Christoph still had a far-off look in his eyes.

'You do not have to protect me, you know,' he said quietly. 'From the topic of brothers.'

Daphne's throat spasmed. When she could speak again, she said, 'I would protect you from anything that gave you pain.'

It was the sort of thing she would never have said before Christoph. *Inside thoughts.* But now…now she was here, with him, and he made her feel safe. It was the least she could do, to impart the same sensation to him.

When he spoke, it was quietly, though there were no

other visitors in this part of the art gallery. 'Anton and I…we were close. When we were young, I mean. I did not know then what he was. What he would become.'

Daphne said nothing. If there was one thing she knew how to do, it was how to be silent in a way that encouraged further confidences.

Christoph's jaw tightened. 'He's two years older than me. By the time I reached twenty, I had already decided that I would never be like him. He was—he is—a cruel man. A man who knows only how to harm, not to help, or to heal. He became King a few weeks ago. Our father died in…well… Anton has stated they were not suspicious circumstances.'

Daphne's breathing was slow and steady, but that was only because she was doing a great deal of work to ensure it was so. 'You think he…?'

'Oh, I don't know. Perhaps he did. Perhaps he did not.' Christoph blew out a long exhale and gave a bracing smile as he started to walk along the wall, pulling her along with him. 'It's why I am so grateful to have Laura. She is a sibling more after my sensibilities.'

'I would have loved siblings,' Daphne found herself saying, a truth that she had never shared with anyone. 'But…but then I suppose, if I had done, my father would not have been able to give me such a quantity of money. We would not be married.'

For a heartbeat, she thought she had gone too far, said too much. Been vulgar. Miss Pike had always been most clear that money was not a suitable conversational topic for young ladies.

Christoph chuckled. 'I suppose not. Had you thought much of marriage? Before your father wrote to...me, I mean?'

It was a strange hesitation, to be sure, but then this was hardly a regular topic of conversation. Daphne fought the instinct to drop his hand as she said, 'No. Who would want me?'

He came to a halt. 'You cannot be in earnest?'

She could not bring herself to meet his eye. Another couple had entered the room, exclaiming loudly at the elegance of the art, how clever the artist had been in their use of light, and she could not think of what to say.

How was one supposed to answer a question like that?

'That one looks just like you.'

Daphne started and giggled in the almost-silence as she looked up at a devastatingly beautiful yet severe-looking woman holding a bouquet. 'You cannot be serious.'

'You have the same eyes!' protested Christoph, though he was smiling too—a smile that became a raucous laugh as Daphne brought her hands together before her and adopted the rather haughty expression of the woman in the painting.

His laughter filled her with honey, with liquid gold, with sunshine. Daphne could not help but giggle herself as Christoph walked on to the next painting, of a general holding aloft a sword, and held up his hand in a similar way, puffing out his chest just as the portrait sitter had done.

'The likeness is uncanny!' Daphne whispered, still

laughing as she grabbed Christoph's hand and pulled him to the next painting. 'Oh, look at this one, that could be you again!'

Her husband collapsed into chuckles at the astonishingly gruff-looking gentleman seated on a resplendent green arm-chair, holding what must have been a squirming puppy. 'You cannot think I look that austere!'

'I think it is the very same look you give Henderson when he does not bring through your post at breakfast!' Daphne found herself teasing, half-astonished at her own bravery.

When had she ever spoken to a person like this?

'Oh, and here you are,' Christoph said, tugging on her hand.

Daphne almost snorted with laughter as they stood before a painting of an elderly woman who was either seriously constipated, or had been painted by her greatest enemy. 'Cheek!'

'Well, you never know, you might look like that when you're old,' Christoph retorted, his laughter fading but his smile broad. 'I can't wait.'

'What? To see me look like—?'

'To grow old with you.'

Daphne swallowed. Somehow the laughter had disappeared from their conversation yet the warmth remained. Christoph's eyes were fixed on hers, warm, caring and… and something else.

'To grow old together,' added Christoph with a wry smile. 'Maybe we shall have our portraits painted then, and be amazed at how old we are.'

'I... I would like that,' Daphne murmured, suddenly painfully conscious that there were other people in the art gallery.

They spent another ten minutes or so viewing paintings in a third room, but they did so in silence. It was not an awkward silence. It was one of warmth, of understanding, even if she did not quite understand it herself.

When they walked out into the autumn sunshine, Daphne said quietly, 'Thank you. For the adventure.'

London had grown busier since they had entered the art gallery. There were many people bustling along the pavement, so Christoph was forced to step closer to her to continue their conversation.

At least, that was what Daphne told herself. It could not be for any other reason.

'This is an arranged marriage,' Christoph said heavily.

The warmth started to fade.

Of course it was—how could she have been so foolish as to think, as to hope, that it could be more?

'But it is for the rest of our lives,' continued Christoph in a gentle voice. 'I want us—I want you—to be happy.'

It was a challenge not to become deflated at the reminder that theirs was no love match, but one of practicalities. She needed a home, a protector. He needed money. They each could provide what the other was lacking, but it was not a match made from passion.

You are clever, and beautiful, and wise, and brave, and I've never wanted anyone like I've wanted you.

Daphne swallowed, trying to forget the moment when they had become one, when the marriage had been consummated. It had happened only because they'd had to do it. He had not spoken of enjoying it—and she was selfish in the extreme for having enjoyed it so much.

'Daphne. Daphne, look at me.'

Blinking back tears that had come from she knew not where, Daphne looked up. There was such an expression of tenderness on Christoph's face that her cheeks burned in sympathy for him. *Out here, on the streets of London!*

'Daphne, I planned this marriage to…to escape a family that did not care for me,' Christoph said quietly. 'A family that was destroying itself from the inside out. I… I was running from something, but now I have the chance to run towards something. Towards you.'

The burning in her cheeks grew rapidly in temperature but there was absolutely nothing Daphne could do about it. She could just as easily have wrenched her gaze from Christoph's and hurled herself into the sun.

'Now I have the chance to create a new family. A family with you.' Christoph slipped his hand into hers and squeezed her fingers.

Daphne's stomach lurched. A new family, with her. He could not mean…

Oh. Oh…now she knew what was wrong…

When she had awoken, it hadn't been the flowers, lovely as they were, that had nudged the back of her mind. It was something quite different.

Her flux. It was late. Very late. Three weeks late.

'And I know an arranged match is perhaps not what we would have expected,' Christoph was saying, utterly oblivious to the realisation that was currently rocking through Daphne's mind. 'But I think—I hope—we can learn to be happy together. To be companions. To become good friends.'

Friends, Daphne thought weakly. *Friends. But she was with child.*

She needed to tell him. Daphne reached out a hand and placed it on Christoph's shirt, not caring that they were in public, not caring that if the Pike had seen such a thing she would have been mortified on her behalf.

'Christoph,' she said urgently, interrupting him.

Christoph placed his free hand over hers on his chest. 'Yes?'

'Christoph, I'm—'

'Of course, you would get to the Regent's art gallery first!' Gwen Devereux and her husband were pushing their way through the crowd on the pavement. Gwen was grinning, her hand being clutched by her little boy. 'You clever thing, how on earth did you find out about it? I've only just heard!'

Daphne swallowed down her secret as Christoph greeted Gwen and Percy with words of welcome.

It was fine. It was fine—perhaps better this way. The streets of London were not the best place, after all, to tell a man that he was about to be a father. It was not as though they had ever discussed children. Did he want them? What did this mean for their arranged marriage?

She would tell him, another time. She would have to pick the perfect moment.

Chapter Twelve

'Christoph?'

So, you've got the harlot yourself.

'Christoph, can you hear me?'

Unwilling to face me? Sneaking out of the palace like a thief in the night to steal my bride?

'Christoph!'

Christoph started. 'What the…?'

Daphne was staring at him from across the dining table with a most confused expression. 'Where were you?'

Where was he? He was here—had been for the last twenty minutes, since the dinner gong had been rung—seated here, at the dining table. Two footmen stood silently at either end of the room, and here he was, with his wife. A wife he had been ignoring.

Christoph shifted uncomfortably on his seat. At least, here was where his body had been. His mind had been completely elsewhere. But that surely could not be what Daphne had meant…could it?

'My apologies. I am... I am preoccupied,' he said stiffly.

There was hurt in her face at his coldness, but Christoph could not bring himself to tell her the truth. How could he?

The letter was still in his coat pocket. He had not been able to leave it anywhere in the house. Daphne was not the prying sort, but he could not run the risk of her picking it up—or, God forbid, a servant.

The paper was burning within him, the words already seared onto his brain so clearly he could almost recite it.

Christoph,

You bastard. You realised I had a good thing going with this Lord Norbury lout, and you just couldn't bear the idea of me having all that money.

So, you've got the harlot yourself. I hope she's keeping you occupied. I can't imagine she's particularly good in bed, wallflower as she is, and of illegitimate birth. I expected better of you, you coward. Unwilling to face me? Sneaking out of the palace like a thief in the night to steal my bride?

It won't be long before you regret this. Don't think I can't carry out my threats—you saw Katalina. You know what I'm capable of.

When I find Laura, she'll be in for the same fate as you. The pair of you can't hide for ever.

Tell that common hussy that she's settled for the

inadequate brother. The pathetic one. The one that couldn't hack it as a true prince of Niedernlein.

I am watching you.
Anton

Christoph swallowed. *Damn.* Someone had said something. 'I beg your pardon?'

Daphne had been saying something. He knew that because his heart had suddenly been soothed in a way that only happened when she was speaking, though he could not for the life of him recall what she had said.

She was not glaring at him, not exactly. Still, there was an undercurrent of… If Christoph did not know any better, he would have called it frustration in Daphne's eyes.

'I was saying,' she remarked pointedly, 'How distracted you have been this afternoon. No bad news, I hope?'

'Bad news?' Christoph said quickly. Far too quickly. 'What gave you that idea?'

Daphne blinked. 'Only…well, was not Laura supposed to join us today? I hope her travels have not been interrupted.'

Christoph's stomach lurched again. Yes, that was another thing to worry about. A sadistic, murderous brother who had finally discovered Christoph's subterfuge, a threat from said brother that he was watching him—how, he could not imagine—and now a sister who was missing.

Well, not missing, but most definitely late. His brother's threat rang in his ears…

'I imagine she has got caught up with the delights of Paris,' said Daphne quietly, placing her knife and fork down on her almost untouched plate. 'That must be it.'

Christoph's smile was a mite strained. 'That must be it.'

How like her to attempt to allay his fears. That was something else he was starting to realise about Daphne: she truly cared about those around her, and sought not just to listen to them, but to aid them. Henderson had scoffed at his mistress's attempts to get to know the servants, but Christoph knew for a fact that when the maid—whatever her name was—had received bad news from her mother, it was Daphne who had dried her eyes, placed a fresh handkerchief in her hand and ordered the carriage to take the protesting yet grateful girl home to Brighton with a month's full wage—and a promise of her position waiting for her. That was kindness itself. That was his wife.

'But there's something else, isn't there.'

Christoph raised his head with a jerk, momentarily catching the eye of a footman who had been looking curiously at his master. The servant flushed.

Daphne had not asked a question; it was a statement. There was a knowing look in her eye, as though she was able to look through the jacket and waistcoat into his pocket, where lay the letter.

'You have a very curious and enquiring mind,' Christoph said aloud. Yes, that was it—distract her.

'You may think you are throwing me off the scent,' Daphne said with an arched eyebrow. *An arched eyebrow? His Daphne?*

He could not help but give a laugh. 'You know, I couldn't imagine dinner without you, now. You're part of my life. A vital part of it.'

The admission was perhaps too strong. Dark splotches of embarrassment crept across Daphne's arms, right down to her fingertips, and she stared at her plate, shifting in her seat.

And that was how to halt a conversation with his wife, Christoph thought sadly, irritated beyond belief at himself. Why had he done that? Why had he opened up his heart, revealed some affection for her? Affection she clearly did not want.

There came the clearing of a throat. Christoph's attention was drawn to one of the footmen, who evidently had one of those early winter coughs that was going around. A little early in the year, perhaps...

Ah, right. It was not enough for him to ache for Daphne to be comfortable. He had to do something to make sure she felt comfortable.

'Thank you, that will be all,' he said smartly to the two footmen.

For a moment the other footman hesitated. It was not usual to be dismissed from dinner, and evidently he wished to ensure that he had not misunderstood.

Christoph's patience throbbed at his temple. 'Go on, off with you.' He said it with a smile, and hoped the two men knew they had done nothing wrong. Nothing wrong save be there, of course.

Examining his wife as the door closed behind the two footmen, leaving them alone, it came as no surprise to see that she visibly relaxed. Her shoulders loosened, a smile teased at the corner of her lips and there was a brightness in her eyes that had not been there before.

He had so much to learn about caring for this wife of his. This was not a woman who felt comfortable in front of an audience, however small that audience was. The thought was rather discomforting. Was he an audience?

'Why did you send them away?' Her voice lilted, a confidence in it that had not been there before.

It confirmed in Christoph's mind that he had indeed done the right thing. 'So that you can be comfortable—comfortable saying anything.'

'Anything?' There it was again, that raised eyebrow.

It was a good thing that Christoph was seated, for he was not sure his legs would have held him if Daphne had given him that look while he'd been upright. It was suggestive, and delicious, and reminded him of those dreams that made him reach out for her in the night.

His desire, his lust—he could not blame her for that. She could not know, surely, what such an arch expression did to him or would do to any man?

'You look a tad flushed. Are you quite well?'

Christoph coughed, hoping that the movement to clear his throat would help dislodge some of this ridiculous attraction soaring through his veins.

Attracted...to his wife? It was all very well for those

in a love match. He was here as part of an arrangement and, when he had suggested mere friendship to her, Daphne had looked pained. If friendship was too much, then what he wanted—true, erotic connection—would be far too much.

'I'm quite well, I thank you,' Christoph said aloud. 'In fact, I was wondering—'

'Christoph, I need to tell you—'

'It's something I've been thinking for a while,' he said, barrelling forward, for he knew that if he halted he would never be able to start again. 'After all, we have been married for over a month now.'

'Yes, I know, and that's what I need to tell—'

'And, although I am perhaps not the sort of husband you would have chosen, I hope to become that. The sort of husband you would choose, I mean,' Christoph said in a rush.

Daphne's eyes were wide, her cheeks pink. 'Do…do you?'

He nodded. *Oh, hell, admitting that he was starting to fall in love with his wife wasn't supposed to be this difficult, was it?*

'And so I wanted to know… I mean, we have our whole lives, and I am sure things will change in time,' said Christoph, warming to his theme.

Well, she hadn't shut him down immediately, had she?

'And so I thought… I mean, if there was anything I could ever do that would increase your happiness…help you with, even.'

Now her eyes were even wider—which was odd, because Christoph did not consider a single word of his admittedly poor speech to have been that suggestive. Quite the opposite, in truth. He was trying most desperately not to think of Daphne beneath his fingertips, quivering at his touch; Daphne lying on his bed in her naked glory; Daphne squirming beneath him as he poured himself into her…

'I'm actually…' Daphne halted, but she appeared determined to continue. 'Hungry.'

Christoph blinked. They were seated at the dinner table. True, they had not yet finished, but he would have thought the soup and the delicious trout with lemon butter sauce would have been sufficient for anyone.

'Hungry,' he repeated.

Daphne's cheeks were pink and she would not quite meet his gaze, which also suggested he had gone wrong somewhere. 'Hungry. A hunger I have felt for…for weeks now.'

A hunger she had felt for weeks? If it had been any other woman but his wife, Christoph would have said that she was attempting to flirt with him. No, more than that—he would have suspected her of attempting to seduce him.

But this was Daphne. *Daphne.* His wife, the woman who had been absolutely clear on their wedding night that she was enduring their love-making because it was necessary.

She…surely wasn't talking about pleasure…was she?

Daphne lifted her eyes and looked directly at him,

cheeks blazing, but her expression resolute. 'I... I want...'

Christoph swallowed, hard. This was just his imagination. He was getting this wrong because he wanted her so badly, wanted to spread her across this table and plunge himself into her. Because he could not be right in his suspicion...could he?

'Daphne,' he said—or, more accurately, croaked. 'Daphne, I think we are at cross purposes. I... Do you mean—?'

'I ache for you, Christoph,' she blurted out. 'For the way you touched me.'

Silence fell between them in the dining room. Silence, save for the ringing in Christoph's ears, that was.

I ache for you, Christoph. For the way you touched me.

If he had not just heard the syllables drop from her pretty lips, Christoph would not have believed it possible. But he had. And Daphne was sitting there, evidently mortified, and yet she had not lurched away, or fled like a deer in the hunter's glare.

No, she was sitting there, squirming on her seat.

Christoph's manhood stiffened. *Squirming*—as though she wanted...

'We had rules,' he said hoarsely.

'I'm not saying that we break any of them,' Daphne said breathlessly. 'And I can't believe... I never would have thought I would say this, but Christoph, I ache for you.'

Christ, she couldn't keep saying that! He would burst

in his breeches. 'I… I can help relieve that ache, if you want. If you trust me.'

Daphne looked deep into his eyes—a little afraid, but mostly, yes, that was lust. Dear Heaven help him. 'Would you do that for me? With…with no expectations?'

I would do anything for you, were the words Christoph wanted to cry out. But he couldn't. His precious, precious wife was asking something of him that had taken her a great deal of courage, and at any moment she could flee in her embarrassment. He needed to go carefully. Mostly.

'I would,' he said, his voice almost a mere whisper.

Christoph rose, pushing back his chair as his mind whirled. So many possibilities, yet so many restrictions. So many things he wanted to do, yet such a great desire to please her without frightening her. How would he do it?

'You don't have to… It was a foolish thing to say, forgive me.' Daphne had evidently misinterpreted his stillness. 'I should never have…'

'You can tell me to stop at any point,' Christoph said quietly, fixing her with a look that silenced her. 'I'm doing this to please you, Daphne. You are so beautiful. Your body is so…so enticing. As long as what I do pleases you, I… I hope you will let me continue.'

Her eyes were wide and her lips slightly parted as she nodded, evidently confused. She was probably even more confused now, Christoph thought ruefully, when he rose to his feet and clambered over the table.

'Christoph!'

He grinned as he reached his wife, pulling her out of her chair and lifting her onto the table.

'Christoph, what are you...?'

Daphne's voice trailed off as he lowered himself to his feet and knelt before her. In a moment he was able to hear her voice but not see her face—which was probably all to the good, he thought darkly. If he was to see the blissful expression of Daphne as he brought her to climax, chances were he would never be able to stop doing it.

'Christoph, what are you...? Oh.'

Daphne's voice halted as he very carefully, very gently, reached for the hem of her skirts and lifted them above her knees, layering the luscious material onto her thighs. Her legs quivered—in anticipation, he hoped.

'So beautiful,' he murmured.

Christoph wasn't sure whether his voice was loud enough for her to hear. Perhaps it didn't matter. He was faced with the most splendid sight he had ever seen as he gently pressed his palms on Daphne's knees and parted them, moving her feet apart. It was impossible to speak any words, now that his throat was so hoarse.

Dear God. She was glistening, her folds dripping with desire. No wonder she had been squirming on her seat. No wonder she ached.

'Oh, you precious thing,' he murmured, lowering his head to press a kiss on Daphne's inner thigh. 'Let me help you. Let me take care of you.'

Daphne squirmed again at the kiss, or perhaps his words; he wasn't sure. All Christoph knew was that her squirming was not aimless. Her buttocks had moved forward, bringing her centre closer to his face, and Christoph swallowed hard as he readied himself for the tastiest mouthful he had ever experienced in a dining room.

There was a clatter of cutlery the moment Christoph pressed a kiss against the slit of her quim, as though Daphne had suddenly grasped the table.

'Christoph!'

It was not a cry of disgust, pain or discomfort. It was one of surprise—of delight—and it made Christoph slip his tongue deeper to gain a true taste of the woman he was starting to adore more than anything in the world.

He groaned. God, she tasted incredible: honey and spices, her wet folds parting, welcoming him in.

Daphne's breathing was quicker. 'Oh, Christoph, that—that...'

It was his delight to make speech impossible after that. At least, coherent speech. Daphne's whimpers, moans, mutters to a deity and cries of his name were precisely what Christoph wanted to hear as he worshipped her quim with his mouth, licking, tasting, sucking and kissing, building a rhythm of sensual delight that eventually brought her hands to his head, her fingers tangling in his hair, pulling him closer.

It was all Christoph could do not to come in his breeches. The scent of her, the taste of her, the knowledge that he was giving her precisely what she wanted, thanks to her tugging his head closer and the mewls of need, were intoxicating.

She was intoxicating.

He had avoided the nub of her pleasure at first, not wishing to overwhelm her with such a sudden climax, but by the rapid, fluttering breathing and twisting moans echoing in Daphne's lungs, she was ready.

By God, he was ready to give it to her.

Grabbing hold of her hips to ensure she did not buck his face away from her quim, Christoph swirled his tongue inside the depths of her, feeling her insides spasming around him, before lifting it to that nub that he knew would give her ultimate relief, giving her both heavy pressure and a slow circling.

Daphne's fingers tightened in his hair, her hips suddenly bucking, thrusting wildly into his mouth. 'Oh, Christoph, yes, yes, yes—eat me!'

And she came apart. It was all Christoph could do to hold onto her, the rush of moisture from her ecstasy almost overwhelming him. The taste was so victorious, the delight in bringing her to climax so achingly sweet.

When eventually Daphne's hips subsided, her moans quietening, and a gentle relaxation of her hands in his hair suggesting that she had taken her fill, Christoph pulled back from between her thighs with some regret.

'Christoph?'

Ducking his head, he emerged from her skirts.

Daphne's face was flushed, her eyes were bright—had he brought her to tears?—and her lips were parted in astonishment.

'That…that was…'

Christoph grinned up at her. 'I hope that sorted your appetite.'

Chapter Thirteen

Daphne picked up her fork, stared at it and put it back down on her plate.

I hope that sorted your appetite.

It was a good thing she was no longer holding it, for she would surely have dropped it when the memory of two days before sparked through her mind. Cheeks aflame, Daphne tried not to think that she had been sitting in this exact seat, at this exact table, in this very room.

Oh, you precious thing. Let me help you. Let me take care of you.

Daphne swallowed. Luncheon was strange enough, eating it on her own, as once again Christoph was nowhere to be found. But, with the memories of that intimate and erotic moment roaring through her mind, it was almost impossible to concentrate. Not that she minded.

'Focus, Daphne,' she murmured to herself, grateful for the privacy that luncheon provided. No footmen. No servants listening in. 'Do not think about it.'

The trouble was, it was the only thing she was able to

think about at the moment. If she had realised such pleasure was to be had, pleasure that did not require Christoph to...enter her, then she might well have attempted to negotiate that into their agreement.

Heat burned her collar bone. Not that she would have had the words to ask for such a thing. In the silence, Daphne's tongue attempted to entangle itself around how she could have asked for such a thing.

And I would like you to kiss me...every day, actually... but not on my mouth...

Daphne shook her head with a wry smile. 'You never could, Daphne.'

No, she never could—but perhaps, if she had known how glorious it was, she would have at least tried. After all, who wouldn't want a repeat, a continual repeat, of what had happened two evenings ago?

Enticing, was what he had called her. The word became bittersweet as Daphne looked down at herself. When she was growing, swelling with child, would Christoph still find her enticing? Perhaps it would be easier to ignore that part of her future if she waited a little longer to tell him. After all, Christoph did not need to know that she was almost certainly with child, did he? Besides, it might prevent him from touching her like that again, and that was definitely to be avoided.

The memories sparked back in her mind, and as she was alone, Daphne decided to indulge herself as her eyelashes fluttered.

Christoph, on his knees. Christoph, parting her own. Christoph, kissing her.

Daphne knocked over her glass of lemonade.

'Oh—oh, no!' she cried, lurching to her feet and picking up the glass, far too late to prevent the sticky yellow liquid rushing across the spotless white tablecloth.

Her cry appeared to summon another, for footsteps echoed in the hall and the door burst open.

'What has—? Oh. It's just you.'

Daphne had not thought it possible for her cheeks to burn any brighter, but apparently so. Henderson stood by the door, his expression fading from worry to disdain.

'Good afternoon, Henderson,' she said to the butler, in an attempt to ease the moment. 'I am afraid I have had a small—'

'What have you done?' sighed Henderson, shaking his head as though she were a child.

Try as she might, Daphne could not prevent her head from lowering. This was ridiculous. He was a servant—admittedly not a servant she had chosen, but still, a servant. She should not be cowed by him. She should not wish to crawl into a hole. The fact that an apology was creeping towards her lips merely because he was looking at her with such contempt was ridiculous!

Daphne swallowed it. 'Have this cleaned up, please.'

Perhaps she had spoken with too much imperiousness. She had attempted something polite yet firm. It did not appear to have worked. Henderson rolled his eyes but at the very least began to obey.

The man would never have acted like this with Christoph in the room—but, as her husband had been absent for the last day and a half, she was stuck facing the butler alone. Christoph's absence made it impossible not only to tell him that she was with child but that she was starting to feel…something for him.

Preposterous. Why had she not had the duty of choosing her own staff?

'Well,' Daphne said as brightly as she could manage. 'I shall leave you to it. Thank you, Henderson.'

Perhaps another woman could have swept out of there elegantly, and with such refinement that her butler would have no choice but to respect her. Gwen would have managed it. Sylvia most definitely would have. Even Rilla would have had an impact.

As it was, Daphne almost tripped over her own skirts and had to reach out for the wall to prevent herself from launching to the ground, in doing so knocking sideways what was undoubtedly a priceless painting, leaving it crooked.

The butler's muffled snort as she passed him was most unpleasant. But at least she was gone.

A ride… Yes, that was what she needed: the opportunity to get out into the fresh air, away from Henderson, away from the weight of expectation that lay on her as the Princess and just be… Daphne. Just a woman riding a horse through a London park.

The stables were small. London townhouses did not have room for spacious stables, apparently. This had surprised her when she and Christoph had first been married a month ago, the Wallflower Academy being the only place Daphne had ever lived. Yet the stables were sufficiently large for three horses: two for the carriage and one for Christoph. Apparently no one had given much thought to whether Daphne would wish to ride. No matter. She was accustomed to not being considered.

With Christoph gone, Daphne thought as she walked across the lawn towards the stables, she could take one of the horses. No one would mind. She was the mistress of this house, was she not? So it was therefore with great determination that she strode round the corner.

'Oof!'

'Ouch!'

Daphne blinked at the crisp white linen expanse she had walked into. To prevent herself from falling for a second time in almost as many minutes, her hands thrust out ahead of her. They were now plastered onto the linen expanse: Christoph's shirt.

She stared up into her husband's smile.

'You are in a hurry,' Christoph said with a grin.

Daphne's cheeks burned.

She had not seen him since...since he had done that wonderful thing to her. And how she was standing here with her palms splayed against his warm chest, his heartbeat throbbing against her fingertips, and her breath caught in her throat.

'I was about to saddle my horse and go for a ride,' said Christoph, jerking his head behind him in a gesture towards the stables. 'I do not suppose you would wish to join me.'

Was...was that a question? A statement?

Daphne's mind was still whirling from the sudden contact, the memories of their last contact clouding her judgement. That was undoubtedly why she said, 'Why would you think that?'

Christoph blinked, evidently lost. 'Well, I thought... that is, I assumed, from everything you said... Well, you're shy. You're a wallflower, but you have been braver than most—braver, I think, than you have ever realised. I see you, Daphne—see you for more than you see in yourself.'

There it was again, that delicate phrasing, just slightly different from the English way of saying things. And he could not be more wrong.

Daphne swallowed, her mouth dry as she prepared herself to speak.

I want to hear your inside thoughts.

'It's not that I don't like the world,' she said in a rush. 'It's that I don't know it.'

A flash of curiosity flickered in Christoph's eyes. 'You don't know it?'

How could she possibly try to explain—and to him, this man who had travelled hundreds of miles from his homeland and settled in a foreign land where people spoke another language?

Daphne inhaled slowly. 'I...it's... The Wallflower Academy was my whole world. It was where I felt safest because I knew it. Oh, we had short forays into London Society, but for an hour perhaps, and then it was back to the Wallflower Academy. London, England, the *ton*... I don't know it. It's like a foreign land, and I want to explore. I want to adventure, but I don't know the rules, I don't know if I would be welcome.'

'Would you like to join me?'

The trouble was, Daphne thought as she stared up into his dark eyes, that she couldn't say no to this man. There was absolutely no impetus within her to say no to him. Besides, she didn't want to.

'Yes, please,' she whispered.

Christoph's smile softened. 'I do apologise. I did not even ask you whether you could ride.'

Only then did Daphne remember that she was pressed up against the man for absolutely no reason. At least, no reason that she could justify.

She stepped back hastily, almost tripping over her own ankle. 'I can ride! We didn't, I mean, I never owned a horse, I had to borrow. At the Wallflower Academy, if I wanted to, there was always Bramble my favourite horse—but I can do it, I can ride, I… Yes. I can.'

She had expected Christoph to laugh. She had expected him to tease her, to laugh at the way her words had got tangled. Not because he was cruel, but because that was what everyone did.

Christoph merely nodded sagely. 'I can see how that would be a limitation, though Bramble sounds delightful. My first horse—a pony, really—was called Midnight. But you do not own your own horse now. That must be rectified.'

Rectified? Was he seriously suggesting they just buy a horse? Who could afford to just go and buy a horse?

All too late, Daphne realised precisely who could. She could. Or at least, he could, now that upon their marriage her entire dowry had become his own personal fortune.

'Right. Good,' she said vaguely, trying not to look at his hands. Christoph's hands. The hands that had gently, almost reverentially, parted her knees to give his mouth access...

'Shall we?'

Daphne took a hasty step back. 'Shall we what?'

'Go riding.' Christoph's expression was one of pure confusion. 'I am sorry, I assumed that was what you—'

'Yes, yes, I would.'

'Because if you don't want—'

'No, I want to.' Daphne's cheeks were burning so much, she expected someone looking from the house could have spotted the red in the trees. 'Let's go for a ride.'

She had expected it to be awkward. A man couldn't put his face between someone's thighs and lick them to completion without it getting a tad awkward, Daphne could not help but think.

But somehow the most awkward part of the whole thing was just how unfazed the man appeared to be.

Once in the stables, with a smile Christoph helped her up onto a horse, and was soon settled on his own steed with an air of complete comfort. He was a good rider; Daphne noted his almost subconscious direction of the beast as they departed from the stables and rode onto the bustling London street. It was almost as though he belonged there. Almost as though he belonged with her.

Daphne pushed the thought from her mind as Christoph chattered away about the weather, the popularity of London in the autumn, the fine wine they would sample that evening at dinner and—much to her chagrin—she found herself utterly charmed.

It was most unfair. Here she was, desperate to get through life without being castigated or censored for her behaviour, and there were people like Christoph who did not appear even to need to try. Glancing over at him as their horses trotted down the street towards Hyde Park, Daphne smiled to herself.

He was attractive. And charming. And kind-hearted. Any woman would have found it difficult not to find her soul touched by him. She merely had the disadvantage of also being married to him.

'You are very quiet.'

Daphne started. Christoph was gazing at her with just as much affectionate curiosity as she had been giving him. It was disconcerting, to see such an expression reflected on his face.

She looked away sharply as they entered Hyde Park by the Clarendon Gate. 'I was just thinking.'

'And what, may I ask, were you thinking?'

You may ask, Daphne wanted to say. *But that does not guarantee that I will tell you.*

Another inside thought, and one she most definitely kept inside. She could not have Christoph think she was flirting with him—God forbid! She did not want him to feel obligated to reciprocate. *Because she cared for him.*

Daphne had not permitted herself even to think it until this moment, the clamour and excitement of Hyde Park all around them as they slowed their horses to a walk and gently rode through the greenery. Carriages rattled along Rotten Row and gentlemen walked with ladies. A gaggle of schoolboys made their way through the park as a few families sat on blankets eating late luncheons, and still she could not stop thinking about how much she cared for him.

Glancing at him from under her eyelashes, Daphne could not help but smile as she met his beaming grin. There was something so… pure about him. So gentle. So compassionate. Guarding her heart had never been a challenge—not when no man had ever smiled at her before.

Only now did Daphne realise just how much of a challenge it was. How vital it was, how necessary it would be, to ensure that she never lost control. Because what was she supposed to do: fall in love with her husband? Lose herself? Embarrass herself, when Christoph would be forced to admit that he felt nothing for her?

Which was why, as their horses walked along the winding path that veered to the left, Daphne knew that she had to do it. She had to say it. Even if it was going to make her entire body burn with embarrassment.

Daphne cleared her throat. 'We…we don't have to do that again.'

There. It was said. And she had been perfectly clear. There was no need to—

'Do what again?' Christoph said, his grin now wicked.

There it was—the burning sensation. Daphne could feel it rising up her legs, past her hips and across her chest. Anyone looking at the pair of them would presume that Christoph had made an unsavoury remark—they would never suppose that it was she who had spoken so out of turn.

'You know what,' she murmured, agonising over her tone. Too cheerful? Too eager? Not eager enough? 'I just meant,' Daphne continued, forcing herself to speak and gazing dead ahead to avoid Christoph's gaze completely, 'That though I… I appreciate what you did—'

'Which we still haven't spoken of.'

'You don't have to do it again,' Daphne finished, hating the way his teasing voice sparked ripples of remembered pleasure through her body. How did he make her feel such tingling bliss without even touching her?

When she managed to bring herself to look at him, Christoph was smiling—but it wasn't the cruel, teasing smile she had seen on some gentlemen, nor the ignorant, accidentally harsh smile she had witnessed on others. It was something entirely different. A smile that was sincere, tender and…

No, she would not think 'loving'. Daphne managed to pull herself back from the precipice before it was too late.

'You didn't enjoy it?'

Daphne's fingers tightened momentarily on the reins. Christoph had asked the question quietly, so that no one passing them could have heard a syllable, and with a gentleness she did not deserve.

'I…' This was not the time for modesty. 'I have never felt anything like it.'

There. That was not quite answering his question, but, so be it.

Christoph had raised an eyebrow...not that she was looking at him. 'Never?'

Before Daphne could stop herself, before she could remind herself that thinking of such things in public was absolutely scandalous, she was back in that bed, on that night, Christoph's fingers caressing her to a peak, his manhood nestled between her, invading her, and yet what a welcome invasion.

Her cheeks must be scarlet. She certainly could feel their heat. 'Twice before. On our wedding night.'

'If I am any judge of the matter, I would lay good money on the fact that that would have been an inside thought, in times past,' said Christoph quietly.

Daphne tried to take a steady breath but it eluded her. An inside thought—yes, it would have been, and how she had managed to say it she did not know.

'Well done,' came the gentle encouragement. 'You impress me.'

It should not have been possible for such short words to have such an impact on her. It really shouldn't. And yet Daphne could not deny that her whole body was aflame, as though she'd stepped into a midsummer's fire, sparks flying around her.

'Let's talk of something else. It was never my intention to offend you,' said Christoph softly. 'Tell me...about your childhood. At the Wallflower Academy, I mean.'

Daphne swallowed. She was not offended, not as such. In a way, she was disappointed. A part of her had wondered...fine, hoped...that they would somehow meander to agreeing to share such an erotic experience, what once a month?

Once a day, a part of her murmured.

'Besides, I can imagine it would be painful to dwell on times before then,' Christoph continued.

Daphne stared. 'Do you…?'

'Well, you have already shared with me some very troubling memories,' he said delicately. 'I would not wish you to upset yourself.'

He remembered. More, he had not only remembered what she had said, but he clearly wished to make her comfortable. Put her at ease.

'You joined the Wallflower Academy young, I seem to recall.'

That was it, Daphne thought ruefully. *Back to the Wallflower Academy we go, even if it is only in conversation.* 'Yes, I was, oh, about five.'

'Fifteen would have been more appropriate.' Christoph's brows furrowed.

Daphne shook her head, relieved to be on safer ground. 'My father… My mother had died and my father had no wish to keep me around. He was concerned it would detract from his marital prospects, I suppose, so I was sent to the Wallflower Academy. Miss Pike made a special case for me.'

A special case that, in hindsight, probably had something to do with the title of her father, and the amount of coin handed over, rather than anything to do with her.

Christoph was still speaking. 'You must have been

lonely, with so many women older than you, and no other children?'

'Lonely? Yes, I suppose it was,' Daphne said as brightly as she could manage. Her voice wavered. *Bother it.* 'It was. But not because I was so much younger. Many of the wallflowers there had younger siblings, and missed them. They were very good to me. Most of them.'

Hyde Park was starting to empty. The temperature had dipped, the sun scurrying away behind clouds and there was the scent of rain in the air.

'Most of them?'

Daphne could not help but laugh. 'Do you always have to notice the parts of my speech that I most wish you to ignore?'

'You draw attention to it,' Christoph shot back gently. 'I know you, Daphne—or at least, I am getting to know you. And I know that when you speak lightly, just like that, it is because of some great hurt. A great hurt from which you have never healed.'

Once again, her fingers tightened on the reins. 'It...it is most disobliging of you to be so observant.'

'Is that not what husbands are for?'

Somehow Christoph had brought his steed closer to hers. Daphne could feel his proximity, feel it like she could feel the sun, a cold breeze or the promise of winter.

She swallowed. 'Yes, I was lonely. Most of the girls in residence at the Wallflower Academy when I was very small were true wallflowers, there because their families had struggled to find them a match. I was the only... illegitimate daughter there, sent away to hide from Society. Sylvia joined me a few years ago, of course, but for a long time I was alone.'

Try as she might, Daphne had been unable to keep the pain from her voice.

Christoph reached out and touched her arm. Just slightly. The moment was gone almost as soon as it arrived. 'You are not any less because of that. Society's rules are not just. Not fair.'

Daphne tried to laugh. It did not work. 'All I knew was that my father did not want to be seen by me. I truly believe that, until our arranged marriage was announced, there were still those in the *ton* who did not know my father had a daughter.'

'So something changed.'

Changed? Daphne blinked, taking in his words. Yes, something had. Now he pointed it out, it seemed obvious.

'Perhaps your father's remarriage,' Christoph said gently. 'People can change, Daphne. I mean, not all of them—true cruelty, true violence stems in my view from a truly evil character—but people get things wrong and wish to make amends.'

It was a pleasant thought, that her father wished he had done things differently. That he was attempting to make amends. It almost did not matter if it was true.

There was something in the way Christophe spoke. Daphne had wondered precisely why her husband was so aloof at times, so warm at others—but, she could see now, it was not aloofness or coldness. It was nerves—anxiety that he would not be heeded. In conversations like this she could see the damage that had been wrought on Christoph the child, but he was healing. They were healing together.

'Besides,' added her husband with a low chuckle, 'you are a princess now. A princess of royal blood.'

'By marriage,' Daphne pointed out, trying not to smile.

Christoph shrugged. 'And where are those other wallflowers now, eh?'

Such a suggestion should not have made her smile so much. 'You know, I have no idea.'

'Good riddance to them, I say,' returned Christoph. 'And—blast!'

Daphne could not help but giggle as the heavens opened. Rain poured down, a torrent upon their shoulders, and they swiftly became absolutely drenched. 'It's only a little rain!'

'This country, with your changeable weather and your constant rain!' Christoph called out over the downpour. 'Come on!'

Laughing as they hurried from the park and rode through the emptying streets, her pulse quickened by the rush of adrenaline that poured through her faster and heavier than the rain, Daphne was glad when they returned to their stables so quickly.

'Remind me never to go out for a ride without an umbrella in this damp country,' Christoph said with a laugh, dismounting in the dry of the stable and walking over to her. 'Here.'

It was not a request. It was not an order, either, but

Daphne found her body willingly obeying the unspoken invitation.

She descended from her horse, slithering down its wet flank and finding herself pinned between that sodden beast and the equally sodden masculine beast before her.

Daphne swallowed as she looked up into Christoph's eyes. His eyelashes were sparkling with raindrops and there was a look of such heady desire, of lust in his eyes.

Christoph released her, stepping away, his laugh ragged. 'If I had my own way, I would keep you here, but that would be selfish—and you are precious, Daphne.

'You had better call a maid to help you out of those wet things. You don't wish to catch a cold.'

'Christoph I must tell you…'

And he was gone, striding out of the stables before she could tell him the secret she had been holding on to for days. The secret she knew had to be said—and soon.

Chapter Fourteen

Christoph had obviously never had a father-in-law, and his relationship with his own father was nothing much to boast of. He had looked forward to this dinner—but the awkward silences between each conversation would be enough to disquiet anyone. Why was it so difficult to get talk going with these people?

'So tell me,' he said, over the clinking of cutlery and not much else. 'What was Daphne like, as a child?'

'A child?' blinked the Earl of Norbury. 'She...she was...' His voice trailed off and the man glanced momentarily at his grown child, then back to his place. 'I almost took her to the opera once.'

'Almost?' Christoph looked in turn at his wife, but Daphne's own attention was fixed on her cutlery as she very slowly cut her food into smaller and smaller pieces. 'How does one "almost"?'

'I was a little late. A game of cards... I had not realised the time. She had apparently been waiting there, on the bottom step of the Wallflower Academy, for almost an hour,' muttered the Earl of Norbury.

Christoph tried to smile. His lips felt tight and he purposefully did not look to his left, where Daphne sat, silently, unmoving. As unobtrusively as possible.

'But you did arrive eventually,' said the Countess of Norbury with a pat on her husband's arm.

'Oh, yes, eventually,' said the Earl of Norbury with a nod. 'But by that time the little mite had fallen asleep, all curled up at the base of the stairs, and I didn't have the heart to wake her. So we left her there.'

Christoph's jaw tightened as the story drew to a close and his father-in-law sipped one of his most expensive wines. 'I see.'

It had been an evening of 'seeing'.

The idea had been good—at least, his intention.

'We really should have them over for dinner,' he had said just two nights ago. 'After all, it has been over a month since the wedding. We should host them.'

Daphne had looked uncomfortable and yet, unwilling to share her true thoughts, had said, 'Whatever you think best.'

Try as he might, Christoph had tried to encourage her to speak her true mind. Those inside thoughts of hers, he wanted to know them. But Daphne had been circumspect. She would not speak the truth.

And now he knew why.

'Tell Christoph the story of when you intended to take her to the ballet,' the Countess of Norbury said ineptly. 'You wanted to give her such a treat.'

Christoph tried to smile, he really did. But the dining room felt claustrophobic and taut, the tension all the more awkward because their guests did not appear to feel it. He certainly could. He would have bet his entire marital fortune on the fact that the woman seated to his left did.

Daphne had not looked up from her hands for almost five minutes. Clasped as they were in her lap, it was easy for her to avoid the attention of anyone else at the table. She had not spoken. She had not smiled. She had not laughed.

'I don't think…' he began.

'Yes, yes, I did intend to treat her,' said the Earl of Norbury with a little more warmth. 'So, I promised little Daphne that I would take her to the ballet.'

Christoph did not need to listen to the details. He could already tell where the story was heading, the inevitable conclusion. The Earl of Norbury had not taken his daughter to the ballet. It was excruciating. Did the man have no sense? Was it possible that he did not hear himself, that he did not realise just how awful it was to hear story after story in which he had disappointed his daughter—even as a child—in almost all these tales?

'But of course, she couldn't be found. Run off, hidden herself away. We looked for her for an hour.'

Christoph's pulse throbbed at his temple. He had thought the evening would be a pleasant one, perhaps even enjoyable. After all, a father who owned his child, who had appeared during the wedding planning to have a modicum of respect for his child, was something Christoph had never experienced. He had envied Daphne, though he had been loath to admit it.

'And so we didn't go,' finished the Earl of Norbury before he gulped another large mouthful of Christoph's wine. 'Top up, please!'

Henderson stepped forward smoothly and filled up the Earl of Norbury's glass.

Christoph sighed and leaned back against his chair.

Well, this has been a disaster. At least it can't get any worse.

'That's the trouble with Daphne,' the Earl of Norbury said with a shake of his head. 'Too shy.'

Christoph bristled as he glanced at Daphne. Her head remained low. 'I actually think—'

'Oh, it was fashionable enough twenty years ago, but men don't want wallflowers for a wife,' the Earl of Norbury said vaguely, waving a hand about. Wine sloshed over the carpet. 'I certainly didn't expect a daughter who was a wallflower.'

Christoph's jaw was getting tighter by the second and yet he could think of no way to head off the foolish man. He was too in his cups, that was the trouble—and yet the Countess of Norbury was just sitting there! Pink-cheeked, admittedly, and silent the last few minutes. But that was the thing, wasn't it? Silent.

Not that he was any different, Christoph thought wretchedly.

Okay. 'I like Daphne's—'

'And it is very chivalrous for you to say so, Christoph, but you don't have to be polite here, we're family,' the Earl of Norbury cut in with a hiccup. 'Excuse me.'

What was perhaps most infuriating was just how nonchalant the cruelty was. Oh, there was no malice in the man. Christoph had been around enough malicious men to know one when he saw it. But that was perhaps worse. The Earl of Norbury did not intend to be unpleasant. He just could not understand how precious his daughter was.

'Christoph has heard more than enough of your stories,' the Countess of Norbury said, patting her husband's arm. 'Let us discuss that horse you bought last week.'

Christoph shifted in his chair most unhappily. Strange... He had told Daphne several times, until she had truly believed him, that he preferred just to be called Christoph, without any title. Yet hearing his first name spoken so carelessly by Lord and Lady Norbury... It did not feel right, somehow. Perhaps it was only Daphne to whom he wanted to give that particular privilege.

'Oh, yes, a magnificent beast, at least sixteen hands,' the Earl of Norbury said proudly. 'Poor old Daphne would never be able to mount him—if she ever had the bravery to approach him!'

Christoph winced. How was it possible that the man was inadvertently able to slight his daughter even on the topic of horses?

It was agony. From the moment that the Earl and Countess of Norbury had entered their home, Christoph had watched Daphne slowly creep into herself, slowly retreat into her shell from which he had worked so hard to coax her. She had lost her brightness, the shine that he had seen.

Not that she had ever become loud. No, loud was not a part of her character, her temperament. She was not a loud woman. She had stayed who she was, but the *shame*—that was it, the shame—had faded away. Christoph had rejoiced in seeing more of Daphne, more of the woman who thought so boldly, even if she did not say the words aloud.

Now she was gone. Weeks of work, of cajoling, of encouraging, all wasted, after two hours in the presence of her father. And it was his fault for inviting them, for not seeing just how uncomfortable the presence of her father would make her.

'I suppose a pony is more enjoyable to ride,' Daphne said quietly, startling Christoph with her words. 'A pony called Midnight, perhaps.'

Christoph managed not to let his jaw drop, but it was a close-run thing. She had remembered. She had truly listened to him. Why was that one of the most attractive things about her?

'Now then, dear, you'll embarrass your daughter,' the Countess of Norbury said with a fond smile directed at her husband. 'You have to remember, Daphne isn't brave like you!'

And that was when Christoph said quietly, 'How dare you speak of my wife like that?'

The dining room hushed to a silence.

Christoph swallowed, his mouth dry. The Earl of Norbury had frozen, one hand in the air in gesticulation. The Countess of Norbury's hands were similarly still, halfway through cutting a piece of lamb. The two footmen's cheeks were pink, their eyes averted, and Henderson, naturally, was smirking.

But it wasn't any of them that he cared about.

Christoph looked at Daphne and saw her pain. Saw the tension across her brow. Saw her discomfort, her desperate wish to be somewhere, anywhere but here.

'I mean,' he said slowly, trying to feel his way through the sentence. *Hell and all its devils, but he should not have been so rude.* 'I mean, Daphne is quite comfortable on a horse, in fact. We went riding just a few days ago, and I was impressed at her galloping, even through the rain.'

The smile he attempted was slightly forced, but then so was the cheery grin his father-in-law gave him. 'She gets that from me, you know.'

It was not completely salvaged, but the conversation managed to totter on. Christoph leaned back in his chair and took a sip of wine, permitting himself one additional look at the beautiful woman sitting on his left.

Daphne raised her gaze just a fraction and met his eye. 'Thank you.'

The words were not spoken but mouthed, yet Christoph felt as though they had been shouted from the rooftops of St James' Court.

It was ridiculous, how swiftly he'd felt like a knight in shining armour—but was that not precisely what he was? A rescuer, a saviour, stepping in to protect his woman?

His woman. What was he thinking? Daphne no more belonged to him than…anyone did. Oh, she might do in the eyes of the law, but in his eyes Daphne was very much a free woman.

A woman for whom he cared deeply.

'You know, I feel remarkably tired,' said the Countess of Norbury suddenly. 'My love, I think we should depart.'

Finally, thought Christoph wearily.

It was not a very fair thought; they were quite within their rights to stay for dessert, then drinks and further conversation. Thank goodness the Countess of Norbury had suddenly got the hint.

'Tired?' blinked her husband.

'Tired,' repeated the Countess of Norbury firmly. 'Call the carriage, will you, Christoph?'

Gritting his teeth, and hoping she did not notice as he tried to smile, Christoph inclined his head. 'Certainly. Call the carriage, Henderson.'

The two young stable hands had the Norbury carriage ready for departure within five minutes, a span of time in which Christoph attempted to say how pleasant the evening had been without lying. He would have to remember to tip the lads.

'A good dinner with good company is one always to be repeated,' he said jovially, absolutely not pointing out that the dinner had been good but the company somewhat lacking.

His father-in-law beamed. 'Oh, I quite agree! We shall have to invite you to dinner, Christoph, even if Daphne would prefer to stay at home on her own!'

And, chortling once again at a joke made once again at his own daughter's expense, the Earl of Norbury and his wife departed.

Giving a distinct sigh of relief as the door closed behind them, Christoph walked into the drawing room, ordered out the footman who was carefully picking up abandoned glasses, and shut the door firmly behind him.

Only then could he relax.

'That,' Christoph said darkly, 'was awful.'

Daphne's laugh was not forced, thank God. She was seated on the sofa by the fire, and had started to let down her hair, pins collecting on the console table beside her. 'It wasn't that bad.'

'It was worse than bad,' Christoph said, striding across the room and dropping into the armchair next to her. 'I cannot believe it—I cannot understand why that was so impossible!'

'My father is an acquired taste,' came his daughter's unduly generous remark.

Christoph snorted rather than giving voice to his true feelings. It was unfathomable that such a gentle and conscientious woman such as Daphne could have come from a man like *that*! A man who seemed only to seek praise when he was criticising others. His own daughter included!

'However hard it was for me to sit through that nonsense,' he said quietly, 'I can only imagine how difficult it was for you.'

Christoph winced as Daphne laughed with a casual shrug. It was far too casual.

'Oh, you know how it is.'

'I don't think I did, until this evening,' he admitted. 'I mean, you have told me often of the difficulties, the distance between you and your father. You have given me plenty of cause to believe you. But I did not think it could be that…that appalling.'

The beautiful woman before him smiled, most of her blonde hair now cascading down her shoulders. 'It is just his way.'

She was being too generous. Far too generous. 'Daphne, you are allowed to dislike your father.'

'I do not dislike him.'

'He was not kind to you.' Christoph hated how strident his voice had become, his deep-rooted need to protect this woman, even from herself, overpowering his sense. 'You are allowed to say that you did not enjoy tonight's dinner. You are allowed to say "I told you so". You did warn me, in your way, not to extend the invitation.' If only he had listened to her.

Daphne was watching him, serious in her silence. But this was not like the silences of before, when they had first been married. No, these days it was quite different. They were warm, welcoming, comfortable silences. Silences in which they could both sit and think. Sometimes they would read, sometimes she would do some embroidery, sometimes he would read the newspaper. Whatever they did, they did it in a silence that embraced them both.

'You are a prince,' Daphne said faintly, breaking this comfortable silence. 'You grew up in a palace. Why is it so important to you that I accept the difficulties of my past?'

It was an excellent question, and not one he particularly knew the answer to. Christoph swallowed, his voice hoarse. 'I...'

When Daphne looked at him like that, with those bright eyes and heady smile, it was rather difficult to think. So difficult, in fact, that Christoph did not think. He just spoke the truth.

'I was never encouraged to be open about my feelings,' he said simply. 'As a child, and a young man, my family valued pride and stoicism more than anything. And yet, I find... I look back and I see pain—pain I felt—and yet I do not think it has gone through me like a river. I think I am a lake. A dammed stream. I think the emotions I feel build up with me.'

Daphne did not interrupt him, but merely sat there, listening. It was a marvel, the way she was able to listen.

'And now I am older and I do not know what to do with many of these emotions, save permit myself to feel them,' Christoph admitted with a wry laugh. 'It is difficult, being away from my country. Not knowing when I will go back.' *If I will go back*. 'Being apart from my sister. It is isolating, being a prince.'

'I cannot imagine it was that difficult,' Daphne said lightly, something that could have been a flicker of mischief in her eyes. 'A title—a royal title—wealth, and grandeur, always getting what you want.'

'Perhaps it is so for wealthy royal families,' Christoph said with a cynical smile. 'Perhaps it is so for eldest sons. Perhaps I am the only one who feels this way. I do not know. What I do know is, it is lonely. No one else is on your level of rank, which means that other than your siblings there is no one appropriate to play with. You are watched, observed and judged from the moment you can walk and talk. Nothing you do or say is ignored, it is picked apart and critiqued, and your family, your whole family, suffers if you make a mistimed step.'

Where these words were coming from, Christoph did not know. The more he spoke, the better he felt. There was something cathartic about telling Daphne; whether it was the telling, or her generous listening, he did not know.

Christoph blew out a heavy exhale. 'I must sound ridiculous, no? A prince, complaining about his life.'

Daphne's laugh was gentle. 'A little ridiculous, perhaps.'

He had to laugh at that, incredulity in his voice. 'Daphne von Auberheiser, you are telling me what you really think!'

Her cheeks were pink. 'I am. And I will tell you what else I think. I think we had a similar experience.'

Now that was something he had not expected. Christoph could not help it; he leaned forward, eager to be closer to this woman. 'How so?'

'I am not saying I was born a princess—quite the opposite,' she said lightly. 'But, just as no one was able to rise to your level, no one wished to stoop to mine. I was watched and judged too, at the Wallflower Academy, constantly terrified that if the criticism grew too much then my father would be told—or, worse, that news of my existence would get out.'

Christoph's eyes widened. 'I... I see.'

And he did. She was not wrong; they had had much the same experience. From different ends, perhaps, but the loneliness, the fear, the terror that one would ruin one's family, had all been the same.

Daphne was smiling softly, and a rush of affection for the woman soared through him. 'And now you are here,' she said softly.

'Yes, now I am here, far from Niedernlein,' said Christoph quietly. 'And I am happy.'

Now that appeared to be something she had not expected. Daphne flushed, shifting in her seat on the sofa before saying in a whisper. 'Are you?'

How could she doubt it? Could she not see the difference she made to his life? Was it so hard to believe that she brightened his days, improved his evenings and haunted his nights?

Christoph swallowed. He had never intended this. This had not been the plan, and the plan had been perfect. But Daphne was more perfect. She was more... more everything. More beautiful than he had predicted, more gentle than he had hoped, more passionate than he could have believed, more elegant than anyone had any right to be.

And he had fought it—by God he had—but he could not keep denying himself. He could not keep this secret to himself. He could not pretend he did not feel a deep affection for her.

She deserved to know.

Daphne watched him with curious eyes, eyes without

judgement, and Christoph loved her all the more for it. Damn, he did not deserve her.

'Daphne,' he said slowly.

There came a tilt of her lips, just for a moment. 'Christoph.'

He gave a laugh, the tension suddenly melting away. Why was he afraid of telling her this? She was his Daphne. Perhaps she would want to hear it. Perhaps there was a chance, a small chance, that she felt it too.

When he had brought her to climax at the dining table days ago, he should have entered that particular encounter with more than just the physical—he should have told her how he felt.

But maybe the perfect time had not been then, it was now.

'Daphne, I… This was, is, an arranged marriage for our mutual benefit.' Christoph tried to grasp hold of himself. *This isn't going right.* 'You aimed to escape the Wallflower Academy and I aimed to gain access to a fortune.'

Daphne's smile appeared brittle now.

Damn it, man! 'What I'm trying to say,' Christoph continued, readying himself for the rejection that he knew was a possibility, 'is that, despite saying we should not, we could not, fall in love, despite the plan not involving anything so emotional as affection, despite knowing that I have no claim on you, not in this regard, despite—'

'Christoph.'

She was holding his hands. Christoph almost choked;

Daphne was holding his hands, her soft fingers entwined in his.

'I have grown to care for you,' he blurted out in a rush. When he looked up, Daphne was looking deep into his eyes. 'I care for you, Daphne. I hope, one day, you can care for me.'

Chapter Fifteen

I care for you, Daphne. I hope, one day, you can care for me.

Daphne blinked. Then she blinked again. Then she swallowed, very slowly, and tried to replay in her head the words she thought she had just heard. Just to make sure.

I care for you, Daphne. I hope, one day, you can care for me.

No. No, that could not be right. It simply did not happen. Handsome princes did not realise they cared about wallflowers, even if they were their wives. The dreams she had dreamt, the daydreams she had indulged in, had all included something like this. Something devastatingly romantic. Some sort of declaration, usually focusing on his deep obsession for her.

But affection? No, that was not something she had dared to hope for, even in her dreams.

Christoph was looking at her with concern, as though he had accidentally cursed before a lady and was waiting to see what social punishment she would exact from him.

'Daphne,' he said softly. 'Did you hear what I said?'

Yes, she had. She had, and Daphne could not believe it. Gentlemen—any men—did not care about her, about ladies like her. About wallflowers. They did not make declarations by the fireside of adoration and affection. They did not usually wait long enough to discover that she had a mind, passion and interests, and was more than a shy woman who preferred to listen to conversations than contribute to them.

So she must have made a mistake. She must have misunderstood. That was all.

'No,' she said carefully. 'No, I don't think I heard what you said.'

There was a teasing smile across his face, and it filled her with certainty that Christoph could not have said what she thought he'd said. No, there was too much mischief in that smile.

'Only someone like you,' Christoph said gently, 'could hear a declaration of affection from your own husband and believe you misheard.'

Flames licked her skin. Daphne did not need to see herself to know she was flushing a dark red, the heat scalding her face, likely leaving a mark. A brand. A declaration of affection.

She swallowed, mouth dry this time, and said the inside thought almost without thinking. 'A…a declaration of affection?'

'Yes,' Christoph said. There was pink in his cheeks too, now she came to look at them. As though he were…

ashamed? Nervous? Unsure of himself? 'A declaration of…of how I feel.'

Daphne wetted her lips, and tried not to notice how her husband's focus flickered to her mouth. Attraction, yes. They could not have shared what…they had shared without some attraction. And he was willing to give pleasure without receiving it, which was far more than she had expected from any man. But more?

'I'm sorry,' she said, her voice croaking. 'But could you repeat that?'

His chuckle was not malicious, and held no teasing. Still, he did laugh. 'You are not one for hearing compliments, are you, Daphne? About yourself, I mean.'

Daphne looked away, but only for a moment. There was something so accepting about Christoph. She had never felt judged by him for a single moment that she had been in his company, not truly.

And she did not feel judged now.

'I… I did not want to get my hopes up,' she said softly, looking back at him. 'We had been very clear with each other—'

'We did not know each other then,' Christoph interjected.

'We were quite clear with each other—in fact, as I recall, it was you who stated quite plainly that you would not fall in love with me,' Daphne said, her lips curling.

'I am not saying I am in love with you now,' said her husband quietly. 'But I would be a fool if I did not admit that even then, when I first told you that love was not possible in our marriage, I was nevertheless concerned for your welfare. That…that I wanted what was best for you. That I cared for you.'

She'd have been wrong if she'd thought she could not grow any hotter. Tendrils of flaming fervour were curling around her ribs, radiating across her body and making it very difficult to breathe.

Cared…cared for…

'I would rather you did not say such things,' she said hoarsely, her fingers knotting together in her lap, the fire far too close, 'if you have any qualms about… I mean, if you do not mean them.'

Daphne gasped and ceased all speech as Christoph rose from his seat and moved to sit beside her. He was too close—and yet not close enough, their skin not touching, the intimacy far less than she wanted.

'Daphne,' Christoph said quietly, his breeches brushing against the skirts of her gown, and she hardly knew where to look. 'Daphne. You are kind, and patient, and you do not have a bad bone in your body. And you have such depth to you—such intelligence, such wit. You are careful with others because you know the value of them.'

It was impossible to bear hearing, and Daphne could not help but lean closer.

Oh, these words, spoken by this man. It was wonderful, heady stuff.

'You…you cannot mean…?'

'And I would be a liar if I did not admit that I am devastatingly attracted to you,' Christoph murmured.

Oh, saints preserve her. She had known, of course—Christoph had not hidden his desire for her—but still. It was quite another thing for him to say the words aloud. 'Dev...devastatingly attracted? To me?'

When Daphne said it out loud, it sounded preposterous. No man had ever spent more than five minutes looking at her, and the few who had spared a passing glance had never liked what they'd seen. Had they?

'Damn it, Daphne, you cannot be that ignorant of your beauty, can you?'

Christoph had at some point leaned closer. Daphne did not know when, but it was playing havoc with her senses and making it difficult to breathe.

Which was the least of her worries. Before she could stop him, before she could even think of why he was doing such a thing, Christoph had slipped an arm down the back of the sofa to her shoulder and was pulling her into his chest. His other hand was...on her knee! On her knee through her gown, admittedly, but still on her knee!

And when he spoke, which he did in a low murmur, his breath blossomed over her neck, spreading tingles of anticipation for pleasure she knew she would not be given, and it was agony.

Sweet agony.

'Daphne,' Christoph hummed into her ear. 'Daphne, you are beautiful—so beautiful that I want to touch every single part of you. Every part.'

She shivered. She could not help it—the embellished words somehow poured through her like warm water, delicate like jewels, sparkling like sunlight.

'And I want to do more than touch,' Christoph continued, a hardness accompanying the softness in his voice.

'I want to caress, I want to taste. I want my mouth on every part of your skin.'

Daphne swallowed hard, her throat dry, an ache building now between her thighs as she thought of the last time Christoph had his mouth on her skin.

I ache for you, Christoph. For the way you touched me.

Oh, he couldn't say such things—and all she wanted was for him to say these things. All she would want, for the rest of her life, was to be spoken to like this. To know herself to be this desired. To feel Christoph's touch...

His fingers were stroking the bare skin of her shoulder now, gently and with purpose, his fingertips brushing heat through her like a furnace. Daphne tried to speak, she really did, but what could she say? What words would be sufficient? How could she even claim to understand precisely what these words were doing to her? Burning her, marking her for him. As though she could ever be anyone else's now.

'And once I've kissed and tasted every part of you,' Christoph continued, his melodious voice low and urgent, 'I want to pick you up and carry you upstairs, lay you out on the bed with not a stitch of clothing on you and worship you.'

Daphne's eyelashes fluttered, no longer able to remain open.

How could they, with this onslaught of desire?

'And then...'

'And then?' she whispered, unable to help herself. 'Christoph? Christoph!'

Her exclamation was impossible to swallow down—not when she opened her eyes to find that the hand caressing her knee had moved. It was now at the bodice of her gown, the ribbons being tugged, the fabric loosening around her breasts to reveal her stays.

Daphne slowly raised her head to look into Christoph's eyes. There was hunger there, yes, but also devotion. What she thought was devotion. How was she supposed to know, never having experienced anything like this? But Christoph would not lie to her. There were no secrets between them, there had never been any need for them.

'Wh-what are you doing?' Daphne knew it was a foolish question the moment the words passed her lips.

It was obvious, what he was doing, what he wanted. Had he not already told her? Had he not shown her with his eagerness to gain access to her body?

Christoph's smile was roguish. 'Well, this is a real marriage now, is it not?'

'A…a real marriage?'

'Arranged, yes, but no longer merely an *arrangement*,' he said lightly. 'We respect each other, Daphne. Love… love is another matter. I told you, I shall **never fall** in love. I cannot risk the hurt, the pain of loss. But this—perhaps a new understanding? I don't want the rules, the restrictions, the negotiations to still stand. I… I want you as my wife.'

As my wife.

The words rang through Daphne's mind and she could not help but flush.

She needed to tell him—she knew that—and yet the

words had always been impossible to say, getting stuck in her throat, becoming tangled with inside thoughts that never made it to her lips. She'd spent so much of her life never speaking, and it was a difficult habit to break.

I carry your child.

That was all she had to say, but something within her stopped her. They had not discussed children, which had been foolish of them, in hindsight. What would being a child of Niedernlein mean? Would the babe have to be born outside England?

Perhaps she had been foolish to think that merely one encounter could create a child—and yet, that was all that had been required. And now here she was, pregnant with his child, fighting off the nausea each morning, hoping that he would not notice, and she still had not told him.

Christoph evidently misunderstood her silence. 'I know the negotiations, the rules, were to protect us. To reduce complications—let me speak plainly—to prevent ourselves from developing any affection for each other. But affection is what I feel. We cannot fight it.'

Daphne merely stared at him, with a pit in her stomach. She had to tell him. *Just say the words. Say the words, Daphne, tell him.*

'But of course if…if you do not…' Christoph swallowed, a shadow of uncertainty grazing his expression. 'I should have considered, but it did not occur to me until now that you did not… That you might not return…'

She saw the awkwardness in his expression, and his nervousness made complete sense. He cared for her, yes, but she had said no words of love. In fact, she had given no sign that she felt anything for him than the vague appreciation of a companion.

Heat flared. She had to tell him about the baby...but perhaps this was not the right moment. In this moment, when hearts were being opened and they were finally starting to understand each other, with emotions heightened and a vulnerability new to them both? No, this was not the time.

'I... I...' Daphne could not find the words.

Christoph looked at her silently, not demanding anything, waiting patiently, knowing that she needed a moment to get her thoughts in order.

And that was when she knew, without a shadow of a doubt, just how wonderful he was. Just how deeply he had touched her soul. Just how much she did not want to be without him.

That she loved him.

How did she tell her husband that she had fallen in love with him?

Leaning forward instinctively, abandoning the attempt with words and knowing actions could speak far louder, Daphne pressed a kiss upon Christoph's lips.

He froze, just for a moment. Then he kissed her back, his lips parting hers possessively, demanding, eager, but never forceful. Oh, it was glorious; Daphne's mind whirled as the giddiness of his touch flowed through her.

Their first kiss.

When it was over, when she could no longer breathe and was obliged to pull away, Christoph kept a close hold on her shoulder, preventing her from moving too far from him. Not that she wanted to move too far from him.

'I feel... I feel much,' Daphne blurted out, the words running into each other. 'I... You make me feel...you make me feel...'

'I know,' he said, his voice ragged. 'I know.'

And they were kissing again; she did not know how, but they were. Vines of pleasure curled around her body, sparking need in her that she had never known before. A deeper need, a closer connection, was possible now and she craved it as she would have panted for water in a desert.

When they finally ceased the second bout of kissing, Daphne's face was flushed and her hair was mussed. Christoph was panting, and his cravat had somehow managed to untie itself. Her fingers tugging at the knot might have had something to do with it.

'Upstairs?' Christoph whispered.

Daphne did not know where this boldness was coming from, but she said, 'I believe I was promised being carried?'

His low chuckle warmed her as nothing else could. 'My wanton wallflower wife.'

Her lungs caught as she yelped—a perfectly natural reaction to suddenly being swooped up into Christoph's arms as he rose from the sofa. Her legs dangled over the sides of them. 'The servants will see.'

'Let them see,' Christoph said in a low growl, a smile teasing his lips. 'What will they see, but a husband devoted to his wife?'

Daphne shivered with the surprise of it all as Christoph strode across the drawing room and she opened the door. A husband devoted to his wife—devoted to her.

Thankfully, there were no servants to witness this shameless display of open affection as they walked across the hall and up the stairs. It was as though she weighed nothing, Christoph having no difficulty carrying her upstairs, across the landing and to the bedchamber where Daphne had been only once, on their wedding night.

Christoph's bedchamber. It was much the same as she remembered it. The four-poster bed was still huge, the large window still covered with a sweeping curtain.

And Christoph was still the same man. Yet she knew him so much better, knew what he was, what he stood for. How he cared for her. So, in some ways, everything in this room was now completely different.

Christoph carefully lowered Daphne onto her feet and cupped her face as he kissed her. She revelled in the moment, tasting his tongue, exploring the way he gave her pleasure in a way that sparked across her breasts and jolted down to her secret place. This was—this would be—so much more special than anything they had ever shared. And what they had already shared was pretty spectacular.

'Let me undress you, love,' Christoph whispered against her neck as he trailed kisses down to her collarbone.

Daphne shivered. 'Y-yes. Undress me.'

How different was this moment from their wedding

night, when he had helped with her ties but remained distant. Her fingers scrabbled at her ties and ribbons, her gown falling in a shimmer of silk, wrenching her stays from her body as she pulled down her stockings until she was utterly nude before him.

Christoph had not been idle; his own clothes were scattered around them on the carpet in a flurry of cotton and linen.

Daphne swallowed. He was…magnificent. Like a classical statue, all muscle and sinew, straining passion and energy, his manhood jutting out to attention, his face flush with desire.

'You are magnificent,' he whispered.

She could not help but smile. 'I was just thinking the same about you.'

Somehow they both reached the bed in a tangle of tongues and hands, gentle yet persistent, Daphne gasping with the sudden peaks of bliss she found as Christoph lowered her down. One of his hands grasped her hips, pulling her closer, and she quivered as his manhood pressed urgently against her thigh in need. Desperate need.

'I—I don't know anything about this,' Daphne panted, suddenly painfully aware of her ignorance. 'I mean, I don't—I don't know how to make it good.'

Christoph stilled, and for a heartbreaking moment she thought he meant to pull away. That he was dissatisfied with her lack of skill and knowledge—disappointed that she somehow did not know.

'Trust me,' he breathed. 'Trust me?'

It sounded like a question so Daphne nodded, before she yelped with surprise as Christoph rolled onto his back and pulled her hips with him so that she straddled him.

'Christoph!'

'I... I have not done it like this before,' he admitted, his face a mite bashful. 'But I think... Ride me, Daphne. Lower yourself onto me and ride me.'

'Like...like a horse?' It sounded ridiculous as she said it aloud, yet there was earnestness in his eyes. He had never done this before...

Christoph nodded and Daphne inhaled deeply. Well, if it would give him pleasure... This was so intimate, just being naked together, touching and being touched. Perhaps that would be enough.

Slowly, her whole body tingling as she positioned herself over her husband's rather impressive member, Daphne pierced herself with the tip of his manhood.

Christoph groaned, his back arching, his hips clearly fighting not to thrust up into her. 'Oh, yes.'

Daphne continued to move downwards, gasping at the flickering bliss that soared through her body as she continued to impale herself on his manhood. Oh, he was filling her, with something so sweet, so exquisite, she could have wept.

When her hips met his own, they both panted. Christoph's hands were on her hips, caressing tenderly, and Daphne managed a smile.

'And now...'

'Ride,' Christoph whispered. 'You wanted me to eat you, Daphne. Well, now I'm asking you to ride me.'

Flushing at the reminder of the wanton request she had made of the man, Daphne lifted herself until only the very tip of him was still inside her, then thrust herself down.

'Oh, yes!'

'Christoph!'

Their mingled cries of delight soared around the room and Daphne laughed, her delight at finding such sensual decadence in such a smooth, short motion shocking her.

Oh, this was far more than she could ever have expected.

It was pleasant to ride Christoph up and down, up and down, feeling the slick, thrusting force of him within her, hitting a honeyed spot that jolted intense bliss through her whole body, while she watched Christoph's twisting, quivering features as he gave himself up to the ecstasy.

'God, you feel…you feel…'

And, as though he could not help himself, Christoph reached up and caressed her breasts, his finger and thumb finding both nipples and twisting as she thrust heavily down on him, and Daphne cried out with the overwhelming pleasure of it. She was close to ecstasy. She knew it now, she was starting to learn the ways of her body, and as she looked down and met her husband's gaze he seemed to know.

Though one hand remained at her breast, the other moved lower, lower, until it found the place where their two bodies met. Carefully, as she continued to thrust faster and faster onto his manhood, her body quivering with the impending climax, Christoph found that nub and circled it slowly but with intense pressure.

And she fell apart. Hardly knowing how her thighs managed it, her body spasming with ecstasy, her sight disappearing, all senses focused on skin that roared with decadence, Daphne crested the wave as Christoph cried out her name and thrust upwards into her.

'Daphne, Daphne, Daphne!'

When she collapsed onto him, and he kissed her lips, nose, eyelashes and neck, when his arms moved around her, she knew she was home—a true home that she could never lose.

When the quivering of her body had slowed and her pulse had not, Daphne knew. This was it. This was everything.

Christoph pressed a kiss against her temple and said, in a frayed voice, 'Ready to go again?'

Chapter Sixteen

Christoph knew who was knocking at the door in an instant. Only one person knocked like that. 'It's her!'

He dropped the book with a crash and rushed out of the library.

'She's not going to disappear in a puff of smoke, Christoph!'

This wife of his! She had a heart far larger than most people—certainly larger than his would have been, if he had been holed up in a place like that academy.

'Where is that seal?'

'In my desk!' Christoph called down the corridor. 'I'll be straight back!'

Daphne laughed in his wake as he hurtled towards the door, where the knocking continued. Where was that butler of his?

Christoph almost skidded directly into Henderson. 'There you are!'

'I was getting there,' muttered the butler as he reached out to open the front door. 'I am sure it can be no one that important, or—'

'Laura!'

Christoph opened his arms and groaned as his sister launched herself into his hug.

'It has been too long,' said Laura, gripping him tightly and making it difficult for him to breathe. 'Too long.'

There was more of a Germanic accent to her words—her English was less practised than his own—and there was a desperate weariness in the way she spoke. But that did not matter. She was here now. She was safe.

'But—but—Princess Laura!' spluttered Henderson.

Christoph tried not to grimace as his sister pulled away to look at his butler. 'Laura, let me introduce you to—'

'Your Highness.' The butler bowed.

When he rose, Christoph was surprised to see that there was a grim look on the servant's face. Something harsh, something cruel. Something displeased. It was gone in an instant. Perhaps he had imagined it. He certainly did not like the man, but that was no reason to take completely against him.

Ah… Perhaps he should have mentioned to the servants that a guest would be coming to stay.

'My sister will be staying with us for some time, Henderson,' Christoph said. 'Please prepare a room for her and help her servants with—'

'I brought no servants, Christoph,' Laura said quietly, her eyes suddenly downcast. 'There was not…time.'

Not time. He knew well enough what that meant. There had been no time to ascertain just who she could trust and who would betray her plans. She had been forced to move fast, so she had travelled all this way without a lady's maid—without an escort!

Christoph's jaw tightened.

Well, that had most definitely not been the plan. If he had known she would be so unprotected, entirely unchaperoned... Perhaps it was a good thing he had not known.

'Please help with her luggage,' he continued, jerking his head at the door. 'But wait—your arm, your wrist—how have you managed without servants?'

There was a pained look on his sister's face. 'I managed.'

Christoph searched Laura's familiar face, saw pain, distress, and relief that it was over, and decided not to pry. 'But you are healed?'

'I think it will take time,' Laura said quietly.

Time. Yes, it was something the two of them would both need. But here in England, with Daphne, he could heal. 'I wish to introduce you to my wife.'

Taking Laura by the hand and completely ignoring Henderson, he pulled her across the hallway and into the main corridor. The instant they turned a corner, the door to the hall closing behind them, Laura halted. 'It is safe?'

'You're safe here,' Christoph said hastily.

He could well understand the fear. The panic. The uncertainty. After having lived a life looking over their shoulders, never quite sure who was telling the truth, who was repeating their words verbatim back to their brother, it was wise of Laura to ask. But she would never have to ask again.

'This home is safe. It is ours, mine and Daphne's, and I will never permit Anton to come here,' Christoph assured her, seeing clearly that Laura was unconvinced by his words. 'The servants are good sorts. I don't particularly like Henderson; there's something I can't quite put my finger on.'

'I was not immediately impressed myself.'

'But being a foul-tempered person is not a crime. At least, not here in England,' Christoph said, attempting some levity.

His sister did not smile. 'And here you are, having made the greatest sacrifice for me,' she said softly. 'Marrying a stranger, someone you will be stuck with for the rest of your life, for me.'

It was difficult to know where to begin. Yes, it had all started as a way to prevent this Miss Smith from marrying Anton and putting herself into harm's way. Then Christoph had seen the benefits he himself could draw from such a connection: wealth; riches that would give him true freedom. Then he had seen the possibility of rescuing Laura, and a careful plan had been put together.

And it had worked. Had worked far better than he could have imagined. Laura was safe. She was here, in England.

And, despite having expected to find Daphne merely a tolerable enough presence in his life that he could bring himself to consummate the marriage, he had fallen in love with her.

Christoph found he was smiling. 'Daphne is no stranger. She's my wife.'

Laura nodded seriously. 'Yes, I know, but—'

'She is my wife, Laura, and I… I love her,' he said quietly.

His sister's expression was one of utter confusion. 'You…you do?'

'I do,' Christoph said, finding it strange to say aloud to another person. It was, after all, the first time he had done so. 'I love her so much, Laura. I cannot wait for you to meet her. She's kind and quiet, yet strong-willed.'

'It sounds like I should meet this woman of yours,' Laura said with a laugh, slipping her hand through his arm. 'Who would have thought it? You, falling in love—and with your wife!'

It was certainly far beyond the confines of the plan he had carefully constructed, but then Christoph had finally learned to let go of those expectations. Something far better had come from it. Something he could never have hoped to plan.

It was therefore with great excitement that he walked towards the library with Laura on his arm. By now Daphne would have found the seal in his desk, and perhaps the three of them could discuss the last few weeks over hot tea and cakes. Oh, these English knew how to do afternoon tea.

Christoph opened the door to the library and beamed at the two most important women in his life. 'Daphne, may I present to you—?'

'What is this?' Daphne said quietly, straightening up from the desk with a passive expression.

Most strangely, Laura removed her hand from his arm

and took a step back. He did not understand it—but then, neither did he understand why his wife looked so serious.

Daphne was not a serious woman, not in that way. It appeared the two letters she held had something to do with it.

'Nothing,' he said instinctively.

What could she possibly have found? Though swiftly racking his memory, Christoph could not recall anything too untoward. So what was the problem?

'I cannot believe you,' Daphne said quietly.

He heard the click of a door. Christoph turned to see Laura had disappeared. Her dislike for confrontation, or anything verging close to it, had clearly frightened her from the room. But this was just a misunderstanding. The moment it was cleared up between them, it would be simple enough.

'"So you've got the harlot yourself. I hope she's keeping you occupied. I can't imagine she's particularly good in bed, wallflower as she is, and of illegitimate birth",' Daphne read out, her voice a level, cutting edge. '"I expected better of you, you coward. Unwilling to face me? Sneaking out of the palace like a thief in the night to steal my bride?".'

Christoph's stomach turned.

'That was from my brother—you know what he is like. I told you he was cruel,' he said desperately.

Perhaps he had not told her enough. There was a dark look in Daphne's eyes that seemed to suggest it was him she was angry with, not Anton. Which made no sense. He had not written such harsh things about her.

'And here's one from my father,' Daphne said, swapping the letters in her hands so she could read from the second. 'And most illuminating it is too. "Dear Sir, thank you for your letter dated fourth of this month. I can confirm my daughter is a virgin, and though not pleasant to look at, I presume rather biddable".'

Christoph winced. He had been a little surprised at the way the Earl of Norbury had written about his daughter at the time, but had assumed there was some sort of reason for it. Assumed they were estranged. Believed that the daughter the man had written of was truly as awful as he had said. Not that the man was utterly clueless about the value of his daughter.

'"I am willing to place my wealth into her name as her inheritance as I haven't been able to find a better option",' Daphne continued to read, her voice astonishingly calm. '"I do not doubt you will find her dull"—'

'Daphne,' Christoph said hastily. 'Don't.'

'"But as you have indicated your requirement for an obedient wife who will give you no trouble, I suppose my daughter is best placed to suit your purposes",' Daphne read aloud, eyes filling with tears now. '"Besides, when you tire of her, you can always take a mistress".'

Christoph swore under his breath.

He should have burned those letters. He should have burnt anything that spoke of Daphne in such a dismissive way. How could he have believed the Earl of Norbury? How could he have thought that Daphne was anything but perfection?

'I cannot believe you—'

'It does not mean I agree with them,' he said firmly. 'It just means—'

'I thought... Yes, ours was a marriage of convenience, but at least I thought we came to it as equals,' Daphne said, tears sparkling in her eyes. 'I thought we came to it openly, honestly. But you—you have lied to me.'

'No,' Christoph said firmly. 'No, that is—'

'And this is what my father thinks of me, which is hard to hear, even though I almost certainly knew it already,' Daphne said, ploughing on despite the evident pain the conversation was giving her. 'And you wanted a dutiful, dull wife. What a disappointment I must be.'

Christoph swore again. 'That is not—'

'But thank goodness you found me palatable, eh?' Daphne's voice cracked again and a tear fell, and Christoph's heart tightened. He wanted to kiss it away as he embraced her, but he could not move. 'Otherwise you would have had to take a mistress!'

'I would never have! Daphne, I chose you! You, as you are,' Christoph said, his voice strong, hoping to show her through the strength of his words just how firmly he believed it. That he meant it.

His legs managed to stagger forward so that he was now standing on the other side of the desk, but it did not matter. Daphne was a long way away from him now.

'And this—this, from Anton, your brother.'

'You can ignore every vicious word of that letter. He knows only how to harm others,' said Christoph tightly.

'So I should ignore this bit, should I?' Daphne returned her gaze to his brother's letter. '"Sneaking out of the palace like a thief in the night to steal my bride".'

She looked up and Christoph knew he should have been honest with her. But now it was too late. All too late.

'I was supposed to marry him, wasn't I?' Daphne's voice was naught but a whisper. 'The older brother. That would have made me Queen—I can see why my father was so eager for it. You haven't told him, have you, that you're the younger? How long do you think you could wait until your lies emerged?'

She waited, the silence eking out between them in agonising shame.

Christoph swallowed, the noise surely audible.

Say something. Say something, man.

Yet what could he say? She was right. She had found out the truth. He had hidden one of the most important things from her and there was no excuse for it.

Why hadn't he told her?

'You're not even the right brother,' Daphne said quietly.

Christoph gritted his teeth. 'It...it wasn't like that. I couldn't let you—'

'Let me? *Let me?*' Now Daphne stepped past him, round the desk and to the other side of the library, her outrage too much to be penned in by the desk. 'You did not even know me! How dare you say you would not let me?'

'You would have been miserable with him, controlled.'

'Lied to?' Daphne said sharply.

It was a low blow, but one Christoph undoubtedly deserved. He swallowed, trying to gain his bearings, trying to work out a way to rectify this. His stomach was churning, and his pulse was far too quick, but he had nothing else to save. Not even his pride.

'Look,' he said urgently. 'I did not want to stay in Niedernlein. The place was dangerous, miserable. His previous wife had died in mysterious circumstances. I knew what would happen to his next if she crossed him, and I was in a spot of bother.'

'Christoph,' Daphne said quietly.

'I will never let anything happen to you, Daphne,' he said swiftly, marching over to her, ignoring her gasp and bringing her into his arms, into his embrace. 'Daphne, you have to believe me.'

'I do.'

'Because I would never—'

'I don't want to hear any more.'

'I love you,' Christoph said before he could stop himself.

The change was instant. Daphne's face clouded, her whole body tensing, and she retreated into herself as he had seen her do whenever the world was too much, whenever she wanted to be alone or whenever she felt herself at risk of criticism.

Criticism? But all he had said was…

'Do not say that,' she muttered in a cracked voice.

Bewilderment rushed through Christoph's chest. 'Do not say that?'

'Do not—do not say that,' Daphne repeated, her gaze

for some reason unwilling to meet his own. 'Do not say it.'

'That I love you?' Christoph repeated, stepping forward with a hand reaching out to touch her.

'You love me, but you lie to me,' she said sharply. 'You say you love me, but this whole time you have deceived me!'

Oh, hell. 'It is not deceit, it is—'

'What do you call this?' Daphne thrust the letter forward, frustration and pain in her gaze. 'How can I believe that you love me when the very start of this, the foundation of our marriage, is based on a lie?'

'I love you, and I will keep on saying it.' He needed to touch her, he needed to feel close to her, but much to his surprise his adoring wife did not reach out for him in turn but instead retreated. Retreated? From him?

'I cannot… I do not want to hear… You mustn't…' Her words became tangled, the panic visible on her face.

And Christoph did not know what to do. True, he had never seriously thought he would ever fall in love. He had guarded against it, told himself again and again that this marriage would be naught but a show. But, now he felt it, how could he have done anything but tell her?

Daphne, however, looked distraught. Pain seared her cheeks and her hands twisted before her again, as they always did when she felt cornered. Difficult though it was, Christoph forced himself to take a step back. He was not going to encroach on his wife.

'I have to go.'

'Go?' repeated Christoph blankly. 'No—no, you can't

go. I—I've just told you I love you. You need to believe me when I say—'

'I don't have to do anything,' said Daphne quietly. 'And I can go anywhere I want.'

Desperation made him say it, not good sense. 'I order you to stay here.'

His wife looked at him. Her brilliant blue eyes had filled with more tears and there was tension in her jaw. 'And you say you're nothing like your brother.'

Christoph's pulse skipped a beat as ice flooded into him. 'Look, I can explain—'

'I'm going home,' said Daphne, storming past him in a whirlwind of determination and agony.

'Home?' he repeated, unable to take in her words as he followed her out to the corridor. 'What do you mean, home? We are home.'

'My true home. The home I should never have left,' Daphne said, somehow managing to walk quicker than him despite his height advantage. 'The Wallflower Academy.'

Christoph halted in his steps, stunned, desperately trying to catch up. 'The Wallflower Academy? But, Daphne, you can't.'

'I can do anything I want, I think you'll find,' Daphne snarled, a bitterness in her he had never seen before as she flung open the front door and slammed it behind her.

Christoph stood in the silent, empty hallway with her words ringing in his ears.

And you say you're nothing like your brother.

It was a most unpleasant thought, but there was little

he could do to argue against her unassailable logic. He had acted like his brother. To very different ends, but did that justify his methods? Here he was, his wife quite literally running away because she had no wish to be near him…and he thought he was not like Anton?

But he loved her. He loved her, and he had told her, and…it wasn't enough.

How could he have lost love the instant he had realised it was within him?

Christoph swallowed. Despite all he had attempted, here he was, just like his father: his lover gone. Finally she had realised the truth: that she deserved far better, that her elegance and beauty far surpassed the life he could offer her.

She wanted better; she wanted more. And she knew he couldn't offer her that.

And so she had gone.

Chapter Seventeen

Daphne had one thought, and one thought only: *get away*.

The glare of the autumnal sunlight was dazzling but her legs propelled her forward, determined not to slow down in case Christoph caught up with her.

She could not speak to him. She could barely look at him.

A carriage was forced to swerve, its driver shouting obscenities after her, but Daphne did not heed him. She didn't have to listen to him. She didn't have to listen to anyone. Her head was pounding, her pulse throbbing, her mind was spinning and all she could do was put one foot in front of the other.

She had to get away. And though the Wallflower Academy called out to her—a place of safety, a place she had always been able to retreat to—she had no carriage, no money to secure one and no other method of conveyance. She could hardly walk the several miles out of London into the countryside towards it. Besides, she had just told Christoph that was where she was going. It would be the first place he would look.

No, there had to be another option. There just had to be.

It took her about twenty minutes to reach the steps. Daphne had been forced to double back on herself once, her sense of direction lost, and once at a crossroads she had breathlessly asked a woman for the name of the street. She had managed it quite well after that, and now she was banging on the front door of one of the few places in London where she would be welcome.

A butler opened the door. 'I am afraid the Duke and Duchess are not at—'

'They're at home for me,' Daphne gasped, hardly able to believe how forward she was. 'And, even if they're not, they won't mind.'

'But, my lady, what on earth are you…?'

Firmly ignoring the butler, she pushed past the servant and into the hallway. She had been here once before, and knew the way to the drawing room, but she was not interested in entertaining or being entertained. No. She had to escape all prying eyes, all questions, all the sympathy that her marriage had fallen apart so quickly, everything.

'But my lady, where are you…?'

Continuing to ignore the butler as best she could, Daphne staggered forward, hardly sure how her legs were carrying her. She had heard Gwen talking about it, she was certain it was here…

When she tried the door, it was with relief. She had

found it: the Orangery. It was just like the Orangery at the Wallflower Academy. There was something intensely comforting about such a place; perhaps the warmth, the stillness, the delicious scents or the knowledge that no one would think to look for her here.

Daphne stepped inside, shut the door quite resolutely in the face of the butler, who had followed her, and slipped off the main path of the Orangery to sit silently behind one of the huge terracotta pots.

The door opened again. 'My lady?'

Staying very still, attempting to keep her breathing calm—no easy feat, after almost running here from her home, or rather the house her father had given her husband—Daphne waited.

It did not take long. The butler evidently believed she had continued through the Orangery and into the garden, so stepped back into the house. Perhaps he would send a gardener after her. Perhaps he would not. It did not matter. All she wanted to do was stay here.

The tears came swiftly. It was a miracle that Daphne had only wept a few of them in the library during her conversation with Christoph. They swelled, multiplied and now poured down her face, the outward evidence of the inner heartbreak.

Eventually she stopped crying, wiping her eyes with the shawl around her shoulders.

There was no point in moping. So, her husband was in love with her and she had panicked and run away. A completely normal reaction.

It would be simple enough. Eventually she would

speak to Gwen. Gwen and Percy would send over some servants for her things and she would live apart from her husband. It happened, even in the best families. She just...couldn't face him. She wouldn't face him.

The door opened again and Daphne instinctively shrank back behind the pot. There was no possibility of talking. Absolutely not. She didn't want to.

'There you are,' said Gwen softly.

Daphne did not look up. Her friend's shadow covered the feeble sunlight and there was a sense of someone waiting for an answer. Well, she could keep on waiting. She didn't want to talk—she didn't want to say anything.

Slowly, with a quiet creaking of her stays, Gwen lowered herself down and sat next to Daphne. Her friend said nothing. Her presence was welcome, and her silence even more so. As the minutes ticked by, Gwen remaining completely silent, the tension in Daphne's shoulder blades started to lessen, melting away, leaving her feeling nothing but exhausted.

Eventually Daphne lowered her head onto her friend's shoulder. Her shawl slipped but she did not move to pick it up. A tear trickled down her nose. Still Gwen said nothing. She just sat there, allowing Daphne to feel the weight of emotions she still did not totally understand, hoping beyond hope she would not sniffle.

After what felt like at least half an hour, Daphne breathed out a long sigh and lifted her head from her friend's shoulder. 'Aren't you going to ask me about it?'

Gwen shrugged. 'If you wanted to tell me, you would.'

Daphne could not help but smile. It was a very caring and compassionate response from her friend and, in a way, she had expected nothing else. Still, Gwen was a curious woman. She must wonder. The fact she had not interrogated her was nonetheless much appreciated.

'Besides,' added Gwen, a light smile on her face. 'I have not been sent by Miss Pike. We are not at the Wallflower Academy here, Daphne. We can do whatever we want, and that includes keeping secrets.'

Daphne tried to smile, but felt so wretched she thought she would fall apart from the pain of it. A father who thought so little of her. A husband who had lied to her and had stolen her from his own brother. A husband who said he loved her, but surely could not—surely would not?—else he wouldn't have lied to her for so long. A sister of his who she had to trust was not instead a mistress—at least, who she'd trusted was not a mistress, but how could she believe anything Christoph had ever said now?

And a child; a child was coming, but into what sort of family? With a long, deep sigh, Daphne attempted to collect her thoughts, but all she was able to manage was, 'Christoph... He wasn't who I thought he was.'

Gwen nodded sagely. 'He is a brute, then.'

'What?' Daphne moved to face her friend, utterly perplexed. 'No!'

'Oh. It's just, you said—'

'I said he wasn't who I thought he was,' Daphne repeated, still confused as to how her friend could think such a thing. 'Why did you think—?'

'Well, because what I thought was that he was a

charming, devilishly handsome prince from some country which name I can't remember, who is painfully devoted to you,' Gwen said with a wry smile, a smile which only seemed to grow as Daphne's cheeks pinked. 'Am I wrong?'

Gwen raised an eyebrow with her question, a question that Daphne was not entirely sure how to answer. Because he *was* charming. Oh, Christoph was charming. She had never been so charmed in all her life. And he was devilishly handsome. It was most unfortunate, because it had blinded her to the fact that she knew so little about him.

And he was a prince. At least, Daphne had no reason to believe he was not. The letters certainly appeared to suggest that it was true.

As to whether he was painfully devoted to her…

I love you.

Daphne bit her lip. 'He…he told me he loved me. It's unbelievable.'

'And what gave you that idea?' Gwen prodded gently. 'Did he snap at you? Offend you? Was he cruel, or remark unpleasantly on your body, or speak ill of someone you cared about?'

Daphne swallowed. 'No.'

No. No, all in all he was marvellous. She could not have dreamed up someone like Christoph even if she had been given the rest of her life to try.

Here was a man who, each and every time he learned something new, seemed to like what he'd discovered about her. He looked at her and…liked what he saw.

'He cannot love me,' she whispered.

'It sounds like you do not want him to,' Gwen said with another rising eyebrow. 'As though you cannot believe he would love you.'

Daphne swallowed. *Yes*, she wanted to say. *Yes, he can't love me.* It shouldn't be allowed—it wasn't possible. Men like him—charming like him, handsome like him, kind like him—did not fall in love with wallflowers. And, if they did, it was with wallflowers like her friends. Like this Laura. Prettier women, cleverer women: charming women, women with better family connections or sparkling reputations as painters or pianoforte players. Not women like her: plain, old, reliable Daphne. Quiet, and shy, and now only useful for her money.

'All...all these years, I have feared being loved, I think,' she said slowly, trying to untangle in her mind any of what she felt. 'It was easier to hide away, to tell myself it did not matter that my father ignored me, that my mother was lost to me, that there was always a wallflower at the Academy with better looks or a wittier character. Oh, Gwen...'

That was the crux of it, wasn't it? Christoph had deceived her about so many things, it was the easiest thing in the world to believe that his love could be a lie too.

Her friend squeezed her hand, saying nothing, allowing Daphne's thoughts to fill the silence.

Eventually she had to make them audible, even if she did not like how they sounded. 'I have been so guarded for so long. I don't know what to do with these feelings now. I don't... I don't know how to face his love.'

Gwen's smile was not cruel, nor teasing, but it was knowing. 'The love of a good man can be a little overwhelming.'

Overwhelming. Yes, that was it. Daphne clutched at the word, an anchor in the roiling sea. *Overwhelming.* Taking over, drowning her in the possibilities of pain. What if—what if Christoph continued to love her but discovered more of her character and decided he could no longer love her? What if his affection became disdain? Oh, she did not think she could bear it.

How would she live if Christoph took his love away? The panic rose again. 'And he said—he said he loved me. He said it, to my face!'

'Was he supposed to say it another way? A letter, perhaps?'

Daphne's lungs tightened at the mention of a letter. She had been quick to fury, a fury masking the sting that Christoph had lied to her and had made a mockery of all they had built these last weeks. Had she reacted too strongly? Had she?

'Has he...?' Gwen hesitated. 'Has he...? I know that some men, they take a mistress and they are not particularly discreet about it.'

Daphne twisted her fingers together in her lap. 'No.'

Now that she was far enough away from the man, from the moment in the library, she could admit to herself that there had been a strong likeness between Christoph and the woman who had entered the room on his arm. It was possible they were not siblings. But she would not have laid money on it.

Gwen's shoulders had relaxed, her hackles no longer raised. 'Well, then. He loves you. You clearly love him. What is the problem?'

It was so difficult to put into words: nothing, and at the same time everything. Daphne tried to untangle it in her mind. The thought was painful, yet heart-warming. Her husband had married her and been quite clear about his rules, about keeping their marriage one of convenience. It had been arranged. It was not a love match.

It had not *been* a love match.

'Gwen,' Daphne said softly. 'Do…do you believe that a real relationship, a loving marriage, can come about by accident?'

'By accident?' repeated her friend.

Daphne nodded while still staring at her fingers. Because it did all seem so accidental, did it not? Nothing in this marriage had been on purpose, at least not from her perspective. Maybe that said more about her complete lack of ability to wield any control over the situation, but still…

'Yes, by accident,' she said. 'I mean, I was never supposed to marry Christoph—'

'I'm sorry, what?' interrupted Gwen, her eyes wide.

Ah, yes. Daphne realised only too late that she had not actually given any sort of explanation as to the letters she had discovered. Not that she fully understood it herself.

'The way I understand it,' Daphne said slowly, 'is that my father wished me to become a…a queen.'

It was no wonder her friend's eyebrows rose. 'I am sorry, a queen?'

'You know what he is like—though, having said that, I suppose you don't. Rilla will know, I suppose, being my stepsister-in-law now. Oh, it's all so complicated,' said Daphne wretchedly with a dry laugh.

Gwen gave her a sympathetic smile. 'Yes, I suppose so. But isn't all life? Isn't everyone's journey a bit wild?'

'Some of us more than others,' Daphne said wryly.

'Now, now, let's not drag Sylvia into this,' grinned Gwen. 'You were telling me that your father wanted you to be a queen.'

'That...that is why, I think, he wrote to the oldest brother of the Niedernlein royal family,' said Daphne slowly.

Her friend nodded. 'Christoph.'

Well, this was it, and waiting around wasn't going to make it easier to say. 'No, Anton.'

'Anton? Is that one of his myriad names?' jested Gwen. Then her smile faded. 'Ah. I see.'

'I don't know how it happened—perhaps Christoph picked up the wrong letter; perhaps he read it by accident; perhaps he was nosey! I don't know how it started, but I know how it ended,' said Daphne with a stifled sob. 'With Christoph coming here, lying to my father, meeting me at the top of an aisle and gaining my hand and my fortune all under deceit. It all began with a falsehood, and here we are now, married.'

'Oh, well,' said Gwen bracingly. 'Accidents happen.'

Very slowly, almost unconsciously, Daphne untangled

her fingers and spread her palms over her belly. Sylvia was large now, but it would not be long before she herself started to swell. How long would it be before anyone noticed? Should she have found a way to tell Christoph over the last few days, even as they'd navigated these feelings neither of them had ever predicted?

'Yes,' she said aloud. 'Yes. Accidents…can happen.'

She should have expected Gwen's gasp. When Daphne looked up, it was to see that her friend's eyes were filled with tears.

'You're not,' Gwen whispered.

'You cannot tell anyone,' Daphne said hastily. 'I—'

'Tell? Who am I going to tell? Perce?' Gwen grinned. 'My toddler isn't going to understand. I haven't been able to get him to understand to be gentle with Florence, and that Sylvia has a baby in her tummy. Do you think I would tell him something like this?'

Daphne had to smile, although Perce was not exactly the person she was concerned about. 'No. I don't… I don't want *him* to know.'

Gwen's smile started to fade. 'Him?'

Swallowing hard, and unsure exactly why it was so difficult for her to say the name, Daphne managed to breathe. 'Christoph.'

'You cannot ignore him for ever. You can't run away from these feelings for ever.'

'Watch me,' Daphne said darkly. 'It has been done. Plenty of *ton* marriages are conducted apart.'

'And is that what you want?' Her friend's expression was far too knowing. 'What I want to know is how you found those letters. Prince Christoph does not strike me as the lax sort. They were put there.'

Put there?

At Daphne's confusion, Gwen sighed. 'Put there for you to find, to upset you! Is there anyone in your household who wishes you harm, Daphne? Someone who would wish to cause discord between you and your husband?'

There was only one person who immediately came to mind and, at the realisation that she had been manipulated, Daphne swallowed hard, resolution filling her mind. 'Just one. And I know what I have to do.'

'I don't think you do.'

She blinked, her friend coming back into focus. 'But I—'

'I think you are focusing far too much on these letters,' Gwen said decidedly, 'Because it's easier than facing up to your fears. To the fact that Christoph loves you, you love him and you were filled with such panic in that moment that you ran away…from the man you love.'

Daphne swallowed. 'He won't love me for ever.'

One day he would wake up and realise that he did not care for her at all. One day he would tire of her, grow frustrated with her shyness, reach his last straw with her father and decide that he could no longer tolerate her. And then she would be alone.

Love is a weakness. To open oneself up like that, to become so vulnerable, to place all one's happiness in the life of another… I swore then I would never do it. I have kept to that promise.

Daphne twisted her fingers together in her lap. Being a wallflower, she had never thought to be a wife. Now she was a wife—a princess. She knew love: not only what it was to love, but what it was to receive love. To make love. To feel it tingling and sparking at the ends of her fingertips because she was so full of it.

And now…what should she do?

Chapter Eighteen

The dart flew through the air like an arrow, sure and true. The *thunk* with which it hit the board was satisfying in a fleeting way. But the moment passed and all Christoph was left with was a sense of emptiness. He twirled the remaining dart in his hand. Two bullseyes... Could he hit a third?

Lifting his head, Christoph concentrated, pulled back his arm and unleased the dart.

The *thunk* resonated around the library and he gave a tired smile that disappeared almost as swiftly as the *thunk*. Three bullseyes. He was clearly better at this than conversing with his own wife.

The Wallflower Academy? But, Daphne, you can't.
I can do anything I want, I think you'll find.

His eyes itched with tiredness, his head was heavy and his heart weary, but there did not seem to be much point in attempting sleep. It had been two days. Two days of silence. Two days of searching, of dead ends and panic. Two days...

'You're still up?'

Christoph looked up and turned around, a weak smile creasing his lips as he beheld the second most important woman in the world. 'Laura. You should go on up to bed—you should get some rest.'

'I could say the same about you,' said his sister quietly as she slipped into the library, a candlestick in her hand, a robe pulled round her nightgown. 'You look terrible.'

He wouldn't be surprised. Christoph had not permitted the valet his father-in-law had chosen to touch his hair. There was little point, and a bath had not been called for. He was wearing yesterday's clothes—what was the point in changing? Daphne was not going to see them—and his meals had been sporadic.

Now he came to think about it, when had he last eaten?

'You miss her.'

Christoph swallowed hard before replying. 'Yes.'

'Then why not go after her?' Laura moved further into the room, placing her candlestick down on the floor and curling up in an armchair next to it. 'You know where she is—this Wallflower Academy, you said. You could be there in an hour. Go to her.'

Go to her.

Yes, that had been his first instinct. Go to her, the woman he loved. The woman he had married to protect. The woman whose funds had provided a safe passage for his sister.

'I have.' When Christoph spoke, his voice was painfully cracked. 'I went to the Wallflower Academy. She was not there—Miss Pike denied her ever arriving. I went to her friends, Sylvia, Rilla and Gwen, but they denied all knowledge of her whereabouts. I... I went to her father. I went to the Bow Street Runners. God help me, I went to the newspapers...'

Missing—his wife was missing.

The tearing anguish in his chest did not abate—it could never abate while Daphne was somewhere in the world alone, unprotected, without means of support and care. Anything could happen to her...

God, anything could happen to her.

Her absence had broken his heart, and in the intervening hours of pain nothing had mended. He had nothing more to offer her, no explanation that she would accept. Seeing her would only double the pain he felt and undoubtedly upset her—but he had to see her, had to ensure she was well. And he could not find her. He, a prince, with all Daphne's wealth, could not find the woman he loved.

'I do not understand,' Laura said simply. 'You love her. She loves—'

'She loved the idea of me,' Christoph interrupted darkly. 'She loved the ideal of me. When I told her how I felt, she... just...'

He could not continue. How could he? He loved her. Worse, he had told Daphne he loved her, opened himself to her, done the one thing he had promised himself he would never do and fallen in love...and she did not want him. She had walked away.

Christoph's jaw tightened. Daphne had seen the worst of him—his lies, his plan to marry her despite not being the chosen brother—and Daphne had seen quite clearly that she could not love him. That was his punishment. That was the retribution he had brought upon himself the moment he had chosen to lie to her about their arranged marriage.

He deserved this. He had earned this. And yet Daphne was not safe.

Striding forward to the dartboard, he pulled the three darts out and returned to where he had been standing. It was near the fireplace, the position he judged to be eight feet away from the board.

Christoph lifted a hand, holding a dart, and drew it back.

'I know you, Christoph Augustus Heinrich Maximus Anton Philip von Auberheiser.'

'I cannot believe you just used my full name!' muttered Christoph. 'I did not bring you here to castigate me.'

'You would not have to suffer it if you did not give me cause,' returned Laura with a wistful smile. 'Just like always, you take things so much to heart. You always blame yourself.'

Christoph's fingers tightened round one of the remaining darts.

'She could be in danger, even now,' Laura said, eyes narrowed. 'She does not know to be on her guard—she could be kidnapped, taken to Niedernlein!'

Closing his eyes did not make the images of his terror disappear. Christoph tried to swallow, tried to breathe, but a vision of Daphne being bundled into a carriage by someone sent by his brother intruded on, persisted through, his determination.

God, he had not thought of that.

'I will not let that happen,' he said.

Something very large and very heavy whacked him in the face.

Christoph's eyes snapped open. 'Laura!'

'Well!' she said indignantly, holding the pair of cushions which she had just launched at him. 'Do you know the backgrounds of all the servants in your employ? Do you truly know who they serve? How did you choose them?'

Ah. This was not going to be an easy conversation to have. 'I… I did not.'

Laura's eyes narrowed. 'Please. Please, Christoph, do not tell me you were so stupid as to permit someone else to choose your servants.'

Christoph opened his mouth. Then he hesitated and ran through the myriad responses he could offer his increasingly irate sister. Then he closed it again.

Laura groaned and dropped her head into a grasped cushion. 'Christoph!'

'I had no wish to be rude to my father-in-law,' he said hastily. 'He was the one who chose.'

'No, he was the one who *told* you that he selected your servants,' said Laura fiercely, lifting her head from the cushion. 'But you do not know who influenced him? Who actually read through the letters of application, who met with them? You really think an earl takes the time to check a man's references?'

Christoph's stomach clenched uncomfortably now. How many men did he employ—fifteen? Twenty? How many of them did he know? None of them. They all knew Daphne had left the house—he had told the servants she was visiting family, but that lie would not hold for long. Which meant someone knew she was out there, in danger, vulnerable, alone.

'Perhaps I am more like Anton than I ever thought,' he said bleakly.

This time he was prepared for it and caught the cushion, but it did not reduce the ire in his sister's face.

'You are nothing like him, you idiot,' she said brutally. 'Because the mere fact that you are *worried* you are like him tells me you will never live without a conscience, as he does.'

Something unfroze in his shoulders and a trickle of relief dripped through Christoph. Well, he could take small comfort from that, he supposed. But it could not remove the sting that was the truth: that the very worst had happened. He had lost Daphne. And not to death. Or not to illness, as his father had lost his beloved mother.

No, it was Christoph's lies and deceit that had broken the trust and affection between them. His own actions had shattered the chain that bound them together. Now he would never…

'So, now we have that settled,' Laura continued, 'precisely when are you going to find that wife of yours? I would start again at that Wallflower Academy. I cannot believe she would not eventually end up there. Was it not her home for a good many years?'

Christoph glanced at the clock and was astonished to see the time.

'Six o'clock? It can't still be six o'clock in the even—'

'It is six o'clock in the morning,' his sister said succinctly.

'In...in the morning?' he said, dazed. 'It can't be. You're just going to bed.'

'I've just got up, you fool,' said Laura lightly. 'How long do you think it'll take before you're presentable to the outside world?'

It took far longer than he had expected. Christoph's valet insisted on washing his hair, not just coiffuring it, and that seemed to take for ever. Then his man said pointedly that his wife would prefer to see him with a fresh face, so Christoph had to succumb to the most irritatingly slow shave he had ever experienced. Prickling at the back of his mind was the suspicion that this man was the traitor, the one who had been sent to harm Daphne and him. It was rather a challenge to keep still when the man held a blade to his throat.

Then there was the clothing.

'You are hoping to impress, I believe, Your Highness?' his valet said delicately.

Christoph winced. '"My lord" is fine.'

'Not if you want to impress,' said the man with a smile.

It was dressing by negotiation. Christoph was willing to accept a complicated knot in his cravat that appeared to take twenty minutes to tie, but pulled on a waistcoat that did not match and made his valet wince in turn.

'And now the—'

'If you try to powder my hair, I swear to—'

'Fine, fine, my lord,' said his valet hastily, taking a step back before adding in an undertone as Christoph ran for the door, 'But don't blame me if your coiffure shifts before you arrive.'

Precisely how his hair looked, Christoph did not care. He hurtled down the corridor, across the landing and down the stairs. When he reached the front door, Laura was standing there with a greatcoat over one arm and a knowing smile.

'You look far too smug,' Christoph pointed out as his sister helped him into the greatcoat.

'Yes, I did call the carriage for you, you are welcome,' Laura said with a grin. 'Now, would you mind finding my sister-in-law so I can have a proper introduction?'

Christoph blew out a laugh as he kissed her cheek and tore out of the front door.

The carriage was indeed waiting. Thanking his sister silently that he would not have to wait an agonising fifteen minutes for the coachman to prepare the horses, and trying to remind himself to thank her properly when he returned with Daphne, Christoph gave the man the briefest of instructions.

'The Wallflower Academy. Quick as you can.'

Surely she would be there now, two days after her disappearance from their home? It was the only one place she had lived for almost all her life, after all; the only place that had been truly hers, a thought which made Christoph's stomach lurch with pain.

His home, their home, should be the place where she felt safe. And, because he had surprised her with a sudden declaration of love, it wasn't. She'd left, walking—fine, running—away. Was it because…because she was overwhelmed? Because she did not believe him? Something else he had not yet fathomed?

It seemed to take an age to leave London. Despite the early hour, there were a great number of people on the streets. Christoph's foot tapped rapidly against the floor of the carriage as his coachman attempted to navigate their way through.

Perhaps he should just have ridden. Just as he was considering launching himself out of the carriage, running back to the house and saddling his horse, Christoph was relieved to see open road before them. The traffic of London lay behind and the path to the Wallflower Academy was clear.

If only the path to apologising to Daphne and winning over her trust again could be just as clear.

It took an age to get there. Or half an hour. Christoph was not particularly sure; all he knew was that, when the redbrick manor house appeared on the horizon, surrounded by golden-leafed trees, he felt a dark sense of relief.

And fear. Because he had to hope it meant that it would not be long before he was talking to Daphne, attempting to explain, hoping she would accept his apologies.

Christoph half-stepped, half-fell out of the carriage just before it came to a stop outside the Wallflower Academy. 'Wait here!'

Was she there? It was impossible to tell from the outside yet the place seemed to have a warmth that he associated with the woman who had brought such joy, such sparkling happiness, to his life.

If she was in there, he would have but five minutes to make his case, and Christoph had no idea how long it would take to explain all this to Daphne. There was so much of him he had to explain, his life, his love, and he did not think he could do it all in one afternoon. He had not been able to do it over the last month. Perhaps it would take a lifetime truly to explain how much she was desired and appreciated.

This arranged marriage… They had not known each other beforehand, but that had to be rectified. And he would start today.

All he had to do was be calm…

'Daphne!' Christoph yelled the minute he knocked on the large front door. Her name had spilled out before he could stop it, his desperate desire to see her overwhelming him.

'Daphne!' he cried again, pulling at the doorbell for good measure, then thundering his fists against the wood. 'Daphne!'

Where was that footman? Why on earth was he taking so long?

'Where is Daphne?' Christoph said in a rush as the door opened. 'Where is my wife?'

It was perhaps not the most elegantly phrased of questions. It certainly earned a raised eyebrow from the footman who stood blearily in the doorway.

'Your Highness?' the servant said.

Christoph tried not to wince, but it was a close-run thing. 'Where is my wife?'

'Your wife?' repeated the footman.

It was growing increasingly difficult to swallow down his panic. 'Yes, Daphne von Auberheiser. Daphne Smith to you, I suppose. Please tell me she is here. I have looked everywhere for her —where is she?'

Without waiting for a reply, Christoph forced himself through the door into the hallway.

'You can't... Really, it is most—you're not supposed to—'

'Daphne!' shouted Christoph, turning on the spot in the hope that he would see a flash of golden-blonde hair. 'Daphne!'

'Really!' exclaimed the footman. 'Now where's the call for—'

'I must find my wife,' Christoph said firmly. 'She is here, I know it. What do you know? Who is paying you?'

Perhaps there was a little interrogation in his voice, but he could not help it. His nerves had grown tighter and tighter with every passing mile from London to the Wallflower Academy, and now he was desperate to see the woman he loved more than anything.

'What do I know?' repeated the footman, wide-eyed. 'Who is paying me? Miss Pike is paying me, but it isn't the day for... Your Highness, it is but eight o'clock in the morning. I don't know anything this early in the morning.'

All too late, Christoph remembered.

Six in the morning? It can't be. You're just going to bed.

I've just got up, you fool.

Ah. Right. Clearly the time spent with his valet and through the slow traffic of London had not actually been an eternity.

'Half of the wallflowers are not even up,' the footman was said. 'And breakfast won't be served until—'

'Matthews, what do you think you're doing, allowing outsiders into my academy before visiting hours?' came a determined voice that Christoph knew. 'It is most outrageous of you to... Oh! Your Most Excellent and Resplendent Highness!'

Miss Pike almost stumbled down the final steps of the staircase as she attempted to curtsey sufficiently low for royalty.

Christoph tried to smile. It was all a tad awkward.

'I did not realise you were planning to visit with your wife,' Miss Pike said, her voice a simper as she remained in a low curtsey. 'I would certainly have prepared for the two of you a most splendid—'

'Where is Daphne?' Christoph demanded, striding toward her, pulse thundering.

'Daphne?' Miss Pike looked blank. 'Princess Daphne, you mean? Your wife?'

'Of course my wife.' Difficult as it was to control his temper, Christoph was determined to do so. *He had to find Daphne.* 'Where is she? At breakfast, perhaps, or still in her bedchamber?'

But, instead of calmly producing his wife, Miss Pike merely gawped in confusion. 'Her bedchamber? Are you under the misunderstanding that she is here, then?'

Christoph's pulse skipped a beat.

No. No, she had to be here, because where else was there to go? Where else was home?

He had looked everywhere—spoken with the authorities, enquired of her father, gone to the papers —and still there was no sign of her. Surely…surely she had to be here?

'If she did not come here,' he asked hurriedly, 'where would she go?'

Most unexpectedly, Miss Pike bristled. 'I believe it would be most outrageous of me to give out that sort of information. Daphne is one of my wallflowers, after all.'

Christoph stared. 'She's my wife!'

'She's my wallflower! And perhaps, if you had taken better care of her, you would know where she is,' retorted the proprietress of the Wallflower Academy sharply. 'Honestly—men! Do you think that merely because Miss Smith has gone off and married that I care any less about her? Do you think I would just bandy about that information for all and sundry to hear?'

Desperately attempting to regain his footing in the conversation once again, Christoph said weakly, 'But I'm not all and sundry, I am her husband!'

Miss Pike's nostrils flared. 'Yes. And yet you do not know where she is. Shouldn't you?'

There was a very witty retort somewhere, Christoph was sure of it, but he could not think of it. Even if he could find it, he was not sure he could say it with feeling.

His shoulders drooped. 'Yes. Yes, I should.'

Ignoring Miss Pike's look of astonishment, Christoph walked past her and dropped onto the bottom step of the staircase, dropping his head into his hands.

'I don't know what to do,' came his muffled voice. 'I don't know where to go. I don't know how to look after her, or regain her trust, or anything. She could be in danger. She could be hurt, cold, hungry and I'm... I'm lost without her.'

The ache in him which had emerged the instant Daphne had left his home, their home, twisted painfully. What was he supposed to do? Who even was he without her? It had happened so gradually, Christoph had not noticed it happening, but he was shaped around her now. There was a hole in his life that nothing else, no one else, could fill, and it was agony. He couldn't bear it.

'You appear,' said a gentle voice that made his broken heart soar, 'to have mislaid a wife.'

Chapter Nineteen

It was a miracle, really, that Daphne could hear her own words, her pulse was thumping so wildly. But perhaps, if it had not been so visceral, she would have supposed that the image before her eyes was merely a dream. Because it could not be true. Christoph could not be here—at the Wallflower Academy.

What on earth was he doing here?

'Daphne.' He breathed her name, he did not say it, rising to his feet with a look of such hunger that she could not help but blush.

'Daphne!' Matthews greeted her with a smile, though it was one that contained a great deal of curiosity.

'Daphne Smith!' barked Miss Pike, striding over to her with pink cheeks. 'What on earth are you doing here? I have been worried sick. Your maid wrote to me two days ago; she said you had disappeared.'

Daphne tried not to smile. 'Well, it's good to know there are two spies in our house.'

Christoph was staring between the two women, clearly perplexed. 'Maid? Spy?'

'Well, I... I thought it would be prescient to have someone in your household that I knew I could trust,' Miss Pike said stiffly, drawing herself up as though she had not conducted a minor act of espionage. 'Daphne is delicate. She deserves to be treated well. I had to ensure that she was.'

It was all Daphne could do not to stare with an open mouth.

Miss Pike cared about her? Cared enough to place a spy within her household?

That knowledge, if knowledge it was, certainly coloured the last few years in a very different hue.

'You placed a spy—your maid?' Christoph said weakly. 'I believe I am lost.'

The instant his attention moved to her, however, it changed. It softened, yet hardened. There was a focus in his eyes that was all-consuming—consuming her.

Daphne shivered. It was astonishing, really; one could go most of one's life without someone, and then they came into that life and one simply could not live without them. Not being in his presence for just a few days was enough to make her wonder how she could go on, not being a part of his world.

That was undoubtedly why her pulse had quickened, her lungs were tight and her skin tingled. Nothing to do with the fact that she wanted his fingers on hers.

'It appears you have much to discuss,' Miss Pike said haughtily. 'Not that I don't have an inkling what it could be about.'

Daphne blinked. That was unexpected. 'Don't you?'

'I have eyes, Daphne Smith—I mean, Your Highness,' said Miss Pike with an air of mystery that was ever so slightly tempered by her next clucking remark, at a gaggle of wallflowers that had collected at the top of the stairs to gawk at them. 'I see the way you look at each other. It's simply a case of… Manners, girls, manners—have I taught you nothing? Really, you simply must not stare at royalty.'

In the wake of Miss Pike's distraction, Christoph eagerly stepped towards Daphne—very eagerly. A part of her wanted him to do what it appeared he was about to do: rush towards her, pull her into his arms and kiss away all concerns and fears about the argument between them.

The part of her that wanted that…was strong. But not strong enough. Daphne put up a shaking hand to halt her approaching husband and he froze, brow furrowed and gaze unabashed in his delight at seeing her.

'There have been too many secrets,' she said quietly.

She expected him to deny it; to say that it had been necessary to have kept it hidden from her. As she watched the flickering tug of war across Christoph's features, she resigned herself to a debate she knew he would win. Or, rather, neither of them would win.

Christoph's face straightened. 'I know. I am sorry.'

His delight in seeing her was evidently at odds with his confusion as to her appearance. Daphne tried not to focus on how greatly she adored him, how much she wanted him to say all the right things.

Tell me you love me again. I need to hear it from your

own lips. But she had to be strong, even when she felt physically weak in his presence.

'I need to know the truth,' Daphne said, working hard to keep her voice level. It did not work. There was a quaver within it that was due not merely to his presence, though that was a large factor, but because it was not in her nature to demand anything. She was not a person who made demands. She was a person who submitted to them.

'What are you doing here?' Daphne added, confusion wrinkling her brow.

It was certainly not where she thought she would find him.

'I was looking for you,' Christoph said in a rush. 'God, Daphne, I have been so worried. Your friends didn't know where you were, neither did your father. I came here to the Wallflower Academy and you weren't here.'

'Girls, decorum, please!'

'The Bow Street Runners said no crime had been committed and I paid a newspaper a king's ransom to put out notices looking for you,' he continued as Daphne stared up at him. 'Well, a princess's ransom, I suppose—your ransom. I… I had to make sure you were safe. Even if you did not wish to be with me, I had to ensure no harm came to you.'

I had to make sure you were safe.

Daphne swallowed hard. He had not attempted to order her to his side; he did not wish to possess her as an object. 'You…you wanted me to be safe? Do you care about me that much?'

Christoph looked down at her, his expression simple. 'I need you.'

Need you. Her breath caught in her throat at the intimacy of his words. Not wanted—needed. Somehow that was more potent. He relied on her, craved, perhaps in the same way she craved him.

'And stop that whispering, girls, I'm trying to listen!'

Daphne smiled, her cheeks pinking with the embarrassment. Miss Pike's voice carried down the wide, sweeping staircase, and undoubtedly theirs carried up it. The gaggle of wallflowers had not gone away, but evidently the proprietress of the Wallflower Academy was attempting to keep them quiet enough so that they could all eavesdrop on the Prince and Princess of Niedernlein.

Well, that couldn't continue.

'Come with me,' Daphne said softly. She turned without waiting to see if he would follow her. She did not need to look to know he would.

Christoph's presence warmed her side as they both walked to the front door. Matthews stood aside silently, though he smiled briefly at Daphne as they passed.

The fresh morning air was almost stifling in its coldness. A deep inhale only provoked her lungs to shock, and Daphne slowed both her breathing and pace as Christoph fell into step with her across the gravel drive.

'Where are we going?' he asked quietly.

'Out,' Daphne said simply. 'Away from pricked ears.'

They walked in silence for a good ten minutes. Daphne knew the way; she would have known the way blindfolded, having meandered along these paths almost all her life. She knew a path for whenever she needed solitude, whenever she knew she needed time away from everyone else around her.

The parkland of the Wallflower Academy was mostly ignored by the wallflowers. It offered little in the way of obvious entertainment, and was too far from the house for Miss Pike's liking. It was therefore her domain. It always had been.

Daphne glanced at the man by her side through lowered eyelashes and saw him gazing about the parkland with amazement at its ancient oaks and towering beeches.

'It is beautiful out here,' Christoph said quietly.

'I have always liked it,' Daphne agreed. 'When I… when I needed to think, or merely have no noise around me, I would come here. No one ever thought to look for me here.'

In fact it was strange to bring someone else here at all. This was her place, one of her special places, and now Christoph was here. Yet it felt right. So right.

'Daphne,' said Christoph suddenly, halting in his tracks.

Daphne halted too, turning with a warily. 'Yes?'

For a moment they just stood there, a few feet apart yet miles apart in understanding. There was so much unsaid, so much misunderstood. So much affection but unexpressed, poorly expressed and poorly received. Daphne could feel every breath, every flutter of breeze, her skin somehow heightened. And he was looking at her as though he wished to ravish her against a tree instead of talk.

'You have to know… I must tell you how much you mean to me,' Christoph said in a rush, more a growl than a statement. 'Daphne, you are—'

'No, Christoph—' She tried to stop him.

'But it is destroying me, the idea that you do not understand how I feel about you,' he said desperately. 'And I understand if you cannot love me in return— Lord knows I do not deserve you— but you must know… Daphne, you must know that you are the centre of my world.'

It was flattering, hearing such things. It was wonderful, hearing them from Christoph's lips. Daphne swallowed; but it wasn't enough. Or at least, it wasn't the right time. There would be time for that, later, should all go well. But they couldn't start there, tempting as it was.

'I need to know other things first,' she said quietly, hating once again that her skin betrayed her, a deep blush rising. 'Things about…about your past. About your family. About how this marriage truly occurred.'

She had gone round and round in her mind on these topics, desperately attempting to understand, hoping to guess the truth. Gwen had had her own theories, of course, and the instant Sylvia and Rilla had visited the three of them had suggested a wide variety of ideas, most of them hilarious, a few of them deeply sad and none of them particularly right.

There was only one person who knew the truth. The whole truth. There needed to be two.

Christoph hesitated, then sighed heavily with a wry smile. 'You deserve the truth. But I am not sure... I do not think I come out of the story particularly well, in hindsight.'

It took a great deal for him to admit that, she could see. But it wasn't enough. 'I need to hear it.'

'I know you do,' he said quietly. 'But it's...it's hard to say.'

This was the hardest thing that Daphne had ever done, but she needed to do it. She owed it to him. She owed it to herself.

'I am sure it is hard to say,' Daphne murmured, her gaze not leaving Christoph's face. 'But I need you to tell me.'

The wind whistled through the trees, causing several golden leaves to fall to the ground, and she waited. Daphne waited, because she knew that if he did not wish to tell her, if Christoph could not bring himself to, then what they had, this marriage, was at an end. She would have this child, and she would love it, and she would be Christoph's wife in name only.

But she did not want that.

'I told you before that Anton...that my brother...' Christoph cleared his throat. 'I told you that he was an unpleasant man. Cruel.'

'A harsh man, cruel—like your father, as I recall,' Daphne said, her mouth dry.

He nodded, his hands clenching and unclenching into fists. Daphne fought the impulse to take them and kiss them.

Christoph was finally talking. Finally explaining. She could not interrupt him now.

'It is a strange thing, to discover that a person who has the same parents as you, who is to all intents and purposes the most alike to you in all the world, is a monster,' Christoph said finally.

Daphne nodded, but said nothing.

'I was happy, when Anton married Katalina,' Christoph said with a bitter laugh. 'I thought he was...untethered. That he needed an anchor—something, someone, to ground him. I thought Katalina could be that person. I hoped she would be, and for a time it seemed she was. For a time, we all breathed a sigh of a relief. For a time, I thought things...things could be different.'

She could see the difficulty, the pain in his words, the way Christoph's whole body was reacting to the telling of this tale—and she was proud of him. Daphne had never felt prouder.

Christoph blew out a long exhale. 'An accident, he said. She tripped down the stairs—that was what he told me. I didn't ask more questions, and I am ashamed of that now, because I should have known—I should have guessed. Katalina was asking for more freedom, more opportunities to serve our people through a charity. That would mean more time alone, more independence, and that is just not something Anton could have accepted.'

Daphne shivered at a cold breeze that she could not feel on the outside, but which she felt deep within her, iced within her chest.

'I vowed I would not let him hurt another woman,'

Christoph said, his eyes piercing into her. 'And then I found it. A letter. You.'

His voice cracked and Daphne fought the instinct to step towards him, to pull him into an embrace.

He was poison, this brother of his. It had to be drawn out, all of it. The truth had to be told. Only then could they move forward.

'I panicked,' Christoph said simply. 'I could not, I would not, allow a poor, unsuspecting woman to come into our family and be subjected to... I could not just sit by and watch a woman have her spirit broken—and, when she tried to find a life for herself, for her neck to be broken as well.'

Daphne's throat knotted painfully. It was shocking, to hear such a thing spoken of.

'And so I thought—I could leave.' Christoph's eyes lit up, and he laughed bitterly. 'You do not realise a cage is a cage until the door opens and you realise you can leave. And this Miss Smith, a woman I had never met and had no loyalty to—she had money.'

This was hard to hear.

'Money that would give me independence. It would give me the chance to save Laura, to provide a home for her, an alternative to staying with Anton. He broke her wrist just before I left Niedernlein,' said Christoph bleakly, and Daphne raised a hand to her chest as she gasped. 'And I thought, I can create a new life. It would hurt to leave Niedernlein, my people, but I could serve a new nation in some way, any way. I could build a life, find a way to belong.'

'You could have told me this,' Daphne said, unable any to restrain herself any longer.

A trio of deer meandered into view just over Christoph's shoulder, but her attention was regained by her husband as he laughed bitterly. 'You might have taken it as a threat! You may not have believed me. You may have written to him, God forbid, to someone in Niedernlein.'

'I would not have.'

'You do not know what you would have done,' Christoph countered in a kind voice. 'I... I intercepted your father's letters. Made the arrangements. Ensured that I covered my tracks as best I could. I left Niedernlein knowing I would probably never return. I married you...'

Daphne tried to smile. 'And you fell in love with me.'

'Much against my will,' said Christoph with a laugh. 'I had everything I wanted: freedom from Anton; distance from Niedernlein; safety for my sister. Wealth... more riches than I would ever have had as the secondborn prince. The opportunity to start again. But now... now I have so much more to lose. And...and you're smiling. Why?'

Daphne could not help it. His confession was precisely what she had expected it to be: loving, considerate and kind. Outraged at cruelty and struggling to hide devotion. It was terrifying to consider that she had walked away from such a man. That she could have lost him, in her terror and instinct to shy away from love in case it hurt her, a flame burning so bright it burned.

Daphne caught Christoph's gaze and smiled, warm affection replacing the chill of fear.

He shook his head. 'I do not deserve your smiles. There must be a spy in our house, someone who placed those letters exactly where you could find them.'

'What, these letters?' Daphne said innocently.

She pulled the letters from her father and Anton from her bodice and tried not to laugh as her husband's eyes widened.

'Firstly, what else are you keeping down there?' he said with a grin. 'And secondly, can I have a look?'

He reached out a hand and Daphne batted it away, but she did so with a chuckle, and could not deny the spark of pleasure that crackled between them as she did so.

'These letters,' she said firmly. 'They were placed there for me to find, weren't they?'

'I would never have left them lying around,' Christoph said, wincing. 'Which I know does not say much in my favour.'

'Which means they were put there specifically to drive a wedge between us,' Daphne said softly, watching his eyes to see whether he would draw the dots together. 'Someone in the house who has power over the household. Who can go where they please. Who has never particularly liked me.'

She saw the moment Christoph made the connection. *Had her face given her away?*

'That damned—Henderson! He works for Anton?'

'I am sorry to say that my father is not the most discerning of men,' said Daphne with a wince of her own. 'I do not believe it would have been difficult for Henderson to impress. When you left Niedernlein, perhaps your brother wished to keep an eye on you. It would have been only too easy for one of his connections in London to recommend Henderson to my father. Your brother has probably been using him for information for weeks. But you do not have to concern yourself. I have dealt with him.'

Christoph's eyes widened. 'Should…should I be afraid of you?'

It was difficult not to laugh at that. 'Perhaps. But, as it happens, I merely informed my father that our butler had been spying on us and selling our secrets to our enemies.'

Evidently her husband had not expected such a response. 'Daphne von Auberheiser!'

She shrugged. 'I told naught but the truth. He is gone. We do not have to worry about him again.'

'I am sorry, Daphne. Not because you found out about the circumstances of our marriage, but because I was not the one to tell you.'

It was precisely what she wanted to hear. What she needed to hear. And that was why Daphne allowed the letters, meaningless as they now were, to fall to the ground as she launched herself into her husband's arms.

Whether or not he could have known such an embrace was coming, Christoph certainly leapt into action. Daphne found herself lifted bodily from the ground as his hungry kiss overwhelmed her, making her head spin and her heart soar.

Oh, it was bliss to be within his arms again, to be touched by him, his hands cupping her buttocks as he lifted her from the ground. It was splendid to be kissed by him again, his knowledgeable tongue teasing instant pleasure from Daphne as she gasped in his mouth. It was intoxicating to know that, whatever forces had conspired to harm them, they were safe and they were together and, if they weren't careful, she was going to pull him down onto the slightly damp lawn and make love to him.

When they finally broke apart, Daphne could barely breathe and Christoph's lips were bruised with the passion of their ardour.

'I love you, Daphne,' he growled. 'And even if you cannot love me in return—'

'I love you,' she interjected, heart singing.

'Would you mind not interrupting as I make this declaration?' Christoph said with a grin.

Daphne laughed and the laughter freely flowed through her as it never had before. 'I do apologise, Your Highness.'

'Right, where was I?' Christoph lowered her slowly back onto the ground, though she could not help but notice that his hands kept a tight hold on her buttocks. 'Ah, yes. Daphne, I love you.'

'You've said that bit,' she teased, delighted to see the way his face worked at the second interruption.

'If you're not careful, I shall have to kiss you again,' he warned. 'If only to prevent you walking away from me.'

Daphne quivered at the mere suggestion, sensing a pressing rod of iron against her hip.

Christoph groaned. 'I'm trying to think clearly here.

The least you could do is not…not be so damned alluring.'

It took a great deal of self-control, but somehow she managed to step out of his embrace, though Daphne did not meander too far. She never would again.

'I am sorry,' she said quietly. 'For leaving. I… I panicked.'

'I had never thought a confession of love would cause such a thing,' her husband said quietly, and Daphne's heart broke at the pain, the self-judgement, it contained.

'It was… I have never allowed anyone to…see me. I had no intention of letting you do so,' she admitted with a wry smile. 'But, before I knew it, you knew me better than anyone in the world. Better than myself. Any moment, I thought, you would find me out.'

'Find you out?' Christoph frowned.

Daphne swallowed. 'Realise…realise that I was not worthy of your love. I am just a wallflower, and—'

'Just a…? Daphne von Auberheiser, you are a wallflower and you are my wife,' Christoph said fiercely, taking her hand and placing it on his chest. 'Worthy of me? What about me being worthy of you? When you walked away—' and here his voice cracked '—I thought—I thought you'd finally realised how much better you were without me; that my character had convinced you that your love was undeserved.'

It was difficult not to stare in wonderment. Christoph thought she could not love him…

It was preposterous. It was ridiculous. It was…entirely understandable.

Daphne breathed a laugh. 'It appears we both love each other and fear losing the other. I am not sure if there is a word for that.'

'I think it is "marriage",' said Christoph with an answering laugh of his own. 'Dear God, the depths of our love could have caused us to have lost each other. We fear being known, my darling, because we assume we are unlovable but it is the pair of us together that makes me feel as though I could conquer the world!'

'You are a prince, I'm afraid—not king of the world,' Daphne teased, her lungs tightening.

Christoph grinned. His smile was warm and welcoming, the only thing she wanted to see every morning and the last thing she wanted to see at night. 'As long as I'm king of your world, Daphne.'

She had to laugh at that. 'Is love going to turn you into a terrible poet?'

'God knows, and I hope you and I find out,' he said with a lopsided grin. 'I… I cannot imagine being married to anyone else. Come back with me, Daphne. Build a life with me. Love me even through my shortcomings. Love me even through my failings. Love me. Please.'

And she kissed him, pressing up on her tiptoes to reach him, and tried to show him through her kiss that she would, she would, she would…

When the kiss was over, Daphne breathed into his neck. 'I love you, Christoph. And I intend to stay married to you and be your wife for a very, very long time. Your wife…and the mother of your child.'

There was a strange blankness in his eyes, then sharpness. 'Child?'

'It's early, I know, but my flux—'

'A child?'

'And Gwen had her doctor see me and he seemed certain—'

'A child!'

Daphne shrieked with laughter as her husband, the man she adored, swept her off her feet and spun her round, his words spilling out in a rush that mingled with the air whistling past her ears.

'And they'll be loved, Daphne. They'll never have to worry. They'll have a life of safety and peace. A child!'

'Christoph Augustus Heinrich Maximus Anton Philip von Auberheiser, put me down!'

Christoph halted, lowering her to the ground with an abashed face. 'Yes—yes, of course. We must be careful of you.'

And Daphne fell in love with him a little more. Was this what true love was—a constant exploration of the person before her as she realised that there was always more of him to discover, always more of him to find, always more of him to love?

'We must be careful of each other,' she said quietly, cupping his cheek and adoring the look of affection he gave her. 'And we always will be.'

Chapter Twenty

'I cannot believe that you talked me into this,' said Daphne forebodingly.

Christoph grinned. Then, because his wife could not see him, he said, 'I am honoured by your trust.'

His wife snorted. 'Excellent. You fill me with confidence.'

The carriage swung to the side as it turned a corner and Daphne put out a hand to steady herself. Her other hand rested on her stomach, which was swollen only slightly. Only someone like he, who knew every inch of her by heart, would notice.

'We are almost there,' Christoph said quietly, trying not to fidget in his seat due to his excitement.

Daphne raised an eyebrow over the blindfold that she had put on before they had left the house almost half an hour ago. 'And where precisely is *there*, exactly?'

It had taken a great deal of planning. For the first few days after Daphne had returned home, Christoph could not put his idea into motion firstly, because he had not wished his wife to suspect something and secondly, because they had spent almost the entirety of that time in bed. Naked.

But as the weeks had gone by, and Christoph had realised he had never been happier in his life than he was now with Daphne, he knew that he had to do it. He'd known the planning would be a little complicated. But she was worth it.

The carriage rumbled to a slow stop. She was so trusting. The way she had accepted the blindfold this time when he had proffered it... They had come so far. And, if he was careful, they would continue to grow in love and trust with each other.

And today was part of that.

'You know, when you said that you were taking me on a magical mystery tour,' said Daphne with a small smile, 'I thought that would mean that we would actually...you know...go somewhere.'

Christoph stifled a smile. 'What do you mean? We have been in the carriage for over half an hour.'

'For all I know, we have gone round and round in circles through London,' Daphne pointed out. 'All to bring me back to our home where you have something... interesting prepared in the bedchamber.'

For a swift moment, Christoph saw stars. It was a brilliant idea. Why had he not thought of that himself? He returned to earth and tried to remind himself that this plan, his actual plan, was perhaps even better than that.

It would be a close call, though.

'Well, sadly I am not about to lead you back up to our bedchamber and ravish you,' Christoph said with some regret. 'We'll be doing something else. Something better.'

Even though her eyes were covered by the blindfold, he could see Daphne's surprise. 'Something better than what we share in the bedchamber?'

It was all he could do not to pull up her skirts and take her right here. They had certainly discovered a great number of things in the bedchamber that delighted them, and he had a feeling that their enjoyment of each other was only going to grow with time. Something else to look forward to.

But he had to be careful; he had timed this perfectly, and if he found himself dilly-dallying outside because his wife had said the word 'bedchamber', then all his planning would have been for naught. It had been his planning that had brought them together. Now, Christoph hoped, his planning would bring them even closer together.

'Are you ready to disembark?' he said aloud.

Daphne's cheeks pinked. 'Are…? We are not going on a ship, are we?'

'No! No, I meant the carriage,' said Christoph with a laugh. 'Come, give me your hand.'

Without being able to see him, and not knowing precisely where he was going to be in the carriage, Daphne trustingly put her hand out in the air.

Christoph took it with a lump in his throat. This woman had taught him more about trust in the last few months than everyone else in his life combined over the last thirty years. There was something so delicate about her, yet as strong as iron. There was nothing like her. No one like her. And she was his.

The carriage door was opened by a footman and Christoph carefully led Daphne down onto the pavement. There were far more people about than he had expected, and a few of them stared curiously at what the strange couple were doing. After all, it was not often that a woman stepped out of a carriage wearing a blindfold. At least, not in this part of London.

'Can I take this off now?' Daphne said quietly, her cheeks red.

How did she know that people were staring? It was another one of his wife's wonders, her ability to sense when she was being looked at. Christoph had so much more to learn about her. And there was so much time for him to enjoy discovering it.

His voice shook just a tad as he said, 'Yes. Yes, you can take the blindfold off.'

Her delicate hands removed the cravat silk that he had used as a makeshift blindfold, and Daphne blinked in the wintry sunlight. Then she frowned. 'It's…it's the church. The church where we were married.'

Excitement fizzed through Christoph's blood. 'It is.'

'And we are here, because…?' Daphne's voice trailed off, confusion on her face.

Christoph grinned. Oh, this was far better than he could ever have dreamed. 'Because…because our wedding was not what it should have been.'

There was a flash of panic on Daphne's face. 'Was it not legal? Are we not actually—?'

'No! No, nothing like that,' he said hurriedly. *Blast, he hadn't explained himself properly.* 'No, I just meant...it wasn't what I wanted it to be.'

There was still a crease of confusion between Daphne's beautiful eyes as she glanced up at the tall building. 'It does not seem that long ago that we were last here.'

'In a way, it wasn't. Two months.' Christoph inhaled deeply. 'But in many other ways it was a lifetime ago.'

Daphne fixed him with her enquiring stare and said nothing.

Well, here goes.

'Daphne, I learned so much in the last few months—not just about you, though that has been wonderful, but about myself. About what sort of world I want to live in, what sort of man I want to be. You've taught me that, and helped me discover it for myself and... I love you. I want you to know how much I love you. And so I wanted to go back to the beginning.'

He evidently had not explained it sufficiently, because Daphne still looked puzzled. 'So we're...back. At the church.'

'I wanted to make it up to you. Our wedding, I mean,' Christoph said gently, pulling her forward through the door of the church and into the vestibule. 'You married a man you did not know in a wedding which was all about me. My needs. My requirements.'

Daphne was flushing now. 'It was an arranged marriage. I did not mind.'

'I mind,' Christoph said simply. 'And so I thought... why not do it again?'

Her eyes widened. 'Get married again?'

'Not married, as such. I couldn't find a reverend who was amenable to such a thing, try as I might to explain it to them,' Christoph said ruefully. They were infuriating, these English vicars, nothing like the ministers in Niedernlein. 'But I thought we could commit to each other again. Properly, this time—knowing each other as we do, knowing our faults and our qualities. Promise each other things with real meaning. We can start again.'

Daphne's flush was deepening, and Christoph could not help but notice just how beautiful she was: the flicker of pink at her collarbone, the way her cheeks brightened her eyes, the soft swell of her curves. She was all Daphne, and she was all his. He wanted to do this, to show her just how much he loved her. How much he appreciated her. Knew her and wanted to keep knowing her.

'You would do that?' she whispered.

Christoph exhaled. 'I would do anything for you.'

They walked into the nave in silence, Daphne's hand intertwined with his own. They walked forward, stopping at the end of the aisle just before the altar. They stood facing each other, hand in hand. Christoph revelled in the sense of her closeness. Daphne's hand pressed into his, their bodies so close he could feel the delicate exhale of her breathing.

'So,' whispered Daphne. 'What did you have in mind?'

Christoph swallowed. What he'd had in mind had felt perfectly reasonable at the time. Now that it was time to tell her, show her, he felt...exposed.

'I thought... I mean, it was just an idea...but I thought we could make each other new vows. Vows not of the church, but of our hearts,' he said hesitantly.

Daphne's beaming smile released much of his tension. Much, but not all. 'You have given this a great deal of thought, haven't you?'

'I have given you a great deal of thought,' said Christoph honestly, his soul singing. 'Shall I go first?'

'I think you may have to, as I have not yet had any time to prepare my vows,' Daphne said with a small laugh that rippled around the church. 'Go on, then.'

Christoph cleared his throat as though about to address a royal court. And, in a way, he was. Daphne was a royal, at least by marriage, and she was the person he wanted to court for the rest of his life.

'Daphne, I vow to always listen to you,' Christoph said softly. 'To always hear you, no matter what you say. I vow to protect you from the world as best I can, in the full knowledge that you are more than capable of looking after yourself.'

'I should think so,' murmured Daphne with pinking cheeks. 'Who was it that discovered the spy in our household?'

Christoph squeezed her hands. 'I vow never to underestimate you, then. I vow to cherish you as the treasure you are. I vow to worship the very ground you walk on because it is precious. And I vow to come back here with you, every year, and make new vows. As I get to know you better, as we grow in our marriage, we will come here and make new vows so that I am always thinking of new ways to love you.'

All the prepared statements had disappeared from his mind the moment he had looked at Daphne, but that did not matter. Christoph had spoken from the deepest part of him and it seemed that Daphne's heart had heard him—had heard his intentions.

There were tears sparkling in the corners of her eyes. 'How am I supposed to follow that?'

'Just tell me whatever you want,' Christoph said awkwardly. Perhaps he should have told her in advance. It wasn't exactly fair to give her no time at all to think of such things. 'In fact, don't worry, you don't have to…'

'Christoph, I vow to love you as you deserve,' Daphne said quietly, her attention steadily fixed on him. 'And that means to love you because of who you are, without fear, with complete truth and with curiosity about the world. I vow to ask you for the truth rather than presume the worst, and to listen to you—truly listen to you.'

There was some sort of knot in Christoph's throat. He had no idea how it had got there, and absolutely no idea how he was going to remove it.

'I vow to challenge you when you are wrong and apologise when I am wrong,' Daphne continued with a wry laugh. 'I vow to work hard to know the difference. I vow to adore you as the best person I know. And I vow to endeavour to be that for you.'

It was impossible for Christoph to hold himself back any longer. Such happiness, such understanding between them, was something that had to be celebrated.

He leaned forward, celebrating in the only way he knew how, moaning at the sudden rush of affection that poured through him as their lips touched. Oh, she was his Daphne, his wife, his woman, the person he...

'Put that woman down, man!'

Christoph sprang back from a furious flushing Daphne and looked up into the outraged face of a vicar. 'Ah. Ah, yes, I can see how this misunderstanding—'

'Do not desecrate the house of God!' the vicar shouted, his words echoing loudly around the church before he strode away, shaking his head.

When Christoph turned to his wife, it was clear to see she was utterly mortified. 'Christoph!' she muttered. 'We'll never be allowed back! There'll be talk all through the *ton*, we'll never... You are laughing!'

He was. Christoph could not help it—it was absolutely the most ridiculous thing to have occurred, though he should have known something would.

'Desecrate the church, indeed,' he murmured into Daphne's ear, rejoicing in the closeness, the way he could breathe her in. 'I'd like to do far more than that in here that would desecrate the church.'

It should not have been possible for Daphne to flush any darker, yet the crimson colour that was spreading down her neck and encouraging Christoph to look at her décolletage was quite something.

'Christoph!'

'Thankfully,' he said hurriedly, 'we do not have to resort to such a thing. The carriage awaits us outside, and our home is not too far away.'

'But it took us half an hour to—'

'There was an element of going around in circles,' Christoph confessed with a grin, tugging Daphne back up the aisle with him. 'Subterfuge.'

Daphne rolled her eyes good-naturedly at him, still pink, as she walked with him out of the church. 'Perhaps we should leave subterfuge behind.'

'Perhaps. Right,' Christoph said bracingly, trying not to think of the rigid manhood in his breeches that made walking difficult. 'Into the carriage and home, where I can make love to you.'

'Home?' repeated Daphne as he helped her into the carriage and swiftly followed her, shutting the door behind them. 'You know… I don't think I can wait until home.'

For a moment, Christoph stared at his blushing bride and wondered how on earth he had managed to be so fortunate.

'Well, that is a terrible shame,' he said in a low voice in the carriage, moving to sit beside his stunning wife as she looked at him with desire-filled eyes. 'If only there was something I could do to you here, in the carriage…'

Epilogue

Daphne couldn't help it. She meandered to the large bay window that overlooked the sweeping lawn. Again.

'Daphne von Auberheiser!'

'I can't help it, I'm so excited!' she said, the words spilling from her lips. For a moment, just a moment, she tried to catch them. Tried to hold back her excitement. Tried not to allow her voice to thrum with anticipation.

Then she looked into the grinning face of her husband and the hackles on the back of her neck subsided.

'I know you are,' Christoph said with a laugh, turning the page of his newspaper as he spoke. 'But you looking out of the window every five minutes is not going to make them arrive any sooner.'

'It might do,' she shot back with a giggle. 'You never know. And they were due here an hour ago!'

The longcase clock just to the right of the mantlepiece did indeed show the time was past two o'clock, and the letter from Gwen that had arrived that morning had been most clear: one o'clock was when they expected to arrive.

Yet here they were, waiting.

Her husband turned another page. 'It's Niedernlein at Christmas, Daphne. What did you expect? I would bet they've been caught by the weather.'

'The weather?' Daphne looked up into the sky. It was blue, a dark blue she had never seen in England. She had not been able to stop marvelling at the sky since they had arrived here two weeks ago. 'But the sun is—'

'The weather could be entirely different three miles down the road, and I would bet good money that it is,' said Christoph vaguely, his attention drifting away from their discussion and back to the newspaper he was examining. 'They say here I'm an absent monarch!'

'Well, you did clandestinely leave your nation for England to marry me, dear,' Daphne pointed out, trying not to smile.

'I wasn't the monarch then!'

'I suppose not,' she said, her stomach twisting at the very thought. 'But you are now.'

It had come as a shock to all of them. The news had arrived by royal courier who had travelled all the way from Niedernlein. He'd been half-dead with cold, exhausted, and yet desperate to bow low to the man who was now King of Niedernlein.

The sudden disappearance of the heir to the throne had apparently caused quite some consternation. Even more consternation had followed when King Anton had been charged with murder by his own soldiers—the murder of his wife. Before he could be arrested, however, a duel had been fought with the lady's brother and the King of Niedernlein had been killed.

And that meant...

'They're full of praise for their new queen, however,' Christoph said with a grin over the top of his newspaper. 'Quite right too.'

'Christoph!'

'Well, with my brother gone, they didn't have any choice but to accept me,' he continued, just a hint of tension in his jaw as he spoke. 'But they've embraced you.'

Heat splattered over Daphne's cheeks, but she did not argue with him. It was impossible to do so. It had all been a whirlwind, the news of Anton's rather disgraceful death accompanied by the startling news that Christoph was the new King of Niedernlein. And that made her a queen—Queen Daphne.

It had all been a little ridiculous. Her father had been thrilled.

'We don't have to live here all year, you know.'

Daphne looked up. Christoph had laid aside the newspaper with a most serious expression on his face.

'Don't you want to stay here?' asked Daphne quietly. 'I thought you missed it when you were in England—Niedernlein, I mean, not...not him.'

Him. They didn't need to say his name.

Christoph sighed. 'I did miss it, far more than I had predicted. But this is not your home.'

He still didn't understand. Perhaps he never would. Daphne could hardly articulate it, which would explain why *he* didn't comprehend.

'You are my home,' she said softly, stepping over to sit on the sofa beside him. 'Wherever you are, that's where my home is. We could travel all over the world: Persia, China—'

'I don't think our subjects would want to lose you for that long,' he quipped with a grin.

Daphne blushed. 'I suppose not. My point is, we could live anywhere, in a box for all I cared, and it would be home. As long as I could share it with you.'

Christoph placed a hand on her cheek. 'My beautiful, clever wife. I don't deserve you.'

'Probably not.'

Christoph laughed and Daphne's cheeks burned—not with shyness, but exhilaration. 'And I love you more and more with the more I learn of you. I suppose there's still more.'

'I suppose so. I hardly know myself,' she confessed. 'But I know that I love you. And that's all that matters.'

She couldn't help it. Really, Daphne thought, she should be congratulated for holding back for so long.

Pressing a kiss against his cheek, she was not surprised when Christoph turned and met her lips with his own. His ardent kiss parted her lips and Daphne squirmed, trying to get into his lap without falling off the sofa as his hands pulled her closer.

'Presenting Her Highness, Princess Laura to Their Majesties... Oh. Oh, dear.'

Daphne sprang apart from Christoph with flaming cheeks and downcast eyes. Still, she couldn't quite ignore the scarlet-faced footman and the laughing young woman beside him.

'You two really have got to learn to keep your hands

off each other,' said Laura with a grin as she strode into the room. 'Are they here yet?'

'This is our palace, Laura,' muttered Christoph as Daphne surreptitiously attempted to check that her gown was straight. As straight as it could be over the growing swelling. 'You could knock.'

'I brought a herald, what more do you require?' chuckled Laura, peering out of the window. 'Where are they?'

'Late. Sylvia's with them so I suppose they got into an adventure,' Daphne said, her cheeks still pink as the footman, or herald, or whatever he was—she really had to learn the different liveries—backed out of the room with a deep bow.

'And Rilla, of course. And the children,' Christoph reminded them. 'Perhaps they had to stop for them.'

Excitement flooded back into Daphne's chest at the thought of her three closest friends arriving for their visit, and with their children: little Perce and baby Florence. And Sylvia must be edging towards her time by now! And Daphne was almost certain the husbands were coming.

'They were meant to be here over an hour ago,' said Laura, stepping away from the bay window and sighing as she dropped into a chair by the fire. 'Where are they?'

Then came a noise. A clatter. Hoofbeats.

Daphne rushed to the window. 'They're here. They're here!'

Laura launched to her side and squealed with delight, grabbing Daphne's arm. 'They're here!'

Turning, Daphne said excitedly, 'Christoph, they're—'

'Yes, they're here, I heard,' Christoph said, rolling his eyes dramatically. 'I would imagine half the kingdom knows they're here.'

Daphne grinned. 'Don't pretend you're not excited to show off Niedernlein.'

Laura had swept off into the hallway in eager anticipation to renew the acquaintance of the ladies she had first met in London, leaving her brother and sister-in-law momentarily alone.

Christoph rose and walked over to Daphne, pulling her into a tight embrace. 'I am looking forward to "showing off Niedernlein", as you put it. But their visit does have a distinct downside.'

Pulling back so she could look into his eyes, but not so far as to step out of his arms, Daphne frowned. 'Downside?'

There was a quirk on her husband's lips. 'I have to share you. I'd much rather keep you to myself.'

Daphne kissed him hard and swiftly on the mouth. 'I'm yours, Christoph. No one else's.'

'Yes, but—'

'And we'll find plenty of time just for the two of us,' Daphne said, pressing on. 'I can hardly imagine any of my friends not wishing for a little…well…alone time with their husbands.'

In the past, the mere suggestion of such a thing would have had her cheeks aflame. They were boiling, to tell the truth, but she had said the words directly, without stuttering or hesitating, all while keeping her gaze fixed on his.

Christoph smiled. 'The woman I first married would never have been able to say that.'

'The woman you first married would have thought it, very hard,' Daphne said with a dry laugh. 'And it's thanks to you that I can... I mean, without your love, your support...'

He stopped her words with a kiss.

Daphne almost melted in his arms as the sound of delighted people alighting from several carriages rang out from the front of the house. 'Let's send them away.'

Christoph snorted. 'Daphne von Auberheiser! You've been waiting for days for your friends to arrive!'

'I know, I changed my mind,' she said with a laugh. 'I just want you here! I want—'

'Come on, you two, aren't you going to welcome everyone?' Laura poked her head round the door, but it disappeared almost as soon as it appeared.

Christoph blew out a long breath and, though he did not say anything, Daphne could read his expression. He was nervous. Nervous, for he was still growing accustomed to the crown. To the weight of responsibility. To the knowledge that he was the representative of a nation. To the certainty that he would be plagued with questions from all three of her friends, Daphne thought ruefully.

'I love you,' she said suddenly.

And all the tension melted away from her husband's face. 'I love you.'

'There they are!'

The screech was one of delight and Daphne could not help but smile as she turned to welcome them. 'Sylvia!'

'Give me a hug, this minute, then order me the largest hot chocolate this kingdom of yours can procure,' said Sylvia, rushing from the doorway to pull Daphne into a hearty embrace that knocked the wind out of her. 'The weather in this country!'

'I didn't think it was too bad,' her husband Theodore said with a wink at Daphne, holding out his hand to shake Christoph's. 'A great many thanks for the invitation.'

'No, this way... Careful, Perce!'

Daphne grinned. Gwen wasn't yelling at her husband, though it easily could have been. Instead it was the tiny version of him who was toddled towards Daphne with hands outstretched. Very sticky hands.

'Someone clean this child!' The elder Percy managed to scoop up his son before he laid his sticky hands all over the silk furnishings. 'Does anyone have a cloth? Or a mop?'

'I need to sit down,' muttered Rilla, walking into the room on the arm of her husband Finlay, their baby Florence in her arms. 'That carriage is not designed for comfort.'

'Here,' Daphne said hurriedly, pulling forward an armchair.

Rilla groaned as she sank into it, closing her unseeing eyes. 'Is that a fire before me? I need to be defrosted.'

'Let me take Florence,' Daphne offered, stepping forward.

Her friend pulled her baby closer to her and snorted

with laughter. 'Absolutely not, she's like a hot brick! Where's that husband of mine?'

'Still here,' Finlay said with a smile. 'Hot chocolate for you too, my love?'

'Hot chocolate for everyone,' Christoph called out over the chatter. 'I'm sure someone can arrange it?'

'I'm not sure how I feel about a king waiting on me,' Sylvia said with a laugh, throwing herself onto the sofa. 'Laura! How the devil are you?'

Daphne moved through the room, not part of any of the conversations but revelling in the laughter and joy. Laura and Sylvia were seated together, the former placing a reverential hand on the latter's swelling belly.

'A few more weeks, they tell me,' Sylvia was saying. 'Are there any special perks from being born in Niedernlein? What sort of names do you have for girls, or boys?'

Rilla was slowly rocking a babbling Florence while stretching her toes towards the fire. Without her saying a word, Finlay moved a footstool under her. His wife groaned. 'Oh, Finlay, I don't deserve you.'

'Yes, you do,' he said softly, his eyes so full of adoration that Daphne felt awkward for noticing. 'Now, let me see if I can find you that hot chocolate… Oh, thank you.'

'Not at all,' said Gwen with a smile. 'A footman brought it over. Goodness, that last valley! I thought we might lose one of the coaches down the ravine!'

'You tell me this now!' Rilla rolled her eyes as she sipped her hot chocolate. 'Perhaps it was better that I didn't know.'

'Trust me, it was bad enough for those of us who did,' Percy said dryly. 'Now, carefully, Perce!'

Daphne smiled as she watched the little boy reach out delicately to the babe in Rilla's arms.

'Gentle,' Finlay said, though he nodded encouragingly at the little boy who peered curiously into the bundle.

'You never know, they could wed some day,' Rilla said with a grin. Daphne laughed as she watched Gwen and Rilla immediately coo.

Percy moved away. 'I can't hear it! I don't want to think of little Perce all grown up!'

'It can't be that bad,' scoffed Theodore as he stood by the bay window, accepting a mug of hot chocolate from the footman and clinking with Percy as he joined him.

Percy sighed. 'Trust me, when your little one arrives, it'll be just as terrifying.'

Daphne smiled as she moved over to Christoph, who was standing in a corner and watching the rabble. 'Ready for three weeks of this?'

'Not in the slightest.'

She grinned. 'They're not that bad.'

'Oh, they're wonderful,' her husband said hastily. 'They would have eventually won my affections, I believe, by who they are. They gained them immediately when I realised what good friends they were, are, to you.'

Daphne looked around the room. Her eyes fell on Gwen and Percy, their little boy dancing around everyone's feet. On Rilla and Finlay, their faces so clearly showing their love, the evidence of that love dozing in her mother's arms. On Sylvia and Theodore, their own child due in about a month. And on Laura, her confidence growing with each passing day.

'They are not my friends. They are my family,' Daphne said, not realising how true it was until she'd said it. 'I'm glad they're here.'

Christoph was chuckling as he shook his head. 'I suppose there will be more of them soon. Sylvia looks like her child could come at any time!'

Daphne's smile faded, but only slightly. It was difficult to tell whether Christoph's tone was positive or negative. It was more...marvelling.

Was this the time?

'Besides, there'll definitely be more of us soon. Won't there?'

Daphne's lips parted in astonishment as she met her husband's gaze. 'What did you just—?'

'Well, won't there?' Christoph said in a low voice. His smile was steady. 'Daphne, the royal doctor has had a word with me, out of concern for you, of course.'

'He promised me he would keep it to himself!' Daphne blurted out, cheeks flushing. 'How dare he?'

'I mean, I am a fool, but not that much of a fool. I'd known something was different, beyond the child you carry. You'd completely gone off eggs, and you love eggs for breakfast,' Christoph said with a teasing grin, lifting a hand to start counting off fingers. 'You suddenly must have strawberries upon waking—and that is a tall order in an English autumn, you know. And don't get me started on the sickness. It's two, isn't it? Twins.'

Twins. She had hardly believed it when the doctor had

finished palpating her stomach last week and had told her, with a rather shocked expression, that he believed there was not one child growing within her, but two.

Two. *Twins*.

'Twins,' Christoph said with a delightful smile. 'Doubling our family in one go!'

It warmed her hear to see him so delighted. 'You are not afeared?'

'For you. But not for them. Not at all.' There was a faraway expression in her husband's eyes that Daphne knew would take her a lifetime truly to understand. 'A fresh start. A chance for siblings to care for each other, not compete. To support each other, not suffer through their childhood.'

Daphne placed a hand on her stomach. 'Well, at least the sickness is well and truly over.'

'Oh, Gwen had terrible sickness too,' said Percy with a knowing nod. 'Just awful. It passes, though.'

'It was the cravings that did me in,' said Theodore with a sigh. 'I ask you, where was I supposed to find asparagus in September? Even with all the money and will in the world!'

'What are you…? You're not…are you?' Sylvia called loudly across the room.

Ah. Yes, only Gwen knew. Trust Sylvia to make a scene.

Daphne tried to smile. 'I… Well, I was going to tell Christoph today that the doctor believes we will be having twins so that we could all celebrate.'

There was a rush of screaming and arms flailing.

Rilla thrust her child into her husband's hands and was moving swiftly towards her, and Daphne was pinned against the wall by a combination of embraces from Sylvia, Gwen, Rilla and Laura.

'Put my wife down!'

'Oh, Daphne, that's such wonderful news!'

'I can't believe it, all four of us!'

'You must have at least a daughter if Sylvia has a son, then we can marry them off and—'

'Help!' laughed Daphne, cheeks flushed with delight at her friends' responses, but rather uncomfortable against the wall.

Christoph came to her rescue. Politely pulling her friends away from her—Sylvia put up the most fight, but as she was near her confinement and there was not much she could do about it—he cupped Daphne's face and beamed. 'Twins! Two of them!'

'That is what the doctors tell me,' said Daphne with a brave smile. 'It is going to be an interesting confinement.'

'Two new members of the family,' Christoph said softly. 'New life, my love. New life.'

'A new life,' Daphne breathed. 'For both of us.'

He kissed her, and the sound of her friends' delighted chatter, and their husbands chattering about names, faded into the background as Daphne clung to her husband.

Her Christoph. Her prince, now her king, and she his wallflower wife.

* * * * *

MILLS & BOON®

Coming next month

COURTING SCANDAL WITH THE DUKE
Ann Lethbridge

His ire rose once more. 'Listen to me, you little fool, you are one whisper away from ruin. Do you not understand this?'

She backed up until the trunk halted her progress, clearly surprised by his anger.

She frowned at him. 'What does it matter to you?'

What indeed? It shouldn't matter at all, but for some reason it did. 'You asked me for advice. Now I am giving it.'

'Then what are you suggesting?'

'It all depends on whether or not you were recognised.' He removed his hat and ran a hand through his hair. 'Why the devil would anyone think going to a gentleman's club would not be a problem?'

Defiance filled her gaze. A dare. A challenge. 'In Paris a lady is welcome everywhere.'

He stepped closer, forcing her to raise her gaze to his face, reminding her that for all that she was tall, he was taller. Larger.

Her soft lips parted on a breath. Her eyelids dropped a fraction. Her chest rose and fell with short sharp breaths.

His heart pounded in his chest. His blood, a moment before warm with anger, now ran like fire through his veins. Desire.

Only by ironclad will did he restrain from unbearable temptation.

'I—'

She raised her palm, face out as if holding him at bay. He took a breath.

Her hand pressed against his chest, then slid upwards, around his nape, and she went up on tiptoes and pressed her mouth to his.

Luscious, soft lips moving slowly.

He pulled her close, responding to her touch in a blinding instant, ravishing her mouth, stroking her back, pulling her close and hard against his body.

For a moment his mind was blank, but his body was alive as it had never been before. Out of control.

Continue reading

COURTING SCANDAL WITH THE DUKE
Ann Lethbridge

Available next month
millsandboon.co.uk

Copyright © 2025 Michéle Ann Young

COMING SOON!

We really hope you enjoyed reading this book. If you're looking for more romance be sure to head to the shops when new books are available on

Thursday 25th September

To see which titles are coming soon, please visit
millsandboon.co.uk/nextmonth

MILLS & BOON

MILLS & BOON TRUE LOVE IS HAVING A MAKEOVER!

Introducing

Love Always

Swoon-worthy romances, where love takes center stage. Same heartwarming stories, stylish new look!

Look out for our brand new look
COMING SEPTEMBER 2025

MILLS & BOON

FOUR BRAND NEW BOOKS FROM
MILLS & BOON MODERN

Indulge in desire, drama, and breathtaking romance – where passion knows no bounds!

OUT NOW

Eight Modern stories published every month, find them all at:

millsandboon.co.uk

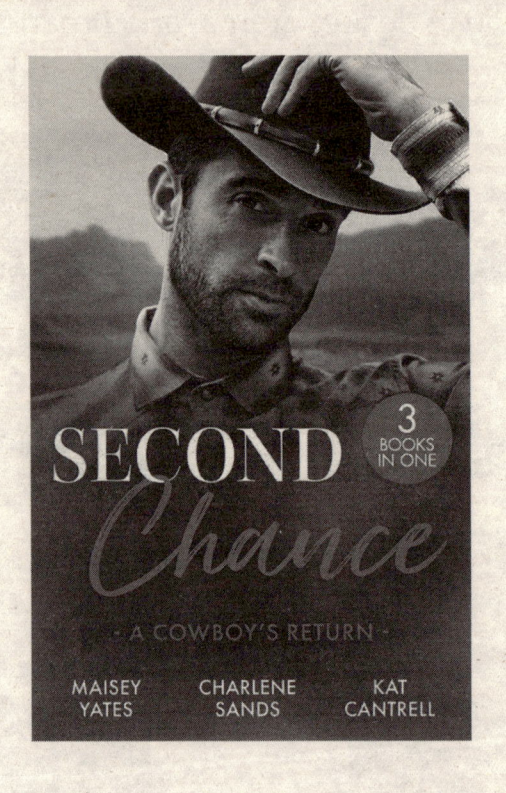

OUT NOW!

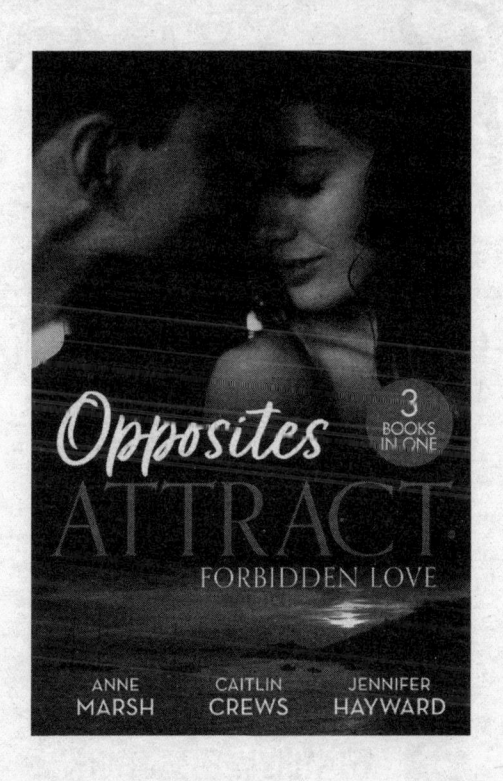

Opposites Attract: Forbidden Love

3 BOOKS IN ONE

ANNE MARSH · CAITLIN CREWS · JENNIFER HAYWARD

Available at
millsandboon.co.uk

MILLS & BOON

LET'S TALK
Romance

For exclusive extracts, competitions and special offers, find us online:

- **f** MillsandBoon
- **X** @MillsandBoon
- **◉** @MillsandBoonUK
- **♪** @MillsandBoonUK

Get in touch on 01413 063 232

For all the latest titles coming soon, visit
millsandboon.co.uk/nextmonth